Across The Border

Lights glowing in early dusk, passers-by rushing to get home. Mai stood on the forecourt of Lao Cai Station as fluorescents on the arch above her flickered bright. She looked towards the carpark just beyond the base of a broad, flight of stairs, assuming Long would come by bus or car to meet her. The last passengers from the afternoon train from Hanoi gradually departed with the carpark slowly emptying. Mai wondered why they were meeting late in the afternoon.

"Mai," she heard from a familiar voice.

Mai turned to face Long. Momentarily she felt startled as if something was wrong, yet nothing was wrong. A few weeks ago they met at the market at her village; since then they corresponded through Facebook, and now Mai was meeting Long as he asked her to. Mai was meeting the man she loved.

"Come with me, please," Long asked.

"Chào buòi chièu," May greeted. *Good evening.*

"Chào buòi chièu," Long greeted in reply. "Now, come with me."

Long with Mai by his side, headed towards the shops across from the carpark. Lao Cai was so big, so modern; so incredible. Even though aged 16, Mai had never been beyond the forests and fields surrounding her village. In silence, Long strode through streets lined by lovely, brick houses a far

1

cry from Mai's home of a timber hut with a corrugated steel roof; surrounded by dirt in the dry season and mud in the wet season. Mai momentarily pictured herself in one of those houses. It was like another world from where she lived, but in reality an hour's walk from home. All Mai had to do was reassure herself Long really was the right man. Mai knew a marriage with the wrong man, like her father, could go bad for her, which was why she agreed to meet Long. But beyond that, to get away from the stuffy confines of her village for a few hours was a good reason to go to Lao Cai anyway.

On and on they walked in silence out of Lao Cai to open country. In the distance in late evening's light, a river shimmered. Long headed along a narrow track between rice paddies towards that river. Mai wondered.

"Long," Mai said. "Is this the right way?"

"Of course this is the right way," he said dismissively.

That really wasn't what Mai meant. "Is this alright?" she asked instead.

"We have to wade across this river, then everything will be alright."

"I understand," Mai said, without really understanding.

They reached the river bank where Mai wondered about wading. She wore jeans, a blue t-shirt and runners; not really suitable for wading across such a broad river. Down and down a graded bank to water's edge.

"Are you sure about this?" Mai asked.

Long laughed which made Mai's heart feel lighter. "You'll be fine although you'll get a bit wet," he said.

Mai was sure she would get more than just a bit wet, but she trusted Long. Down to the water where Long put out his hand. Mai took it as she stepped into almost still water; although broad this river barely flowed. It was nice to be in cool water on a calm evening. Mai liked this experience; especially holding Long's hand as they crossed a river about 100 metres wide. On and on, deeper and deeper, with water reaching Mai's upper arms until the river bed slowly curved upwards. Up and up with wet denim dragging her back. Higher and higher until they were on dry land with water draining from wet clothes. Mai's jeans now hung tight on her body and especially her t-shirt. She felt embarrassed.

"Not so far to go," Long said, as once more he strode on with Mai alongside. Ahead lights glimmered; the lights of Lao Cai. For some reason they'd gone out of town and then back again. Long was from Lao Cai so he must know the sense of this. Closer to buildings now and a little shop too. A little shop with a big surprise. Mai stopped walking. Now she knew where she was.

"This is China," Mai said. "That writing is Chinese."

"How do you know that writing is Chinese?" Long snapped.

"Because that's not Vietnamese."

3

Mai turned to run until Long grabbed her wrist. Another young man, maybe Long's age, ran along the road to grab Mai's other wrist. As much as she squirmed and tried to get away, she had no chance. Mai knew she was in terrible trouble.

* * *

Nuan was about to remove her boots when the buzzer of her door rang. She opened to see Father. That was surprising, given she went to their apartment for dinner last night. After greetings she invited Father in.

"Welcome to my humble home," Nuan said.

Father nodded his head. Nuan's apartment had a living room, with a kitchen at one end separated by a counter where she ate. Through a doorway was her bedroom, while off that was a small bathroom which had a shower, basin and an Asian-style toilet.

"Would you like a cup of tea, Father?" Nuan asked.

"If that's no trouble," he said.

Nuan filled her kettle, and while it boiled she got out her pot, tea, and two cups with saucers.

"We can sit at this counter," Nuan said.

They sat side by side.

"I heard what happened when you were on patrol," Father said. "I heard you handled things well."

Nuan nodded her head. "I'd never imagined so much aggression and sheer, brute strength. I had to beat the...," she

paused. "I had to beat him with my baton while the constables handcuffed him."

"You beat the shit out of him."

Nuan smiled at that. "I had to."

"Methamphetamine, ice, is a scourge. Did you study it?"

"Heroin and cocaine have to be grown, harvested, processed, and smuggled into China. Ice can be made from chemicals available from thousands of factories across China, and especially here in Guangdong Province. It's cheap and freely available, and unlike heroin and cocaine which sort-of zone out users, ice leads to aggression."

"We have a problem with ice addiction which I believe can best be overcome by cutting back on supply and forcing prices up. We can never totally eliminate drugs, but I believe we have to act on ice."

"I'd heard about the aggression, but now that I've experienced it!"

"Ice can be made anywhere, anytime, under the protection of corrupt cadres and corrupt police officers paid to look the other way. What I propose is a taskforce of about twenty whose purpose is unknown except by a few, where in secrecy they're going to shut-down ice production, and break-up the responsible triad gangs so production can't be restarted. I don't want a repeat of Boshe," Father said.

"I understand," Nuan said. In Boshe several years ago now, three thousand from the People's Armed Police Force

raided what was called a village but was actually the town of Boshe, to seize three tonnes of ice while arresting a few hundred and the local cadre in charge, who was later executed. Ultimately 10,000 were arrested, but that raid, publicised far and wide and even internationally, made no discernable difference to the production or availability of ice in Guangdong Province. Triad simply continued doing what they were doing at Boshe, elsewhere in the province.

"This has to be done in absolute secrecy," Father said. "If one member of this task force takes one bribe, we may as well not bother. Triad will find out and everything will be moved somewhere else."

"A secret and totally non-corruptible task force?"

"Yes. I have three or four who I absolutely trust, and you. I trust you, Nuan, of course, and you have your degree with honours which already puts you in the upper echelons of our police force. Would you be interested?"

Nuan barely believed that! "Yes I am," she said.

"I can have you transferred, temporarily promoted to Detective-Sergeant Grade One. Also, are there fellow graduates you absolutely trust not to take bribes, no matter the amount?"

Nuan knew one. "I know one male graduate posted to Lufeng."

"Good. Any others? Any women?"

Nuan frowned. "There were very few women so we stayed together, and particularly we did our assignments together. But I don't know them well enough to absolutely trust them that way." Nuan thought. "Men are more straightforward, I think. Men have an objective, solve a case, or in their private lives, find a girlfriend, and then they set out to do that. Women have the same objectives, really, yet it's not so straightforward, if you understand. More mysterious."

"I absolutely trust you."

"That's because I'm your daughter! Why do you want more women?"

"To stop men from acting before thinking."

"That's the same as having an objective and straight away setting out to do it. Women will pause and think."

"I need more pausing and thinking. I intend to infiltrate triad gangs and take them out at the top. There's no point arresting those at the bottom, because these gangs will just restart production somewhere else."

"To infiltrate triad gangs you need women?" Nuan asked; quite surprised.

A pause. "No, I would never ask a police officer to do that. My plan is to negotiate the purchase of large quantities of ice to import into Australia."

"That won't work, Father. Triad import into Australia now, so they won't sell ice to a competitor. Same with New Zealand, the Philippines and many other places. Let's go with places more obscure, like Fiji, Samoa, Vanuatu and New Guinea."

"Good idea. Do you know any women?"

Nuan thought. "Possibly there's one, but I would like to speak with her first." Nuan thought more. "Do you actually need a taskforce of twenty?"

"What are your thoughts?"

"You could have a smaller taskforce of six or seven or even eight, where they bring in other officers just before they take suspects into custody, but those officers don't know where, what or why until the very last moment."

"That would work."

"When does this start?"

"I'll have you and the other officers I've selected, transferred on Monday week."

Nuan finished her tea. "I'll give you the name of the graduate in Lufeng."

She went to her bedroom to grab a notebook and pen. Nuan returned to the counter to write 'Constable Grade One Zhang Hu – Lufeng'. She tore out the page before giving it to Father.

"Thank you, Nuan," he said. "While you'll be transferred temporarily, this doesn't have to stop there. If things work well, what's temporary might become permanent."

Nuan nodded her head in understanding, while her heart raced. So much happening so fast! She thought.

"On Monday week, I'll take a car to drive to Fuzhou," Nuan said. "With luck you may have another woman for your taskforce."

"Thank you."

Father put the page in the pocket of his shirt before standing. "I'm sorry to interrupt your day off with police work, but I'm sure you understand why. I didn't want to discuss this yesterday when you came for dinner. Today with a clear head and time; this has been fruitful."

Nuan stood. "I'm looking forward to this very much, Father."

Those simple words didn't express how Nuan really felt. Father left while Nuan couldn't get her head around what had just happened. Just last week she joked she wouldn't be aiming her gun at triad bosses anytime soon, but now she may well do that. So amazing! So incredible!

Across The Border

by

Mark Morey

Mark Morey

http://markmorey.blogspot.com

978-0-6484246-6-6

Published In Australia

July, 2020

Other Works by Mark Morey

The Red Sun will Come - June 2012

Souls in Darkness - August 2012

The Governess and the Stalker - July 2014

Maidens in the Night - September 2014

One Hundred Days - September 2015

The Last Great Race – April 2016

The Adulterous Bride – October 2016

No Darkness – March 2017

In Our Memories – November 2017

Blood Never Sleeps – March 2018

Ketsumeidan – October 2018

Yuejin – Aim High! – July 2019

Wenge – Destroy The Old! – July 2019

Ice – February 2020

- Chinese names are always expressed as family name – given name.

- Hanyu Pinyin has been used to transliterate Mandarin Chinese to our Romanised alphabet. Most names and places in this story are pronounced phonetically, except words commencing with 'X' sound more like Zh but not exactly, and words commencing with Q are more like Ch.

Chapter One

Nuan stood in the doorway of that apartment, the home of Dewai her boyfriend, but now her home too. But it didn't feel like her home. She walked slowly across the living room with the heels of her boots noisy on burgundy-coloured ceramic tiles. She reached the wall of floor to ceiling glass with a great view of Guangzhou, as to be expected on the 31st floor. Although there were many skyscrapers taller than 31 stories, they were in the distance so Nuan could look down to smaller buildings, busy roads, freeways, parks, and the Pearl River lazily curling past the city. She turned towards the door to face a burgundy leather lounge suite arranged around a low, dark-tinted, glass-topped metal table, a big television set onto a grey-painted wall, and further around, a kitchen of grey cabinets and granite bench tops separated by a counter with three black, metal stools. Nuan headed past the kitchen to the dining area which had a table with a dark-tinted glass top, and six, black-framed steel chairs; matching the kitchen stools. Further to the second bedroom, home to a computer with two screens, important for a man who owned his own information technology company, and exercise equipment. Further again to a bathroom which unusually had a bath, and of course a shower, a washbasin and a toilet. Then to their bedroom of a wardrobe on one side with mirrored sliding doors, and floor to ceiling glass opposite.

Like the rest of the apartment, walls were painted a medium shade of grey. Their bed was big, larger than king-sized, with a dark grey quilt cover. Nuan went to the window to gaze upon Guangzhou from a different aspect while thinking she had to make her new home seem like her home. But a pretty, floral quilt cover would look totally out of place. Lights were recessed so she couldn't do anything with light fittings, but maybe cream-coloured cushions on the bed when it wasn't being used, especially if those cushions were embroidered; perhaps dark blue. She went to the dining room where a vase and flowers would make a big difference, and also on the low table in the living room. What else? The kitchen, with a small vase of flowers on the counter separating it from the living room. Nuan went to the kitchen, where the view across that counter and across the living room through floor to ceiling windows was magnificent. It would be a pleasure to cook there. Her next shopping trip will be for three vases, flowers, and cushions.

"You seem deep in thought," Dewai said.

Nuan turned to face her boyfriend. "I'm just planning," she said.

"What?"

"A surprise."

He came alongside. "I'm glad the way things worked out," he said.

Nuan thought: *wait for my surprise!* No, what she planned was simple and tasteful, to suit simple, masculine elegance.

"I know you can't tell me," Dewai said. "But seeing as Office 1.10 is now public with your arrest and now charging the six leaders of the Axe Gang triad group, I assume you'll be targeting more organised crime?"

"I don't know for certain," Nuan said. Like Dewai she assumed Commissioner Shui of the Guangzhou Public Security Bureau, who also was her father, had something like that planned. "Whatever's in store, I'm looking forward to a new case."

"There's one question I've never asked, I suppose because you were already a detective when we met, but why did you become a police officer?"

"My father is a police commissioner while my mother is an economist, so I could have studied economics or finance if I wanted to, but I studied policing to help make China better and safer for the many good, honest people who live here."

"That's worthy."

That was Nuan's motive, despite policing being more dangerous than when her father was on the streets. Nuan walked along the small kitchen while thinking there were times she liked cooking, especially when her mind was busy and she wanted to relax, but not that day. Besides, it wouldn't hurt to define expectations.

"Now that today is closing, where would you like to eat?" Nuan asked.

Dewai rubbed his chin. "Let's go for a walk and see what takes our fancy."

Yuexiu Park was nearby with many restaurants close to there. Nuan took his hand to head out of what she would soon make her home, to find somewhere nice to eat.

* * *

The door to the dark room creaked open. Mai retreated to the corner as far away from those men as she could get. Mai smelled masculine sweat which made her retch, and different odours which meant more than one man.

"Get up!" Long ordered.

Mai stayed where she was, so Long grabbed her wrist to literally drag her to her feet.

"What do you think?" Long asked.

The door was open wide now, revealing an old man with a deeply lined face. The man nodded his head while speaking in Chinese. Then the old man reached into his pocket for a thick wad of banknotes, but not Vietnamese dong. He handed the notes across while Mai felt ever sicker. Mai felt sick enough to throw up. With those notes in his hands Long pressed his palms together to bow. Then Long turned to face Mai.

"This is Deng Wendong and he's taking you to marry his son," Long said.

16

"How can you do this to me?" Mai asked incredulously.

"Are you so stupid to think what I wrote in Facebook was real? I just wrote that to get you here."

"To sell me."

"I'm sure these are good people, and I'm sure you'll have a wonderful life as the wife of this man's son."

Mai doubted that. She couldn't even speak their language.

"We have a long way to travel," Long said. "If you need to go, go now, and then we'll leave."

"I'm fine," Mai said. It hadn't been so long.

"Let's go."

"Can I have my phone?" Mai asked.

"When you get to your new home, then you get your phone."

Long pulled Mai's wrist for her to follow him outside, where sunlight was especially intense after two days of near-darkness. A white car, dirty and dented, sat in that sun. Long opened a back door to shove Mai onto burning brown vinyl. Mai realised that was the first time she'd had ever been in a car, but it wasn't a trip she was going to enjoy. Remember with dread, maybe, but never enjoy. The old Chinese man sat alongside Mai, while Long and the other young Vietnamese man, Li Van Hong, sat in front. The engine made a terrible racket before they lurched into the Chinese city of Hekou. Mai wound the window glass down to get comfort from terrible heat, before staring blankly at Hekou Chinese peacefully going about their daily business without realising a tragedy was playing so close. Totally unaware of one girl's tragedy. Soon they left bustling Hekou to speed past countryside very much like home, but where every minute, and even every second, took Mai further and further from those she loved.

Chapter Two

The high speed train eased into Zhuhai Station with many readying to leave that second-class carriage, Liko amongst them. He didn't want to get caught in the inevitable queue. As door locks were released, they poured out across the elevated platform and down escalators to street level, and then outside to the left towards the border crossing with Macau. The border crossing buildings hadn't changed for decades when few Chinese were able to travel, so now could barely cope as queues already formed. Liko stood at the end of the shortest queue, his passport in his inner pocket as they eased forward. In the distance were many skyscrapers like much of southern China: Macau, Hong Kong, Shenzhen and Liko's home city of Guangzhou. Liko made it to the border guard, got his passport stamped; then walked to his usual foreign currency bureau to change his wad of yuan notes to Macau patacas. After that, Liko walked along the line of buses until he saw the courtesy bus to his favourite casino, the Golden Dragon, where he'd booked to stay for one night. Liko joined the many on board, to sling his backpack onto a luggage rack and wait. Soon they were on their way to the hotel and casino not very far. It was too early to check-in so Liko left his bag at the luggage room before entering the gaming room, semi-darkened with no natural light, and an unreal air of hushed busyness.

As always Liko bought 2,000 patacas, or MOPS as they were known, of chips before joining the mahjong table. He wasn't a bad player of this game of skill and luck, but luck had deserted Liko during his past few visits. Yet Liko was sure his luck would turn and he would be able to eat into his debts. Surely one or two good visits would see him repay that money he owed? Liko was certain as he bet one chip, 100 patacas or MOP, on his first game. Mahjong was not a game for the impatient as the traditional tiles, seemingly as old as China itself, were kept or changed as the game unfolded and more bets were laid or players dropped out. Indeed Liko's luck had changed and he won, scooping a huge pile of chips to his corner before betting just one chip for the first round of his second game there. That second game didn't go so well, nor the third, nor the fourth, but at the end Liko was ahead rather than behind, thanks to his early win, so he cashed his winnings.

At the luggage room Liko exchanged his receipt for his backpack, went to the reception desk, so bright after the gaming room, and checked in to get room 1410 on the 14th floor. That room held no surprises as Liko unpacked the few belongings he needed for an overnight stay, before going down to the Dragon Palace restaurant, where the food was good and not too expensive. Liko took a table for two before browsing the menu, but he sensed something. He looked up where two men looked down. One took the menu from Liko and laid it aside before sitting opposite.

"Kam Liko gambling again," he said.

"Who are you?" Liko asked.

"More like what are we, but you know that already I'm sure. You owe us a lot of money, Kam Liko, more than you'll earn even in a year of honest work, especially if you keep losing."

"So far today I've won."

"That's a nice change but until you've won the 300,000 you owe...."

Liko was shocked. "Do I owe that much?"

"With interest, of course. With interest rates being what they are, it's to your advantage to pay sooner rather than later. How much did you win?"

"Not that much. Three thousand, one hundred MOP."

He laughed. "How about we do a deal to wipe your debt? You have access to valuable information, so when we ask you simply tell us."

Liko felt sweaty despite cool airconditioning. "I don't think I can do that."

"If you don't then the consequences, for you and for your family, might be unfortunate."

"My family has nothing to do with this," Liko said.

"Until your clear your debts, your family is in the picture. Either pay with money or pay with information."

"When?" Liko asked.

"When we ask, you tell. When you've told us enough there will be no more debt." The talkative man leaned forward. "I have advice; just don't come back here. You've lost a lot and even if you're lucky and make a few thousand in a day, you'll never win. Give us information instead."

Liko had a thought. "How did you know I was here?" he asked.

"A police officer asks me that?"

He looked up at the ceiling so Liko did too, to see surveillance cameras. That's how they knew, and in the gaming room too. Every time he came they knew. Liko was played by these men, played for a fool, but he had no choice.

"I'll pay you with information," he said.

"Be prepared for a phone call when we're interested." He stood. "Enjoy your meal."

Liko watched them leave while thinking he was in terrible trouble unless he gave them what they wanted. He didn't want to, but that man was right; Liko would never pay his debts honestly, nor would he win 300,000 yuan at a few thousand MOP for a good few hours. If he went back to the gaming room after dinner, he would lose that quicker than he won it. Really he wasn't any good so it was the best way, the only way, to give them what they wanted, when they asked for it.

The waiter came so Liko picked up the menu to order, and a beer too. While he waited, Liko wondered when he got to work on Monday, if his colleagues would suspect something. He had to behave as straight as possible until this mess was over. For sure Liko had got himself into a terrible mess.

Chapter Three

Mai stared out of the window of the old truck as they sped along flat countryside, leaving that city behind. When Long and Hong took Mai to Kunming some distance into China, Mai never imagined a city could be so big, so busy, so noisy; so much of everything. But that was just the start. She was taken onto a train which travelled further north for more than four hours, to the city of Guangzhou. Guangzhou made Kunming seem like nothing. Mai couldn't imagine surviving in such a place of chaos, but fortunately that wasn't the case for her. Instead they caught a bus for a two-hour ride to yet another city, but somewhat smaller. Now they left that city behind as they crossed between rice paddies with many waterways nearby, and mountains in the distance reminding Mai of her home so far away. A home she was sure she would never see again. She could have escaped from that man at either of the stations, when they went to the bus, or when they arrived from the bus; but that would have been pointless. She didn't know where she was, she didn't speak the language, she couldn't read signs and she had no money to get home. Simply, she couldn't ask for help to get home. So with every hour of travelling Mai was taken further and further into this land of rice and rivers.

The truck slowed as Mai saw old houses built of dark-coloured bricks fronting a lake lined with stone walls and crossed by two old, stone bridges. Brick house after brick house after brick house, all with odd, curved tiled roofs, and all but touching each other. They travelled along that road to stop at a square of rough paving surrounded on all sides by houses. There the driver switched off the engine of the truck and the old man climbed down. He beckoned Mai who climbed down too, to be surrounded by ancient bricks covered in moss, with narrow, dark lanes, also covered in moss, branching between these old, old houses.

The old man pointed to himself and said, "Gong Gong."

Given she was bought to be married, that probably meant 'father' in Chinese. Mai pointed to him and said, "Gong Gong," to get a great, big smile in reply. Although this old man had bought her and taken her away, he wasn't so bad.

He said something before walking along one of those narrow, dark, moss-covered lanes while carrying his bag retrieved from the back of the truck, so Mai followed to reach a dark, heavy, timber door. This the man opened to go inside, followed by Mai.

It was dark inside and old. The walls were in dark brick like outside, while the floor was stone. Mai's eyes slowly became used to the darkness where she saw long, cloth-covered benches for sitting, but with backrests, a table and chairs, a kitchen with a stove, pans and plates, and brown timber doors leading from that room to other rooms. Pictures hung on walls, a man and a woman in bright clothes, a photo of another man and another woman, the same man with a child on his knee.

There was an older woman but not lined like the old man, not as old but clearly his wife. The old man, Gong Gong, pointed to her.

"Po Po."

Mai bowed to this old woman. "Po Po," she repeated, but received an angry looking frown instead of a smile. Mai didn't like this woman.

The third person in the room was younger, her husband to be. The old man, Gong Gong, pointed to him. "Yuanfu."

Husband maybe or his name. Whichever, Mai bowed and repeated, "Yuanfu."

Gong Gong then pointed to Mai and said, "Ma Thi Mai."

The young man, Yuanfu, bowed and repeated, "Mai."

The young man talked earnestly but Mai could only say 'I don't understand', which she didn't understand, and he didn't understand her. He took Mai's wrist which she snatched away, before the old woman pushed Mai from behind while speaking in Chinese. Mai knew she was to go with this man, her husband to be, who opened a door.

The small room had a big bed; too big for one person, and two chests on the floor. Mai had a terrible, terrible feeling as the young man, Yuanfu, closed the door to this room. He grabbed both of Mai's upper arms while she tried to pull away, but he was too strong. Just too strong, he literally pushed Mai to sit on this big bed. When he let Mai's arms go, she punched his chest with a fist for which he slapped her. That stung! Mai rubbed her cheek as he climbed onto this bed to push her flat, while she punched him again. This was wrong! This was wrong, wrong, wrong as he pushed her flat with one hand while his other hand was at the button on the waist of her jeans. She punched him and punched him and punched him, even as he loosened her jeans and pulled them down, and her panties too. She put her hand between her legs to stop him but he simply took her hand away, he was too strong, and held it above her head, but still she kicked at him. Mai had no chance, she knew that, but she was going to fight this man, Yuanfu, all the way.

* * *

Yuanfu only wanted one thing, for Mai to take her clothes off so he could fuck her. After a night, a morning and a night again, Mai knew it was pointless to fight him. She had no way of stopping him, so if he wanted to fuck her, she lay there and let him.

The old woman Po Po was as bad as Yuanfu. Mai was given a brush and a bucket, then made to scrub those old, stone floors on her hands and knees. Not well enough because the woman got angry, said things in Chinese, and even hit Mai who realised she had to scrub them again. Every room in the house. Then Mai had to get fresh water from a tap in the square to scrub kitchen benches. Again not to Po

Po's satisfaction so she had to do that again too. After scrubbing and scrubbing so hard all day, it was almost a relief to lay in bed to be fucked by Yuanfu. Mai wondered if he realised she hated him. She doubted he cared. She was silly, no childish, to be tricked by Long, but she wasn't stupid. Mai hated Yuanfu because she knew he could have treated her better.

The most horrible thing was not the scrubbing or the fucking but being unable to communicate. She had one t-shirt, one pair of jeans, one bra and one pair of panties, and nothing to sleep in. She needed more clothes and underwear so she could wash one and wear the other, she needed a nightgown, she needed lots of things, but when she asked all she got was blank looks.

The third morning there, after for once not being fucked, Mai went with Yuanfu to sit at the table for their usual breakfast of rice porridge with tea. Some hours after that Mai had the greatest surprise; Gong Gong carried a lovely, long, white dress and fresh underwear too. Gong Gong draped the dress over Mai's arm and spoke quietly but nicely. Mai could barely believe it; it was the most beautiful dress she'd ever seen.

Yuanfu carried a basin of water to their room, with a towel and a cloth over his arm. Mai followed carrying the dress and her underwear, to wash, dry and dress. It was good to leave her dirty clothes aside, as she returned to the main room of the house now dressed in a pretty, white dress; tight at her bust and waist while then long and flowing to the floor. Gong Gong smiled brightly while speaking, but once more Mai had no clue. Perhaps he said the dress was pretty, which it was. Gong Gong opened the front door to beckon Mai to the lane, and then to the square.

This had been transformed with red ribbons everywhere, lengths of red material too, pots boiling giving off many delightful scents much nicer than rice porridge, while long, timber tables and benches were in place. Mai knew what this was. Then she recognised what she thought were two Vietnamese women. They came to Mai.

"My name's May Thi Na," one said in Hmong. "This is Do Thi Hu."

Mai bowed. "My name's Ma Thi Mai."

"Welcome to your wedding."

"Am I really getting married?"

"You can't get married here. You don't have the right papers to get married in China."

"What's the purpose of this?"

"This is a pretend wedding. They'll celebrate, eat, drink, pretend it's real, and everyone in this village will regard this as real, even if it's not."

"What is this village?"

"This is Fusi Village. You're marrying Deng Yuanfu."

"What does Gong Gong and Po Po mean?"

"Father and Mother."

"I thought so. How did this happen to us?"

"Things are what they are so don't fight it."

"I'm trying not to but Po Po isn't nice to me."

"Your Po Po is a horrible woman," Do Thi Hu said.

"What can I do to make her like me?"

"Have a son but don't have a daughter."

"As if I can make that happen. A child yes, a son – well.
Do you have these problems?"

"Not so much for either of us."

Mai's bad luck. Then Gong Gong interrupted to beckon
Mai to their house where Yuanfu wore really smart clothes of
a style Mai had seen on the internet, a grey suit, a white shirt
and a black tie. He looked handsome even, as she stood by
him in her white, flowing dress.

Suddenly loud explosions with Mai quite startled, but none
of her now new family were the least concerned as smoke
drifted along the lane. Yuanfu took Mai's hand to lead her to
the square filled with Chinese villagers, and the two
Vietnamese women and their pretend-husbands. In the
square an older villager had a red book from which he read
Chinese, before Yuanfu put a ring on Mai's right hand. Now
she really was pretend-married, while Yuanfu gave her a glass
to drink from. It was horrible, whatever it was; Mai coughed
from this drink while Po Po glared angrily at Mai for that.
Yuanfu took the glass from Mai to drink from it too, before

he led her to sit on a bench at the end of one of the long tables while food was served. Mai was given her food first, then Yuanfu, then many from the village. Despite being pretend it was a happy event, in fact the first time Mai had felt – unburdened if not even a bit happy, even though it was pretend. She had some more of that terrible drink, ate the food which was tasty and very different to Hmong food, and all in all in that village square, it was – well, happy. May Thi Na said don't fight it, so Mai didn't. If her pretend wedding was happy then she felt happy. Later she expected Yuanfu to fuck her, given they were now pretend-married, and she would try to enjoy that too. There was no point in forever being angry at that which couldn't be changed, as Mai looked along the table at Po Po glaring at her.

Chapter Four

Nuan was never first to work, so when Superintendent Ma wasn't in she suspected something was happening. Office 1.10 was based in a large, windowless room on the 18th floor of the Guangzhou Ministry of Public Security, where each of the eight officers had a desk, chair, and a laptop computer with a large screen. Nuan greeted her colleagues who represented a broad diversity with six men and two women: Nuan and Detective-Sergeant Xiong Jia; different ages with Superintendent Ma and Detective-Sergeant Suo Shen in their 40s, Detective-Sergeant Kam Liko in his 30s, and Detective-Constable Zuo Huang in his late 20s. The youngest were the three graduates of the People's Public Security University: Nuan, Jia and Hu; all aged early 20s and all recruited by Commissioner Shui through Nuan's recommendations. As a graduate with honours, Nuan was Detective-Sergeant Grade One; equal-second in rank at Office 1.10 with Liko. Kam Liko was alright but there was something about him. As a university graduate Nuan didn't want to put Liko down because he didn't have her theoretical knowledge or technical skills, but she did put him down because he lacked the ambition to rise to challenges and simply get difficult things done. Then Superintendent Ma entered the room where all eyes turned.

"Ah, I see you've missed me!" Superintendent Ma exclaimed. "Sergeant Kam and Sergeant Shui; could you please attend a meeting now?"

Nuan followed Superintendent Ma and Kam Liko to the big office of Commissioner Shui, her father, where she and Liko saluted before shaking hands formally. Commissioner Shui beckoned all to sit at his meeting table close to big windows with a lovely view over Guangzhou.

"Now that the leadership Axe Gang has been charged," Commission Shui began, "we still have an ongoing methamphetamine problem here in Guangdong Province, and indeed across all of China. Our original plan was to target a known triad group by buying methamphetamine or ice, to sell in bulk to markets not yet covered by triad, being Fiji, Samoa, Vanuatu and New Guinea. Do you have ideas on how to get this started?"

That was originally her father's idea although Nuan refined it. In past weeks she'd thought of a strategy. "Commissioner Shui," she began. "One place to start is the bottom, by making contact with a 49er, a triad foot soldier, and through that contact make the offer to buy methamphetamine in bulk. One way to make this contact would be to pose as secondary dealers to buy drugs. Once we're sure we've gotten a genuine triad 49er and not just another secondary dealer, we can make this offer and see where this leads us."

"Does this mean working undercover?" Commissioner Shui asked.

"Yes it does. One place to purchase drugs is through the dark web."

"Can you do this?"

"Yes I can, as can Sergeant Xiong and Constable Zhang."

"Superintendent Ma?"

"I understand this idea," he said. "What I propose is an undercover team of two: Sergeant Shui supervising Constable Zhang, while Sergeant Xiong's technical skills can assist us while her colleagues are undercover."

"Anything else?"

"I suggest an undercover team could be based near where I used to live," Nuan said. "This is the sort of place I would expect to find drug dealers and drug users."

"That's true," Commissioner Shui said.

Nuan knew he knew, having visited her there many times.

"We'll need money for expenses, and to buy drugs," Nuan said.

"See my personal assistant for whatever you need. Are you comfortable working undercover?" Commissioner Shui then asked Nuan.

"I know the theory, we all read case studies, and really this is a low-level infiltration which requires common-sense more than anything else."

"If that's all, I'll leave you to this." Commissioner Shui stood, which was the end of their meeting.

Nuan walked back to Office 1.10 with her head spinning, even though going undercover was her idea. Facing reality was different to thinking things through. One good thing she had Hu, who even though was her ex-boyfriend from their Beijing days, they worked well together, especially when issues became difficult. Nuan suspected Superintendent Ma, although not knowing their background, recognised they formed a good team.

At Office 1.10, Superintendent Ma briefed all officers before gathering Nuan and Hu to an informal meeting at his table.

"You said you should be based near where you used to live?" Superintendent Ma began.

Renhe to the north of the city centre was an older part of Guangzhou. As the population of the city grew to more than 14 million, more valuable areas to the south and closer to the Pearl River were torn down and rebuilt with modern skyscrapers, making Guangzhou the skyscraper centre of China. Renhe to the north remained as first developed, with older, brick apartment buildings of a lesser standard, or more accurately of a substantially lesser standard, but cheaper for rental which originally attracted Nuan. What also attracted Nuan were the many shops, cafes, restaurants and markets, where everything she needed, from her groceries to a meal out if she didn't feel like cooking, were available at modest prices.

"We shouldn't use my old apartment because they know me there, but we could rent another apartment and then use my furniture."

"Are you sure?"

"I intend to put my furniture into storage but I haven't had the chance."

"Alright. We need names. Sergeant Shui you will be Kinling Lo, and Constable Zhang you will be Liu Wen. The code word for your operation is 'Red Sun'. If you have problems, tell anyone here 'Red Sun Is Blown'."

Nuan had more pressing issues than an undercover name and code words. "If we're to infiltrate triad at a low level by posing as secondary dealers, we need to be better than ice addicts. I propose we purchase a quantity of ecstasy for the party scene."

"Good idea," Superintendent Ma said.

"One last thing. In this operation we may need to break the law. Most likely we will break the law."

"Does Commissioner Shui know this?"

"Commissioner Shui knows we'll be buying drugs but we may need to break other laws."

"I'll make sure he knows."

Nuan nodded her head. She grabbed a piece of paper to write the address of a real estate agent she knew but didn't use herself. "Hu, or I should say Wen, we'll be boyfriend and girlfriend. Meet me here which is a real estate agent, tomorrow morning at eight-thirty. We'll rent an apartment and take things from there. Superintendent Ma, I'll need a clean laptop without our surveillance programs."

"Get one from Commissioner Shui's personal assistant. Anything else?"

"We can use our current police mobiles." Nuan put her head down while she thought things through. As a low-level dealer it would be better for her to dress as she normally dressed out of hours, with tight jeans and her usual ankle-high boots with five centimetre heels. There was one other thing which she had to deal with, that evening. "That's all I can think of," Nuan said.

"Thank you both," Superintendent Ma said.

They returned to their desks.

"It's going to be odd to be your boyfriend again," Hu, or Wen, said quietly.

"Not too odd, I hope."

"We'll manage."

So far they had managed working together, but living together was going to be somewhat different. Nuan knew she had to go undercover for this case, but at the same time she wanted this to be over as quickly as possible. She went to the tea room to buy a milk coffee from the vending machine, and while she drank she thought. Everything she could think of was covered and they were only a half-hour away from the public security bureau anyway. *What could possibly go wrong?*

* * *

Nuan sat in the leather armchair while the ingredients for dinner were ready for her to cook. She heard the click as Dewai swiped his security card, before the door opened. She stood to face him.

"How was work?" Nuan offered.

"Good. Busy. And you?"

"I have something to tell you. Please sit and we'll talk."

He sat while Nuan gazed through floor to ceiling glass. "Office 1.10 has been given a new assignment, which will require me to be away from home for a time. I don't know for how long but this may be a few weeks. I'll be here in Guangzhou so I can contact you from time to time, but if ever you see me on the streets, ignore me. I'm sorry to leave you at short notice like this." Nuan shrugged her shoulders. She wanted to say more but the words weren't there. Then they were. "I love you and I'll miss you."

"I love you and I'll miss you too.'

Behind on the counter, dinner waited. Dinner could wait. Nuan stood to reach for his hand. He stood to let Nuan lead him to their bedroom. There she let his hand go to unbutton her blouse. She watched him watching her as she removed her blouse and then unfastened her bra.

Chapter Five

Liko's personal mobile rang but it wasn't a number in his contacts. He swiped his phone.

"Wéi," Liko greeted. *Hello.*

"This is our call for information from where you work. Office 1.10 if I'm not mistaken."

Liko gasped.

"What are you investigating?"

Liko wondered what to say. "I'm still working on the old Axe Gang case while others are doing something else, but I don't know what that is."

"You should find out."

"I don't want to be suspicious."

"Alright. We'll call again."

The call ended.

"Who was that," Biya asked.

Liko looked to his wife frowning. "Nothing," he said. "Just – nothing."

Liko knew Biya didn't believe him.

Chapter Six

Mai knew how to make rice porridge, or congee as they called it. So every morning she made rice porridge for four by cooking on a stove run by electricity. However the stove was run she knew how to make good, smooth, congee. When the porridge was almost ready Mai got four bowls from the bench to ladle it, before taking those bowls to the table, already set with pottery spoons and cups of tea. Mai sensed affection from Yuanfu, more as time went by. Little things like making congee brought a smile to his face, an affectionate touch of her arm, and just a sense that even though they were pretend-married, he now regarded her as his wife. Of course if Mai would leave she could. She hated Po Po, she hated not being able to communicate despite learning some of their language, but mostly she hated being away from home. She wanted to see her mother and her brothers again.

After breakfast, Yuanfu and Gong Gong set off for work while Mai washed the bowls, spoons, teacups, and the saucepan, before putting them all away. She knew to ask Po Po if anything needed to be done, but in a small house scrubbed clean there wasn't so much of that, except cleaning the house once a week, and washing, drying and ironing twice a week. When there was nothing Mai went to the square where she met Na and Hu most mornings. Without Na and Hu, Mai doubted she would be able to get by.

"How are you, Mai?" Na greeted.

"I'm good, and you both?"

"I'm good," Hu said. "Anything to report?"

"No, I'm fine. I cook for this household, I do all the work in the house, and I share a room with my husband, so I've settled into this routine. You two have your own houses?"

"We both do."

"Yuanfu is nice to me and I'm sure if I had my own house my life would be better. But I'm getting by. I have you both to thank for that."

"How?"

"You said not to fight it, so I didn't and that made a difference, especially with Yuanfu. Po Po is beyond redemption but Yuanfu likes me."

"Are you pregnant yet?" Hu asked.

"I had my period last week."

"Now I must warn you. Unless something is wrong you will fall pregnant, and if you give birth to a son, most likely they will take it from you and sell it."

Mai couldn't believe that. "Why?" she gasped.

"They can get back the money they spent on buying you through selling your son."

"That's wrong. How can a husband do this to his wife?"

"The next son you have you can keep."

"What if I have a daughter?"

"When you fall pregnant they will take you for a test. If it's a girl they will abort it."

Mai suddenly felt dizzy and would have fallen had Na not grabbed her. Slowly things came into focus.

"What is it with these people and daughters?" Mai asked.

"Sons are more valued than daughters where we come from," Na said.

"But not like this. If they don't have daughters they have nobody to marry," and then it hit Mai. "That's why we're here."

"That's right. With luck if you fall pregnant with a daughter, they may let you give birth to it."

Mai couldn't imagine Po Po ever doing anything decent. "I don't think so. How about you two?"

"I had a son but my husband's family sold it," Na said.

Mai grabbed her friend and hugged her. "I'm so sorry."

"Don't worry. We'll have another son and then I can keep my child."

"I'm pregnant," Hu said. "Normally that's a happy time, but not here."

"I'm sorry," Mai said. "Your family seems nice. If you're pregnant with a daughter you might have a child to keep."

"Maybe."

"But never in my family," Mai said.

"I know."

"If only I could speak with Yuanfu and talk him into having a daughter. Better if we had our own home instead of just a room. If only I could ask him to get his own house."

"If only we could speak their language instead of a few words," Na said.

That was their biggest problem. If Mai could run away she would, except she couldn't speak Chinese and she had no money, so she would never be able to get back to Vietnam so far away. She was stuck as good as if they put chains on her.

"If you could go, would you?" Mai asked Na.

"Yes."

"Even though your marriage is alright?"

"My husband is no worse than a Vietnamese husband, but I miss my family. I miss them terribly"

"Me too," Hu said.

"I feel the same," Mai said.

"Let's sit by the lake," Na said.

The lake was nicer than the square, especially with ducks swimming across the water leaving little trails. Mai wished she was a duck rather than a pretend-wife. They sat there for a long time before Mai realised she ought to get back to help with lunch. She bid her friends farewell before going home. Mai spent as much time outdoors as she could, not only to be with her friends but to be away from Po Po. Inside, Po Po told Mai to make spring rolls, which Mai did. While she cooked she didn't have to look at Po Po or even think about her, as she made those rolls and then fried them. By then Gong Gong and Yuanfu were back, so Mail set the table with bowls and chopsticks before brewing tea. When that was done she served those spring rolls into a bowl and carried them to the table. She then sat and ate too.

Yuanfu smiled brightly as he ate her spring rolls. Mai knew what that meant. He liked them and he was proud of his wife, or he liked his wife, or something like that. Even though Ma and Hu had their own homes, and even though their husbands most likely liked them too, both would go home tomorrow. Mai wondered if Chinese men realised the women they bought, despite being civil, just didn't like them. Yuanfu took Mai's hand affectionately, but still she would leave, even that day, if she could.

Later when they finished eating lunch, Mai stacked all plates in the kitchen to wash later. She sat beside Yuanfu to at least feel his affection as he held her hand once more. Then Po Po shouted at Mai. Eyes met eyes as this horrible woman wanted to come between husband and wife. Po Po dragged Mai to her feet while shouting, and then she slapped Mai. Mai stood there, shocked, as Po Po spoke at her fast while punching her. *What did she want?* Po Po slapped Mai again, that stung, as Mai backed away to the kitchen to avoid those punches and slaps. Again and again but Mai was hemmed by the bench with the stove and still Po Po hit her. Was anyone going to help her? The stinging and pain was terrible as Mai tried to get away from punches and slaps, but couldn't. Mai reached behind to feel the handle of a saucepan. She grabbed that saucepan and belted Po Po over the head. Po Po collapsed to the ground while Gong Gong raced to his wife and Yuanfu pulled Mai away to their room. There he closed the door.

Mai tried to make up the words. "What want?" she said in their language.

Yuanfu spoke fast.

Mai shook her head. "No understand."

Yuanfu put the palm of one hand flat and used the other hand to scrub it, and then Mai realised. Po Po wanted her to clean the plates there and then.

"Sorry," Mai said in Chinese while Yuanfu hugged her. "Sorry."

Po Po burst into the room to speak with Yuanfu, who pulled away from Mai while speaking loudly with his mother. Then he spoke to Mai who shook her head. Yuanfu took Mai to the front door and opened it, to take Mai to the laneway and point towards the square.

"Not there again," he said.

Mai understood. She wasn't allowed to see her friends just for protecting herself from Po Po's attack.

"Sorry," Mai said while Yuanfu took her inside. Now Mai was trapped inside with Po Po all day. Although it would be difficult Mai had no choice. Now she had to run away.

Yuanfu was always tired after he fucked Mai and always he slept well. Mai knew she wouldn't have to wait long, that night or the night after, because he fucked her every night or every second night, except for when they couldn't. In fact it was that night, and while Mai tried to get enjoyment from their fucking, that night she couldn't. She knew Yuanfu couldn't go against his parents wishes, not in their home and not if they had their own home. More, Yuanfu was understanding and protective when Po Po attacked her. But Mai had too many thoughts to ever get enjoyment. Indeed, Mai felt sorry that she couldn't make Yuanfu's experience nicer that night.

Later with Yuanfu fast asleep and bright moonlight flooding through cracks in their curtains, Mai used that light to dress before gathering her possessions, her other t-shirt, her other bra, her other panties, her other socks, to take them to the kitchen where she took one of the hessian bags they used to store rice. With that bag folded over, Mai crossed the stone floor, slowly opened the big door, and headed outside while carefully closing the door behind her. She went to the square, peaceful and still, before walking along the road they used that day in the truck. With so much moonlight Mai felt exposed as she left Fusi behind to trudge along a road bordered by rice paddies, before entering a forest. On and on through the forest and then returned to rice paddies again.

Mai was tired and sore from walking so she sat beside the road with her legs stretched over a gully for a while, until she was sufficiently recovered to continue her walk. Mai knew a little Chinese, not help but other words, so she might have a chance. Regardless, she had to leave Po Po. On and on Mai walked while remembering a town they passed shortly before they arrived at the village. At that town she might get help, from police even. To keep a woman prisoner was wrong and the police might help her, as Mai walked on and on to reach that town quiet and still at night. There was no point going further and she couldn't do anything late at night with everyone asleep. Mai found a lane beside a shop where all was peaceful. She unfolded her hessian bag as a kind of bed before lying down to sleep. In the morning she would get help but for now she would sleep.

* * *

Mai woke where light was much brighter than a full moon. She got up, rolled her bag, took her bearings, before heading along the lane to the road. There she stood to see a street market already trading. A little way along Mai saw a Chinese man in a blue uniform, surely he was police; enter a building, surely a police station. Mai followed this man to go inside where there was a timber counter, a timber bench to one side and the man at a desk while speaking on a mobile phone. Mai went to the counter until she finished his call.

Mai pointed to herself. "Ma Thi Mai," she said. "Vietnam."

The man looked surprised before speaking while Mai shook her head. He took his phone from his pocket to make a short call, before leading Mai outside and around the back of the building where there was a white car with a blue, zigzagged stripe. The policeman opened a door, Mai got inside and the policeman got inside too. Soon they were away but almost immediately Mai realised this was wrong.

"No," Mai said in Chinese.

But he kept on driving, all the way to the square in Fusi. There he made a call on his mobile, for moments later Yuanfu to be there. Yuanfu led Mai from the car, put his arm around her shoulder, apologised with "Sorry" as he took Mai to their house.

There inside Gong Gong looked as sorry as Yuanfu but not Po Po. First Po Po abused Yuanfu and then abused her husband, before grabbing Mai by her wrists and taking Mai into her room. Mai didn't resist because she didn't want to provoke Po Po further, even when Po Po pushed Mai down on her bed, undid her jeans, took them off and her panties too, and rolled her onto her face. There Mai lay with her heart running very, very fast.

The first lash across her bottom was shocking, terrible, and not a hand but something like a rope. No, the belt from a man's trousers. Again and again and again while Mai's bottom was on fire, worse and worse and worse, until Mai heard Gong Gong's raised voice and the blows stopped. They left Mai alone on that bed; face down in so much pain. Mai didn't want to die but she wondered what there was to live for. Po Po hated her, for what Mai didn't know, maybe because she came between mother and son. Maybe Mai was hated for just being there. But worse that they fucked every night or every second night, except when it was Mai's period. What for? If it was a son it would be taken while if it was a daughter it would be aborted. What sort of life was that? Mai wasn't going to kill herself but she didn't want to live like that. The only thought that brought comfort was that she tried to get away. It didn't work but she tried. Even her bottom burning hot didn't matter when she realised she tried.

Chapter Seven

Older apartment buildings, anything from five to ten stories, crowded streets and roads. Those streets and roads bustled with many shops, cheap restaurants, a wet market, and more. Looking up, airconditioners at many windows drained water from Guangzhou humidity onto streets below. It was busy, even exciting, and although living at an address in Renhe was looked down upon, Nuan felt that shouldn't be the case. Those buildings were basic but comfortably habitable, as were the many profitable small businesses. One of those businesses was Yabang Real Estate, where the proprietor led Nuan and Hu, or Lo and Wen, through what seemed like a maze until they reached a seven-storey building. There Liu held the doorway open for his potential customers to enter a white-painted foyer, but marked and stained. Nuan followed Liu up four flights of stairs to where he opened a door. In that building nobody stirred as they entered a basic, two bedroom apartment not too dissimilar to where Nuan lived until recently. A living room with a counter separating a small kitchen with a sink and cooktop, while through two doors were two bedrooms; sandwiching a bathroom with a shower, an Asian-style toilet, and a basin.

"This is good," Nuan said. Hu lived nearby so he would have known it was good, too. That apartment was just a bit grubby with stained white walls, while the carpet in the living room had seen better days. She expected that for the age of the building and the price of their rent.

Hu handed across 800 yuan as their first month's rent, while Nuan realised they could have haggled but she wasn't in the mood for it.

"Do you know any furniture removalists?" Nuan asked Liu.

"I'll send two men around," he said.

"Thank you."

Liu gave Hu the key while Nuan made a mental note to cut a copy for herself. The two, twenty-something men, tattooed and perhaps even triad, showed up shortly after. A few hours later her bed, lounge suite, stools for the counter, and a box of crockery, cutlery and cooking items, were relocated. By then Nuan had hung her clothes from her backpack, and secreted the new laptop in the wardrobe. Now sleeping arrangements.

"We'll buy some food now," Nuan said. "While we're out we'll find an inflatable mattress or something like that. We can take turns sleeping on the mattress and the bed."

"You can sleep on the bed," Hu said.

Nuan wanted to take turns, but she didn't want to argue with Hu so said nothing. Besides, an air mattress might not be so bad. There was one thing she wanted to know."

"Do you have a girlfriend, Hu?"

"No I don't. I know you have a new boyfriend, but girlfriends are harder to find."

That was true. Nuan knew Hu wasn't going to rape her or anything like that, but she would have preferred Hu to have a natural outlet for companionship, friendship and sex. That knowledge made their living together somewhat more awkward. Nuan sighed.

"Let's go," she said.

Down and down the stairs to buy the last of their requirements, after which they could explore the dark web.

* * *

Nuan sat on her old couch with Hu by her side. Already she was outside of the China firewall by using her favourite VPN, and now she waited for the install of Tor to complete. Less than 10% of the web was visible to normal users; the rest was encrypted, needing a special browser like Tor to access. Of that 90%, only a tiny proportion, well less than 1%, was truly 'dark' or illegal. That was the place Nuan intended to explore, and explore it would take. She opened Tor where from her notes, she typed the random series of letters that made up the URL of The Hidden Wiki. Page Not Found. Clearly the URL had changed, as was common in the Deep Web. Nuan searched for 'main page' in the Tor search engine to find it that way.

"What do you think, Hu?" Nuan asked. "Drugs or China?"

"Which tech-savvy user in China doesn't use the Deep Web?"

"I can but I don't," Nuan said. "There's enough for me inside the firewall, especially Weibo, not to bother with Deep Web discussion forums, or even using a VPN to get to Twitter or something like that. Do you use a VPN alone or with the Deep Web?"

"No I don't."

There. Nuan thought she would concentrate on drugs, starting with the first forum on the first page of The Hidden Wiki. There she got a terrible shock! She backed out.

"I wish we could do something about that," Hu said.

Nuan wished that too. Videos of men abusing girls, for girls they were, were too terrible. Protected by VPNs and encryption, a few bitcoins could get anything on the Dark Web, but to link that video to an actor producing such material, or other actors purchasing it, because without those purchases there wouldn't be a need for that product, was virtually impossible. Usually, arrests for buying illegal materials on the dark web came from conventional policing methods. Nuan went to the next forum where she discovered she could buy American social security numbers, but that wasn't what she wanted. She continued scrolling posts while thinking her brilliant plan was unravelling. She knew drugs were available, virtually to delivery, on the dark web, but that didn't mean triad were the retailers.

"You're thinking about something," Hu said.

"I'm thinking our Guangzhou-based triad groups might not even be here," Nuan said.

"That's possible, although if there's money to be made, then organised crime could be there. Triad bosses might be in their 50s, but their 49ers can be our ages. Some of those will be tech-savvy. We both know about the Shanghai drugs market which may still be operating."

"That was true," Nuan said while thinking. "This might take ages to find something, so we should do this in shifts. Instead of watching me, take a break. After a few hours you can take over. If after a few days we don't get anywhere, we'll buy drugs more conventionally."

"Being?"

"True Color on Saturday night." Nuan then giggled. "I just know how much you love to dance!"

"Buy some E?"

"Yes."

"That sounds like a plan," Hu said. "In the meantime while we're browsing here, if we see something really bad that we can do something about, like Chinese sexual abuse or Chinese sex slaves, we should make a note of it."

That was a good idea. No, that was a great idea. "We should, Hu."

"I'll go for a walk to clear my head."

Hu headed out while Nuan returned to browsing forums and markets, while thinking there were sick people out there. They turned beauty into ugly. Nothing on that forum, where really Nuan was looking for hanzi of which there was very little. So much drivel in various languages, but little Chinese. By the time Hu returned, Nuan really needed to take a break to clear her head. Then she saw it.

"I found a site in hanzi," Nuan said, as she scrolled posts. "What's this?"

Hu sat beside. "That's Singapore-based and a market for drugs," he said.

It was too. Heroin, cocaine, ice, ecstasy, GHB, ketamine, fentanyl: the usual suspects. Nuan went on and on but found nothing but selling, buying and bitcoins. She reached the end, exhausted. She handed the laptop to Hu.

"Two issues there," Hu said. "One is they could be fake, that is pay a few bitcoins but get nothing delivered, and the other is we don't know if the sellers are triad-type ice manufacturers. On the other hand if that is legit, it could be the Singapore equivalent of what we're looking for."

"Could be," Nuan said. "Your turn; I need a break."

Nuan powered up her personal smartphone to send a text. 'Be home in half an hour for a few hours. Interested?' She sent it. Seconds later the answer. Ha! Nuan felt uplifted, although a little sad that Hu hadn't yet found love.

"I must go," Nuan said.

"Enjoy."

Did he really mean that? Nuan headed out the door while thinking that although they made a minor breakthrough with that Singaporean drug market, the most likely next step for their operation will be True Color on Saturday night.

Chapter Eight

Mai was well overdue which meant only one thing. After dinner they always watched television, and later went to their room, where Mai didn't know that word in Chinese. She knew how to show, though.

"Cev xeeb tub," Mai said while using her hand to show a pretend growing stomach.

A big smile from Yuanfu. "How long?"

"Six or eight."

"Weeks?"

"Yes." Mai grabbed his arm. "Kuv xav kom nws," she said.

Yuanfu looked really confused while Mai searched for the right words.

"Keep baby," she said.

He shrugged his shoulders.

"Please."

Mai decided to bribe him. While he watched she took her t-shirt off and her bra too, before her jeans. Then she took his t-shirt off and loosened his jeans where he was already hardening. It was safe when pregnant, at least until the very end, so Mai decided to do that really nicely to make him like her. Make Yuanfu like her enough to not abort her or sell their child. When Mai removed her panties, Yuanfu literally picked Mai up, her arms wrapped around his strong shoulders and her legs wrapped around his waist, while his erection grazed her bottom. Yuanfu carried Mai to their bed like that, laid her down like that, and with Mai still holding him like that he filled her. She stayed like that, close and loving, all the way until he came and then she kissed his cheek. She hoped that would be enough as he buried his head between her breasts while still she held him tight to her.

Chapter Nine

At 11 in the evening, True Color could be described in one word: purple! An older style building in stucco, bathed in purple light with a queue at the door. Nuan, dressed in her new, black minidress tight across her upper body and frilly from her waist, joined that queue with Hu. To get into a club like True Color you had to be passed by the security guards, but Nuan knew, dressed as she was, she had no problems with that. Indeed, guards beckoned Nuan and Hu, or Lo and Wen, inside to more purple! Music, dancing, happiness, showgirls in leotards dancing on stages and around poles, and more happiness. The showgirls were European which was one thing Nuan didn't like about True Color. If Chinese girls were half their customers then Chinese girls were pretty enough to dance as their entertainment. Never mind, Nuan went to the bar where, with loud music, she had to bend close to speak. She asked for a gin and tonic and a beer while handing over 40 yuan. She got two glasses, where she gave the beer to Hu who looked out of place. Nuan knew clubs weren't his thing. Nuan moved away from the bar to give others a chance to order, while discreetly surveying the crowd as she sipped her drink through a straw. The queue for the ladies was her best bet. Nuan gave her drink to Hu to mind before easing away to join that queue, where one young woman stood discreetly to one side. Nuan reached into her cross-shoulder bag for a loose bundle of notes, and peeled two away. She drifted close to the young woman to place two 100 yuan notes in her hand. The woman placed a small packet in Nuan's hand. Nuan moved closer.

"I want to talk with you," Nuan shouted in the young woman's ear over the noise of the music.

The woman pulled back so Nuan peeled away two more notes and held them high. The young woman snatched those notes before heading to the ladies with Nuan following. Inside was crowded but there was an empty stall. They squashed in.

"I want your dealer," Nuan whispered in her ear.

"Why?"

"I'm a party girl, like you."

"You're not police?"

Nuan took the packet, stuck her tongue out to put one tablet on the end, and swallowed. She opened her mouth to stick her tongue out with a bright smile as the MDMA took effect. Awesome! The young woman smiled brightly too.

"Alright," the young woman said.

Nuan reached into her bag for the small pad and pen she placed there earlier. The young woman wrote quickly. Nuan read a name, Peng, and a mobile number.

"Thank you," Nuan said. "Great stuff too!"

"It's the best."

"Enjoy your night."

"You too."

Nuan danced her way out of the ladies ready to really dance! Fuck if Hu didn't like dancing, there were plenty of guys and girls who did!

"What have you been up to?" Hu shouted in Nuan's ear.

Nuan felt like kissing him and only massive self control prevented that from happening. "I have what we need," she shouted back.

"Now we can go?"

"You can go; I'm staying."

It was typical that men stood around in groups or ogled girls, and especially ogled heavy-built European showgirls, while women danced alone. Nuan danced her way into what seemed like a group of girlfriends, but she felt so happy she knew they wouldn't mind her joining. She liked men, not women except as friends, but she felt like hugging and kissing them all! One tablet and every single happiness gene in her body was ignited. True Color bathed in purple, loud music, and a happy crowd dancing the night away. What more could a girl ask for, expect that other E? It took great self control, almost as much self control as to not molest her dance partners, to leave that tablet in its packet still in her hand.

* * *

Nuan rolled out of bed, went to the bathroom and splashed her face. She felt a bit down which she guessed was the after-effect of that ecstasy. Still in her pyjamas, although short they

61

were decent and actually showed less leg than the night before, Nuan crossed the kitchen to switch on the kettle.

"Making a coffee?" Hu asked.

"I'll make you one."

"Thanks."

Nuan took two mugs to spoon coffee and sugar into both. The kettle switched off, so she poured and stirred. She sat at a stool.

"What happened last night?" Hu asked.

"I got details of a dealer," Nuan said before sipping her coffee. "We're undercover so I went deep undercover."

"Ah. How was it?"

"Nice. I like nightclubs, I like dancing, but it was – more."

"Be careful."

"I know."

"Does your boyfriend dance?"

"Not so much. My best friend from school does, and her boyfriend. And Jia."

"Really?"

"Jia's awesome! I took a tablet to get a name and number, but I don't need drugs to be happy dancing with my friends. It was a nice experience, I won't deny that, but I don't need that."

"I'm glad."

"What did you do last night?" Nuan asked.

"Mostly I watched you. Then I came home."

Nuan didn't quite know what to say, but then thought. "I think we were too young," she said. "You don't know what you don't know, until you find it, if that makes sense."

"So you're happy?"

"I was never unhappy with you, but now is more intense. More that you can wrap your fingers around it and hold it in your hands. More than you can squeeze it tight and never let it go." Nuan thought more. "Perhaps there's a lesson to be learned."

"I know what you're implying. I don't know what you know, but now I know to look for, whatever that is."

"Love."

"We were great friends."

Nuan giggled. "We still are great friends and I hope we always will be."

"Yes we are, Lo," he said.

"That's right, Wen," she said. Nuan finished her coffee. "Stay here and I'll get my mobile. You can listen in."

Nuan went to the bedroom to rummage through her small bag. She returned to the stool with her pad in one hand and her smartphone in the other. Feeling a little breathless, she dialled the number.

"Wéi."

"Wéi, Peng. I was given your name by a girl at a nightclub."

"And...?"

"I'm a party girl like her, but my income covers only so much partying."

"What can you offer my other girls can't?"

"Meet me and we can talk this through."

"Alright. Als Gong Cha in Renhe in one hour."

"I'll be dressed in blue. Blue blouse, blue jeans and a blue cap."

He ended their call and only then did Nuan realise her heart was racing. She put her phone down.

"I'm to meet Peng at Als Gong Cha here in Renhe," Nuan said. "He must live nearby." She thought. "I'll shower first."

Nuan went to the bedroom where she closed the door to undress and shower. She decided not to wash her hair, just brush it, so it didn't take so long to shower away her tiredness. If she felt down when she woke that was gone by the time she went to the living room to wait for Hu to shower. Dressed in blue with a blue peaked cap, her favourite colour and also something Peng would recognise. Hu emerged in jeans and a black t-shirt over white runners, which was a look that did him no favours. They headed downstairs and outside to mid-morning Sunday somewhat less busy than other days of the week.

"You go in first," Nuan now instructed Hu. "Get a table near the back to watch over us. I'll follow a bit after you to sit nearer the window."

"Alright."

They reached the distinctive burgundy-coloured facade of Als Gong Cha where Hu went inside to darkness while Nuan studied specials on a blackboard on the footpath. After a few moments she went to the counter to order and pay for her favourite, a flat white, before taking a table near the door. The decor was simple with a glass-fronted timber counter, and polished timber tables, chairs and benches. Nuan's coffee arrived, so she slowly sipped her drink. Nuan was half-finished when a young man, like Hu in jeans and a dark t-shirt, took the timber chair opposite. He put out his hand to shake, where Nuan stood to notice tattoos on his forearms and around his neck. Not a guarantee but promising.

"Peng," he said.

"Lo," she replied.

They both sat.

"What can you offer?" Peng asked.

"Any nightclub, any night of the week."

"I'm short of sellers at Xi Gong."

Nuan sipped some coffee. "I can do there." She put her coffee down.

"E is 40 yuan a tablet, two per packet. Clearly you know the price and your cut."

"I do. How many can you supply?"

"Twenty packs per delivery."

"Pay now?"

"We'll do this out the back."

"Alright." Nuan finished her coffee. "I'm a party girl so only E for me, but I might be able to move other product during the day."

"Ice?" Peng asked.

"Ice users are losers, but if they want I'll sell it."

"Where do you live?"

"Not far from here. Give them my number and we can do it near my place."

"Let's go."

Peng led the way to the busy street, then along a lane between a clothing shop and a budget hotel. Further around to a lane running parallel to the street of shops. There Peng reached into his rear pockets for two bundles of small bags tied together with elastic bands. Nuan reached into her bag for the wad of yuan notes, where she counted 16, 100 yuan notes. She exchanged her money for the two bundles where she counted 10 each. She put those bundles into her bag and zipped it.

"What about ice?" Nuan asked.

"Five hundred yuan per gram, 10 grams per bag."

Street price was 560 to 600, which was fair. "I'll take two bags."

"Here in one hour."

"Alright."

Peng put out his hand which Nuan shook.

"Do you have a boyfriend?" he asked.

Nuan pondered her response. "I have a friend but we're not attached, if that's what you want to know."

"You're a free agent."

"I am but I'm picky."

Nuan touched his smooth face with the tips of her fingers. He took her hand and put her forefinger in his mouth to suck. Nuan wondered if she was going too far. She let him suck her for a while before easing her hand out of his grasp.

"One hour here," she said, before turning for home.

By the time Nuan returned to busier Sunday crowds, she spotted Hu's dark t-shirt ahead. She followed him home.

"Done," Nuan said. "I have 20, two-tablet packs of E, and I've ordered ice. I'll meet him in an hour to take delivery."

"Did he look triad?"

"He had tattoos on both arms and it seemed he had tattoos on his upper body. One thing, he's interested in me."

"No surprises there!" Hu exclaimed.

Nuan removed her cap before shaking her head to get her ponytail to hang straight. Sexual attraction could be handy but Nuan would never go that far for a case.

"I'll string him along as much as I can, or I'll bring you in as my boyfriend." Nuan frowned while she thought. "Now I need to call someone."

She scrolled her contacts before selecting one. It rang twice before Jia answered.

"Wéi Jia," Nuan greeted.

"Wéi Nuan, or should I say Lo."

"Call me Lo. I don't have much time but I've made a contact. Track this number and monitor his calls: 173 8822 9617. He goes by the name of Peng. If you hear him speaking about Lo, that's obviously me. Let me know if he does."

"I will, and congratulations for this."

"Thank you. Sorry about this being Sunday."

"That's alright. I'll go in now and set it up."

"Thanks."

"Be careful."

Jia ended the call. Nuan glanced at the time on her smartphone. "Hu, follow me. The deal is in the same place, and after we'll have lunch in the cafe."

"Are you good with this?" Hu asked.

"I don't like dealing ice, but I took the decision to buy in order to establish his relationship to the drug. If this goes well, the minute we've connected him to someone useful, we're out of here. Just, disappear."

"I understand."

Nuan then thought of another option rather than just disappearing. She decided to keep that in the back of her mind, as flirting with Peng was an option for her, although she suspected a young criminal like Peng wouldn't have much patience before he expected results for his efforts. Nuan counted 20,000 from the stash under her mattress to stuff into her bag, slipped her cap on; then headed out with Hu now trailing. Peng waited in the same lane, so Nuan unzipped her bag while walking to hand him the wad of notes. He quickly counted before reaching into the back pockets of his jeans for two packets of white crystals. Innocent-looking yet terrible.

"For a party girl you're well resourced," Peng said.

"That's from my friend who's not really my boyfriend," Nuan said while she put the packets into her bag and zipped it. His capital and we split the profit. The E at Xi Gong will be ongoing, but this ice might be once-off. That's his call, not mine."

"But you're still available?"

Nuan rubbed his smooth cheek again. "Remember I'm picky. I'll call you when I need more E. Zài jiàn." *See you later.*

Nuan left along the lane between the clothing store and the budget hotel, aware Peng's eyes were on her. So far so good. Nuan met Hu in the cafe looking forward to eating, given she hadn't got around to breakfast. But in her bag safely on their table, Nuan was well aware of 20 packets of E and two packets of ice inside.

Chapter Ten

Baby Face had two clubs where Xi Gong was for younger people. Like True Color, Nuan's favourite, purple was the theme at Xi Gong. Seven nights a week they partied at the nightclubs of Guangzhou, all dressed in their best, girls in their shortest best, with Nuan staked just beyond the end of the bar while looking as anonymous as possible. She didn't know who else dealt for Peng so she had to go through the motions, and even sell if someone slipped a couple of hundred yuan into the palm of her hand. That didn't happen very often but she couldn't afford to make a fuss. After a few hours of that, logically sales were earlier in the night anyway; Nuan had a chance to dance. Western guys were more of a feature of Xi Gong, and were more ready to dance than Chinese guys. Better that Nuan studied English to university level which made their initial greetings flow more naturally, and also allowed Nuan to set her rule of a dance only. That rarely stopped them from trying to pick her up when their dance was over.

After a few hours of dancing to make her night worthwhile, Nuan got to bed by about three or four in the morning. Sleep came easy to rise by about midday. There Nuan noticed a missed call from Jia; she slept straight through the racket, so she returned it.

"Wéi Lo," Jia greeted.

"Wéi Jia. Sorry about missing your call."

"What have you been up to?"

"My cover is a party girl selling E at a nightclub, so I'm going through the motions of that each night. I also bought some ice from Peng but I haven't had a buyer contact me yet. I have a plan to deal with my ice by not selling it through Peng. It'll take a day or so before I can execute that."

"So Peng deals ice?"

"Absolutely he does. How have the traces on his calls gone?"

"Mostly personal calls and a few from girls wanting refills of E."

"Soon I'll throw the E I bought away, and then I'll buy more so he isn't suspicious. When you hear me call him, you'll know what that's about."

"I understand. Superintendent Ma wants you and Hu to stay undercover for now, and even if Peng is triad he'll probably keep you undercover just in case."

Nuan didn't really want that but she had to do her duty. Besides, Jia was more than capable of handling the technical side of their investigations. "That's fine," Nuan said.

"I'll call when we come across something."

Jia ended the call. Clearly Superintendent Ma recognised the three university graduates formed a team within his taskforce, so he made the Jia her handler. Nuan looked at the date of her smartphone: Tuesday. She'd lost track of time!

Three days was long enough. She scrolled her contacts to find Peng and then called him.

"Wéi Lo," he greeted.

"Wéi Peng. I need a refill of E."

"Same place, one hour."

"Alright. One other thing; I sold the ice and I won't need any more."

"I understand. One hour."

He hung up.

"We're going out to buy more drugs, Hu."

"Do you realise how that sounds?"

"That's why I said it!"

Nuan went to her stash to count 16 notes to stuff in her bag. She headed through weekday crowds to eventually end up in that sequence of lanes where Peng waited. Nuan unzipped her bag to retrieve the bundle of notes to hand to Peng, who then reached into his pockets to give the packets to Nuan, who counted before slipping them in her bag and zipping it closed.

"I called around last night," Peng said. "I saw you sell, then move to dancing with a Westerner."

Indeed Nuan had sold last night.

"I got the impression you speak English well," Peng said.

"I do."

"Did he take you to his place?"

"Remember, I'm picky."

"What does it take?"

"If you're asking me then you don't know."

Peng crossed his arms. "You're just a cock-tease like all beautiful women," he snapped at her.

Nuan tilted her head while she contemplated Peng, for who she didn't feel the slightest attraction, but like all men, like Hu even, had to deal with women having the upper hand. "I do apologise if that's your impression," Nuan said. "For me it takes love, and love is one of those things you can't force."

"Can I make you love me?"

"We could fall in love, and if we do then nothing will be off limits."

"How?"

A breeze blew, swirling old newspapers and rubbish. "This isn't the place. Come with me to the cafe and I'll buy you a coffee."

They went to the cafe where Nuan ordered and paid for two flat whites, before leading Peng to a table. After taking their seats, the waitress placed two cups. Nuan sipped.

"Do you have a girlfriend?" she asked.

He shook his head.

"Have you had a girlfriend in the past?"

"It didn't work."

"I'm sorry about that. You know Yin and Yang, the two complimentary forces. Well, women aren't entirely Yin or feminine and passive, but rather women have more Yin than Yang. Not only that, but the balance of Yin and Yang is different in each woman. You might say I have a bit more Yang than many women. Men aren't entirely Yang either, so what attracts me is the man who wraps around me, who has more Yin than most other men, to compliment my more Yang than most other women. Does this make sense?"

"I think so, yes."

"So power and money doesn't do it for me, rather the man who's in tune with his emotions like I'm in tune with my – abilities."

"Perhaps that's what I find attractive in you."

"Perhaps it is," Nuan said, although she knew the real reason lay elsewhere. For a long time she thought she wasn't anything special, just another ordinary Chinese girl, but when she was dating and later when she met Dewai, she realised that wasn't the case. She was tall for a woman her age, fair, well-proportioned, presented herself with clothes and shoes that suited her, and that attracted men well before they knew the real Shui Nuan.

"You strike me as a man who knows what's what, so perhaps your best match is the woman who wants to be pampered and spoiled," Nuan said. "If you know a woman who's more Yin to suit your more Yang, then you might find love."

"I know a woman a bit like that," he said.

"If a woman fits as your complimentary half, then little things like taller or shorter, or darker or fairer, don't matter."

Nuan finished her coffee. She stood. "Zài jiàn."

"Zài jiàn."

Nuan left Peng to contemplate the passive woman he could pamper and spoil, if he had the resources for that. After talking love with Peng, that rekindled memories of her man so close yet so far away. At that moment Nuan would have given anything for intelligent conversation, or better, one of Dewai's spur of the moment massages when he sensed her tension. Nuan missed love and hoped they would be together, in love, soon.

Chapter Eleven

Jia contemplated the map on the screen connected to her laptop. Li Peng lived at Baiyun Qu, and spent most of his time in and around Renhe District. He had very few personal calls, mostly calls from various women dealing in the clubs of Guangzhou. One of those mobile towers he connected to might be the contact for Peng to pick up product, and another might be where he supplied his girls. Jia had an idea. She scrolled her contacts on her police mobile to select Nuan.

"Wéi Jia," Nuan answered wearily.

"Wéi Lo," Jia greeted. "Can you talk?"

"Yes I can."

"I'm tracking Peng's movements. Where do you usually buy from him?"

"In a lane at the back of Als Gong Cha in Renhe. I expect most of his girls see him there."

"Thanks," Jia said. "Are you alright," she then asked; worried by the weariness in Nuan's voice.

"I'm fine, just tired. I now know Peng checks up on us, so I have to keep going every night which is taking it out of me."

"Can you take a break?"

"Not tonight; Friday night's busy. Saturday too."

"Sunday?"

"I'll take a break on Sunday."

Jia was worried about something else. "How's Dewai?"

"Yeah, I know. I'll text Dewai from my own mobile for a date on Sunday. When I see him I'll tell him more about what I'm doing undercover in a general way, but I won't tell him about Hu. Hu's fine but few would understand."

"How is Hu?" Jia asked.

"There's not a lot for him to do, except watch over me when I buy, but there's not a risk with that. No question we need the two of us undercover, and no question Hu's the right person for this. I'm sure he'll appreciate a break on Sunday too." Silence for a moment. "We had a chance to talk," Nuan said. "Not that there's ever been any awkwardness, but now he understands what happened between us, and the difference with what I have now. So that was a good opportunity."

Jia thought that was a great opportunity.

"Jeans don't look good on men, don't you think?"

Jia wondered what that was about, but Nuan was right. "No they don't. Look after yourself, Lo. I'll expect you to be off-line on Sunday."

"That's for sure!" Nuan exclaimed. "Zài jiàn."

"Zài jiàn."

"How are things?" Superintendent Ma asked which gave Jia a shock. She wondered how much of that conversation he heard. "Li Peng is monitoring his dealers so Sergeant Shui is committed to working every night. This is tiring for her, as you can imagine, so I suggested she take a night off. Sunday when it's quiet."

"Good idea. Anything else?"

Jia turned to her screen. "These are the towers Li Peng has connected to, where this one is near where he supplies drugs to his nightclub girls. I think we've gone as far as we can go from here."

"Now we should get on the street. There's no car registered for Li Peng so he must use public transport. We'll follow him around as best we can and see where that takes us. You and Constable Zuo to start. The usual: radios with earpieces, throat microphones and push to talk; pistols and extendable batons."

Jia turned to her screen to bring up the satellite image of Li Peng's apartment building. Close-ups showed an older-style building with barred windows, as was typical for Renhe. The only way in or out would be through the front door. Jia moved the image with her mouse and then zoomed it back.

"This building here," Jia said while pointing. "It's opposite Li Peng's building. We'll monitor the doorway of his building from across the street. I could start this now."

"You and Constable Zuo now, with Sergeant Kam with Constable Tang to relieve you at eight this evening. Sergeant Suo and I will monitor your radios and provide support from here."

Superintendent Ma spoke briefly to Constable Zuo Huang, Jia's usual partner where they formed a good team, unlike Sergeant Kam Liko and Constable Tang Bo together. Jia was younger than Huang but in charge, while Huang followed orders but also made suggestions, which Jia really appreciated. They had a good blend of university theory and hands-on practical experience. They went to the armoury to check-out what they needed, then caught the bus to Renhe and close to Jia's home.

The apartment building where Li Peng lived had a facade of chipped white porcelain tiles, a square arch over the entrance in bright yellow, with double glass doors left open. Ground floor apartments were protected from the street by barred windows. The foyer was carpeted in dark green, with a concrete staircase painted in a lighter shade of green. The apartment building opposite was of a similar style, except for a facade in plain brick and the apartment name in red on a wooden backing. Once more, double glass doors were left wide open. One bonus was the foyer had a grubby, floral couch in shades of brown. Jia sat with Huang, before reaching for her smartphone. She scrolled her gallery until she found the picture she wanted.

"This is Li Peng," Jia said as she showed his ID picture to Huang.

"Low-level drug dealer extraordinaire!" Huang exclaimed. "How many girls does he have working for him?"

"That we don't know but I'm sure he has many. But as you know we're not interesting in low-hanging fruit like Li Peng and his girls."

"We're after his bosses, bosses, boss."

"Yes we are, so now we wait."

"At least we have comfort in a relative sense."

There they waited as a never-ending stream of pedestrians strolled by, and a few cars cruised by too, but fortunately that wasn't a busy street for motor traffic.

"Is that him?" Huang asked.

Jia looked up; then checked the picture on her smartphone still in her hand. "Yes it is."

She got up, and with Huang by her side, joined the swarm of pedestrians as she followed a young man, age 24 or one year older than she, dressed in jeans, a black t-shirt and runners. Li Peng strode purposefully, zipping past slower moving pedestrians while Jia and Huang did likewise, as Jia tried to look as inconspicuous as possible. On and on around a corner, along another street; then around another corner with the burgundy facade of Als Gong Cha just ahead.

"This is where he supplies his girls," Jia said quietly to Huang. "Don't follow him."

Li Peng disappeared up a lane, while Jia led Huang past that lane to the blackboard in front of the cafe. There Jia pretended to read the specials over and over while keeping one eye on the laneway. A few minutes later an attractive young woman in tight jeans came from the lane, followed by Li Peng. Once more into crowds but Jia guessed the route, back to his home. As he went inside, Jia and Huang sat on the grubby couch opposite. Jia thought Nuan's observation was spot-on: the right cut of jeans looked great on women but never looked good on men.

"What are you thinking about?" Huang asked.

"Jeans."

"I don't like jeans," Huang said. "Great on women but not for men."

"Are you into fashion?" Jia asked.

"I like to look smart in my free time. It doesn't take much to look good, and doesn't cost much either. And you? You always look good."

"Thank you. Work is slacks and a blouse, and a jacket to hide our weapons. I like this leather jacket. Weekends might be jeans and a t-shirt, but like you said, we women can do that."

"Yes you can. You're from somewhere else, aren't you?"

"I was recruited from Fuzhou, although rescued would be a better description. After four years in Beijing, I just couldn't come to terms with my home city. But Guangzhou! I totally love this place!"

"Yeah, it's got everything. Daytime, night time, the lot. Nuan's undercover in clubs, isn't she?"

"Yes she is, with Hu."

"Do you like clubs and dancing?" Huang asked.

"Of course."

"Me too."

Jia pondered her partner. He was a few years older, but when it came to men, that was better. "Do you go to clubs much?" she asked.

"A couple of times a month. And you?"

"I haven't clubbed much until recently. Nuan invited me where I met her boyfriend, and her school friend and her boyfriend. We had a great time. We've done that a few times since then." Jia thought. "When this case is over, or when we've gone beyond Nuan working undercover, would you be interested one night?"

"That would be great!"

Jia realised she just invited Huang on a date, at sometime in the future. That was cool. Then Jia had an idea for later. She took her phone out, checked her time, a few hours to go. They sat there and sat there and sat there as crowds got busier and busier with people heading home.

"Nothing's as good as surveillance," Huang said sarcastically. "Although as a former constable on street patrols, this job in Office 1.10 is fantastic. You wouldn't have done much patrolling."

"During semester breaks we patrolled in Beijing, and part of our assessment was three months full-time patrolling in Beijing. After I graduated, I did a month of patrolling in

Fuzhou before I came here. I know enough about regular policing to realise Office 1.10, even when you're waiting for something to happen, is just incredible."

"Incredible, fantastic; however you want to describe it."

Darkness gradually descended on that cool season day. Crowds lessened to almost nothing. Jia checked the time on her smartphone where Liko and Bo would be relieving them shortly.

"Huang," Jia said. "Do you have anything planned for this evening?"

"No I don't."

"I live near here," Jia said. "I'm going home to cook, but I could cook for two."

"Would that be any bother?" Huang asked.

"Not unless it upsets your plans."

"I don't have any plans."

Jia wanted to know more. "Do you need to tell anyone?"

"I'm sharing a place with a couple of friends. I'll text them so they won't worry."

Jia's heart ran faster and faster and faster. Huang effectively lived on his own, he accepted a date to club with her which showed he was available, and Jia had always liked him; especially since they were first partnered with each other. Not send her into orbit like she saw with Nuan and Dewai, but a girl could do a lot worse than Zuo Huang.

Just then Liko and Bo entered the grubby foyer. Jia stood to check, but there wasn't anyone around to overhear.

"We're staying here until about midnight," Liko said. "We know nothing happens before nine each morning."

From his phone movements, they knew that. "We'll get here at eight-thirty tomorrow morning," Jia said.

"If that's the case, we'll be here at four-thirty tomorrow afternoon."

"Zài jiàn."

Jia and Huang headed along a near-deserted street, cool in the evening. Even though it was Renhe, it was magnificent.

"This is the best time of the day," Huang said.

"I was thinking the same thing," Jia said. "Have you had Fujian cuisine before?"

"No I haven't."

"I've got something special planned for you."

"That sounds great."

Jia walked on with Huang by her side. Everything started from something, like surveillance with time to talk and to get to know each other better. Where things might go was really up to – mutual attraction. Something like that.

Chapter Twelve

Jia locked the door of her apartment before joining Huang on the landing.

"From now on, Detective-Sergeant Xiong Jia, we're on a professional basis."

"That's right, Detective-Constable Zuo Huang."

Down and down they walked.

"You must have come across this sort of thing before?" Jia asked.

"Yes, a few times. Usually men are more senior, but you have your degree in everything policing which is fair enough. I've never seen this turn into a problem; besides, if we can't make this work then no couple can."

They reached the bottom, where Huang held the door for Jia to enter early weekend morning streets somewhat quieter than a weekday. The morning after had no awkwardness, apart from Huang going downstairs to buy underwear and socks while Jia cooked breakfast for two. The night before she cooked gua bao, while Huang leaned against her kitchen counter as they talked about their respective pasts. Then they shared her meal, only when it was time to go, somebody hugged and kissed somebody. That part was a bit of a blur but it happened, as did her bed. Jia had a past so she didn't think twice about sex on her first date with Huang, as she didn't think twice about sex on her first date with an ex-boyfriend who then tried to take over her life before she got rid of him. For now, Huang was probably going to be a regular visitor to her apartment; they had a date to go clubbing sometime in the future, while beyond that Jia wanted to take things step by step. Everything started from something. One thing: Jia knew: Huang wouldn't try to take over her life. That was a good thing.

They reached the foyer with the grubby couch. Jia sat with Huang beside,

"Now we wait," she said.

"Indeed we do," Huang said. "What's today?" he asked.

"Saturday."

"True Color tonight?" Huang asked.

"My place, a meal, True Color."

"That's a date."

Saturday grew ever busier with more shoppers, as Jia kept her gaze focussed on Li Peng's apartment building, but focussed in a relaxed way. If she knew Zen Meditation or something similar, then being alert but relaxed to last the whole day would have been easier to do. Jia wondered if she should take lessons, given detectives sometimes, or often, watched and waited for hours on end. Then she spotted him!

"Huang," she said,

"I see him."

Once more Li Peng wore a dark t-shirt, jeans and white runners, although this t-shirt was not quite black; like black in the past but many washes in the meantime. Once more Li Peng strode fast through the crowd which was difficult to follow. On and on; Jia knew where he was going.

"Renhe Metro Station is down there."

Huang nodded while Jia knew their surveillance was now going to be difficult. Li Peng headed straight to the metro station, a steel-roofed, glass-walled shelter on a wide footpath, and amongst swarms of Saturday shoppers, he climbed three steps, and then stepped onto the escalator to descend. Jia, with Huang by her side, stepped onto that escalator with Li Peng three steps in front.

"Have you done this before?" Jia asked.

"No, never."

"The theory is stay alert, keep in communication, and don't stress because you can't do better than you best."

"Understood."

"I'm certain he's heading south. North is to the airport."

"Understood."

Down and down they went to the underground forecourt, where Jia reached into the inside pocket of her jacket for her Yang Cheng Tong card to have it ready, while momentarily revealing her pistol and her extendable baton! She followed Li Peng across the forecourt where he swiped his card to open a gate. Almost in parallel she swiped her card to open a gate; then he crossed the forecourt to the south platform, as Jia expected. There, travellers gathered while a blast of wind announced a train approaching. The silver, blue and red train burst out of the tunnel to stream past and stop sharply. Jia stood a few metres from Li Peng as doors peeled open, and never keeping her eyes from Li she stepped onto the train with standing room only, fortunately with Huang by her side. Doors peeled closed and the train moved away, but her vision was blocked.

Jia put her hand in her pocket for her PTT. "Can you see him?"

"I can," Huang said.

"I can't see him, so communicate."

"He's holding a handrail a distance from the door."

"If he's a distance from the door, we'll have time to respond."

"Understood."

Station stop after station stop after station stop; more and more packed commuters into the train.

"Huang?"

"Still holding."

"Understood."

They stopped at Yantang Station where Jia suspected something. She pressed her PTT. "Li may get off or change at the next stop: Guangzhou East."

"That will be difficult."

"We can't do better than our best."

The train moved away now quite packed.

"He's moving to the door," Huang said.

"Understood," Jia replied.

Jia squeezed, or actually forced her way through the crowd to get to the door. Still the train sped on, until noise changed. They slowed. Now right at the door, the train stopped and the door peeled open. Jia stepped onto the platform with hundreds of others. She followed the crowd to the escalator and up.

She pressed the PTT. "I have him in sight."

"I see you."

"He's heading right to Line One."

"Can't see but I'm heading right."

Huang was doing all the right things, like he always did. There the passage ended at the Line One platform, the terminus of that line. A train waited.

"Li Peng entered the train. I'm entering one door along."

"I see him. I see you."

Huang popped on, right next to Jia. Well done! Only then did Jia realised her heart was running extra, extra fast. But so far so good.

Announcement, doors peeled closed and they were on their way.

"I see him," Jia said.

"I see him too."

Like before Li Peng was a distance from the door, so like before they would have time to move when he moved. Station stop after station stop after station stop.

"I still have him in sight," Jia said.

"Me too."

They moved away from Marty's Park Station.

"Li Peng is moving to the door," Huang said.

"I see him," as Jia pushed her way through the crush. Right to the door as they slowed for Peasant Movement Institute Station. Doors peeled open for about 30 or 40 commuters to step out.

"Heading right," Jia said.

"I see him."

Through the exit gates which sprung open automatically, then to the escalator and up and up and up. To Zongshan Fifth Road; what a surprise! Huang came beside, as they now strode side by side with a faded black t-shirt a little way ahead.

"This must be his destination," Jia said to Huang. "We'll follow him inside, and into a lift to see which button he presses. It'll be too suspicious to get off at his floor."

"I understand."

"Hold my hand like my boyfriend," Jia said, as she straightened her jacket to better hide her weapons.

At number 70, a towering, L-shaped skyscraper, Li Peng strode past shops and cafes to glass doors which glided open. He crossed the tall, polished granite foyer with his footsteps muffled by thick, red carpet, to the lifts where he pressed the 'up' button. Still holding hands, Jia walked alongside to wait while looking as innocent as possible. Lift doors sprung open just along; Jia and Huang followed Li Peng inside. He pressed '22' so Jia pressed '24'. Up and up and up. At floor 22 the lift eased to a halt, doors slid open and Li Peng left. Doors closed and they were on their way to floor 24 where doors slid open. Jia stepped onto a granite tiled corridor where she looked up at the ceiling.

"No security cameras," she said.

"I know."

Jia took out her smartphone to take a couple of pictures of the corridor. "Floor 22 will be the same as this, for what that's worth." She put her phone away. "Let's go downstairs and hide somewhere. We'll see how long he takes."

Huang pressed the 'down' button, for the same doors to open. In the lift he pressed 'G' and down they went.

Jia leaned against a mirrored wall while the lift hurtled downwards. "We know from Nuan that Li Peng, despite his apartment and his appearance, runs a fair-sized operation. Probably he doesn't get much personally, but with maybe 30 or 40 girls pushing E at 20 or more nightclubs, he would be turning over quite a bit. Is he here to pay what he owes for the E he's dealing?"

"That's possible," Huang said. "If he doesn't stay here for long, that's a more probable explanation."

"I'd love to know which apartment the next up the chain lives in!" Jia exclaimed.

"At least we got the floor."

"That's true."

The lift eased to a stop where doors slid open. The lifts were on a curve, where at the far end of that curve they would be out of the line of sight.

"That way," Jia said, while pointing to the left of the lift foyer.

They went to end of the curve to be fairly well hidden. Now Jia waited for a long time or a short time, although she suspected a man dressed in a faded t-shirt, cheap jeans and runners was here purely for business of a financial nature, or a short time. As Jia suspected, it was a short time. She nudged Huang who nodded his head.

They followed Li Peng out of the foyer and past those shops; including a Starbucks for American travellers and tourists who had to have a piece of home in Guangzhou, even if there were better cafes with better coffee all across the city. Peng walked to Peasant Movement Institute Station; there they caught the escalator down to the forecourt with few around.

"Hold back," Jia said; worried Li Peng would be suspicious if he saw them again.

Jia let Li Peng swipe his card well before she swiped her Yang Cheng Tong card. He went to the eastern platform, or the reverse of his journey before. He may be heading home, but that wasn't certain. At the platform, Jia watched Li Peng stand close the edge of the platform while she grabbed Huang's hand to hold him well back. Only when she felt the rush of air of a train approaching did she stride forward, still holding Huang's hand, to enter the train just arrived.

"I see him," Huang said on the radio.

"I see him too."

Once more it was station stop after station stop after station stop until there was only one station to go.

"Most likely we're returning to Renhe," Jia said. "If we lose him, just catch a Line Three train."

"Understood."

The train slowly drifted to a halt, where the crowd split in two general directions: to the escalator to street level, or to the passage to Line Three. In the distance, Jia spotted that faded t-shirt.

Jia pressed her PTT. "To Line Three."

"I see him; I see you."

Huang was really good at communicating. A smart man and a fast learner.

Down the short escalator towards Line Three northbound, Jia pressed her PTT. "Hang back, Huang, so he's unlikely to see us. Move forward only when the next train arrives."

"Understood."

They stood in the background for four or five minutes, until the next blast of wind.

"Now," Jia said.

They strode forward as the train streamed past to stop. Doors peeled open to a packed carriage. Doors closed but Jia couldn't see a thing.

"I see him, about twenty metres towards the front of the train," Huang said over the radio.

"I can't see him so you're my eyes."

"Understood."

So good! The adrenaline rush – awesome!

Station stop after station stop after station stop.

"Next stop Renhe," Jia said.

"He's moving."

Jia forced her way through crowds to be at the doors when they peeled open. She stepped off while looking right, to spot faded black.

"I have him in sight," Jia said.

"I don't."

Through the exit gates which sprung open automatically, then across the exit forecourt.

"Heading to the west exit."

"I can't see but I'm following.'

Up the escalators to where Li Peng emerged from the station, and in his usual purposeful fashion he strode through crowds, with Jia tailing while wondering where Huang was. She put her hand in her pocket for the PTT.

"Heading south from Renhe Metro Station."

"I still can't see but I'll track south."

"Understood." Li Peng took a side-street. "Now heading along Yuying Street,"

"Understood."

At a shop with many red signs with gold characters, Li Peng strode in as if he owned the place.

"Entered Feifan Massage."

"I see it."

Huang came to Jia. "Well!" he exclaimed.

They couldn't stand in the street outside a massage parlour! Jia looked around.

"Over there," she said. "Aishang Milk Tea."

"I could do with a drink."

They entered where the menu was big and bold.

"What do you want?" Huang asked.

"Just a milk tea."

He ordered and paid while Jia took a small, white plastic table near the window with a good view of the massage parlour, and men entering and leaving. Their teas: black tea, evaporated milk and sugar, arrived in glasses which Jia sipped. She really needed that.

"You know that's a brothel," Huang said quietly.

"They had the same in Beijing when I was on patrol. So much for a massage with a handjob, so much extra for a blowjob, and more again for full service."

"Fulfils a need and keeps things safer for women."

Jia sipped more milk tea. "Not safer for women. The majority of rapes of women, and even murders of women, are by men that female victims know. Beyond that, rape is about power, control and even hatred of women; not sex."

"You learned this?"

"Yes."

"But with the one child policy and sex selective abortions for decades, there are many more men than women. Surely men get frustrated, and maybe that frustration could boil over into hatred of women for being constantly rejected."

"I'm not a psychologist, I only know the statistics, and even if that happened, statistically that's uncommon. Personally, if women freely want to sell sexual services and men want to buy them, then to try to prevent that is rather pointless. But I have a problem with women coerced into selling sex in seedy places like that."

"Is there such a thing?"

"Hypothetical number one," Jia said. "She's gotten married, they've had a child, but her husband finds fatherhood isn't what he wanted. So he clears out and the single mother pension isn't enough to live on, and if she wants to work while her parents look after her child, there aren't enough jobs in her town. So she leaves her child with her parents, and does a deal to get residency in the city for a price, the price being a massage parlour selling handjobs and blowjobs and full service, to send money home to her parents to care for her child. Hypothetical number two. It's a poor, coal mining town where the mine is now working half-shifts and there are no other jobs in town. Daughter does a deal to get residency in the city for a price, to support her parents."

"Those aren't hypothetical."

"Those are from Beijing."

"That's sad."

"I wish I could make the single mother's pension, or the unemployment pension, sufficient so that women didn't have to resort to sex work. If women freely choose because it's easier than working in a milk tea shop, or less stressful than being a detective, that's fine, but I do have a problem with economic coercion."

"Me too. He's leaving," Huang then said.

Indeed he was, with a young woman. Short, skinny, darker complexion, scruffy hair; but strangely not unattractive, especially in her short denim shorts showing a lot of slender leg. Jia put her glass down to ease out of her seat, and then to Yuying Street. Now they were tracking a couple holding hands while heading in the general direction of where Li Peng lived. Jia knew what came next. The couple reached his building to enter the foyer under that bright yellow arch and disappear from sight. Jia with Huang at her side; crossed the street to the building opposite. There they sat on the grubby couch.

"I'm sure she's his girlfriend," Jia said.

"I'm sure too. We may not see them for a few hours, or for the rest of the day."

Jia thought. "We made a breakthrough today and I want to follow this through tomorrow. I want to go into Office 1.10 to find and hack the server for that apartment building in Yue Xiu, to see if we can find who owns each apartment on floor 22. If we're lucky, we can cross-reference names to criminal records."

"It's a big building so there will be many apartments on each floor."

"I know, but if I can hack it and there are records, which I'm sure there will be, then it's only a matter of time and resources." Jia thought more. "There's no point in Liko and Bo watching Li Peng with his girlfriend, so they ought to do daytime tomorrow, which I'm sure will be quiet anyway. I'll call them now."

Jia took her smartphone to scroll her contacts to Liko. She quickly explained a bare-bones version of finding something and following it through tomorrow, which Liko understood. Then Jia called Bo who was relieved he wasn't working all night. Time on her phone was four-ten.

"I'm no longer Detective-Sergeant Xiong and you're no longer Detective-Constable Zuo, so this is a suggestion rather than an order. How about my place for a shower to freshen up, and...?" but Jia couldn't bring herself to say it.

"I have a better idea," Huang said. "How about your place for a shower to freshen up, and then we make love?"

"Yes."

They headed into sparser crowds.

"I'm looking forward to this," Huang said. "Yesterday sort-of happened all of a sudden, which was good, but this morning when I saw you after your shower, only then did I realise I missed something. You're a beautiful woman, Jia, and I want to take that in."

Jia glanced out the corner of her eyes at Huang while knowing that wasn't the case.

"Naked you're amazing!" Huang exclaimed. "You're nicely tall with lovely long legs, and you're perfectly proportioned."

That was a nice compliment, but Jia didn't want to respond. She knew new she was taller than most; not as tall as Nuan but she was taller or else she wouldn't have been eligible for the People's Public Security University. Beyond that she was alright and her other men had no complaints, so if Huang thought she was perfectly proportioned, that was fine. Probably not right, but fine.

"Women are beautiful, even that skinny girl from the massage parlour, but what do women think of men?" Huang asked.

"I like men," Jia said, which wasn't what he asked. "You're handsome, Huang, I do notice such things. But what mattered was our friendly conversation while I was cooking, and later when we were eating. In a moment we became good, close and special friends. I don't want to be the gatekeeper always fending off advances, so when I feel something I go with it. Like last night."

"You're a modern woman."

"Yeah."

But that was just the start of a memorable night. When the time came for it, Huang was great. He took his time, he had the right touch – everything. Jia looked forward to showering to get rid of the grime of a busy day, and having Huang admire her proportions too, but she more looked forward to good love-making with a man she cared for, later cooking him a nice meal, and later still, dancing at True Color. What more could a woman ask for on a Saturday night in Guangzhou?

Chapter Thirteen

Jia swiped her security access card to enter dark silence. She groped for the switch, for shaded fluorescent lights to flicker on. She went to her desk, beside Huang's desk actually, to switch her laptop on. She waited for it to power up.

"Each apartment building has a management company who looks after common areas like foyers, lifts, window cleaning, airconditioning; all those sorts of things. I'll find the development company and that will lead me to the management company.

She turned to her browser and bookmarks, to open up the Guangzhou Property Registry. She logged in with the Office 1.10 user id and password, to find 70, Zongshan Fifth Road was developed by Jiale Jiaje Group. Management was then handed to China Real Estate Group. She went to China Real Estate Group.

"Now we hack," Jia said.

"You university graduates are good at that. Nuan especially."

"We can all do it," Jia said. "Most computer systems have one of few common default user ids and passwords, so we'll try them first. Normally live user ids and passwords should be added then the defaults deleted, but that doesn't always happen."

Jia logged in with user id admin, password admin. Denied. She tried admin and password. Denied. She tried admin and Password. Denied.

"Doesn't work," she said. "Now I need a user id. I'll use Google outside the firewall to find email addresses for that corporation."

She searched and scrolled and found quite a few, including a Chief Executive – Marketing. She attempted to logon where the user id was accepted, but the random password she entered, password, was rejected. She then set a brute force attack using that user id, and let it run.

"This may take minutes or hours, depending on how clever that user has been."

"That's it?"

"Let's get a coffee."

They went to the tea room to buy some milk coffee, while the hack ran.

Chapter Fourteen

Nuan swiped her card to enter her home. She smelled Dewai's scent well before he emerged from the second bedroom. He came close and hugged her.

"I've missed you," he said.

"I've missed you too. I have plans but first I want to talk."

"Alright."

Nuan sat on the leather couch with Dewai by her side so close, like he didn't want to let her go.

"Methamphetamine, ice, is a terrible drug. It's freely available, cheap, highly addictive, and when users are high, they have incredible strength and uncontrollable rage. The current ice epidemic is terrible for China. In Office 1.10 we're not so much interested in other drugs because it's naive to think we can eliminate illegal narcotics in Chine, but we are targeting methamphetamine or ice to make it less freely available and force its price up, which should mean less users. To do this we're taking out the top level of organised crime gangs making and selling methamphetamine, as you saw with the Axe Gang arrests, because to take out low-level dealers is pointless. For our next organised crime gang we're starting at the bottom, but we will finish at the top. At the moment I'm working undercover in nightclubs. That's all I can tell you, but really, that's all there is. How long this goes on for I don't know, but I will keep in touch."

"I knew what I was in for when you went away a couple of times with your last case, so I'm good with what's happening."

"That's good," Nuan said. "I don't know if I've said this before, but I love you."

"I love you too, I always have. Our first date."

"Me too. Now, let's make love.'

He stood, took her hand, and led her to their bedroom with floor to ceiling glass and great views of Guangzhou. They didn't need to close their curtains because other tall buildings were far away. Nuan unbuttoned her blouse.

"Do you want a massage?" Dewai asked.

"Oh yes!"

"Undress and lie down."

Nuan quickly undressed. :"You know you're the best," she said.

"I don't know that, but I do know I'm the luckiest."

"Even when I go away for four or five days at a time?"

"But then you texted me."

Now naked, Nuan lay on the bed. Dewai, also naked, knelt astride her hips. He massaged her shoulders, so good.

"Is working undercover hard?" Dewai asked.

"I'm playing a role and that takes a lot out of me."

"I feel your tension."

Nuan felt the same. "A good massage, and love, will make me feel better."

"When your girlfriend's a detective-sergeant; you have her job in your relationship. But that's good. That makes you interesting."

"So you understand why I do this?"

"I know you have an interesting job. I love you, and more, I know you always come back."

Nuan had enough of that massage; it wasn't intense enough. She moved away and rolled over. "Really, I need a good fuck."

"Really?"

"Really! So let's fuck!"

He devoured her, and that's what Nuan needed. Making love was for other times, but after all that stress, dealing E, back lanes with that loser, what she needed was a good fuck! Dewai gave her that, and even more.

* * *

After the luxury of home, that shabby apartment seemed even shabbier, if such a thing were possible.

"You're looking better," Hu said.

"Thanks Hu," Nuan said. "I didn't realise how stressful this is until I stepped away for a day. I really needed a break. Now, back to acting."

Nuan sat on her old couch, pulled out her police smartphone and scrolled her contacts. She pressed 'call'.

"Wéi Lo," he greeted.

"Wéi Peng. I need a refill of E."

"Usual place, one hour."

He hung up while Nuan sighed. "One hour, Hu."

"Alright. How's your boyfriend?"

"I missed him and he missed me, so...."

"I understand."

Nuan pictured Hu alone for the day, while she was massaged, they fucked hard, and later, they made love less frenetically. She felt sorry for Hu but there wasn't anything she could do, other than hope he found a good woman for his life. Nuan slipped her bag over her shoulder and stood.

"Let's go, Hu, although there's probably not much for you to do."

"You never know."

"That's right."

Outside along familiar streets to Als Gong Cha, and the lane out the back. There Peng waited while Nuan reached into her bag for a wad of notes. She counted sixteen to exchange for two bundles of bags, which she counted before placing into her bag.

"Thanks," Nuan said.

"Lo, I took your advice," Peng said. "I knew someone. She's pretty, not as pretty as you but she's pretty, and she's nice. Now she's my girlfriend."

"That's great! I'm so pleased."

"Do you want some coffee?" Peng asked.

"Alright."

Peng led Nuan, or Lo, inside.

"What would you like?" he asked.

"A flat white."

He ordered while Nuan sat towards the back. She looked up to see Hu at table near the door, positioned just right, although she wasn't going to need him. Peng sat.

"What's your girlfriend's name?" Nuan asked.

"Binbin."

"That's a lovely name. What really matters is here," Nuan said as she put her hand over her heart.

"Yes, you were right about that. What about you?"

"Me? Well," Nuan said while she thought. He was triad or an equivalent gangster, so she could spin him a story to see where that took her. "One night you saw me dancing with a Western guy. So, for a night, 4,000."

"That's a lot!"

"That's for all night, and I speak good English. It's just a casual thing for me. We dance, they usually ask me, and I give them a price. If we dance and they don't ask, or they don't want to pay, so be it."

"Binbin works in a massage parlour."

Nuan nearly choked on her coffee. "We have something in common."

"But not 4,000!"

"It's sex for money, just at different ends of the market. Have I surprised you?"

"You're a party girl so perhaps I'm not surprised."

Nuan put her hand out to touch the tattoos on his left arm. "Are you triad?" she asked quietly.

"Why?" he snapped while frowning. "What do you know about triad?"

"Apart from old movies, nothing. It's just your tattoos. I've seen tattoos in movies."

Peng leaned back in his chair while seemingly assessing Nuan, or Lo. "Seeing as you live on the wrong side of things in a few ways, yes I am."

"You're part of a gang and everything," Nuan exclaimed in mock shock.

"Yes I am, but that's all I can tell you."

"Of course."

Peng drank some of his coffee. "This is nice!" he exclaimed.

"It's Australian coffee."

"Have you fucked many Australians?"

"Yeah, a few."

"They're nice?"

Nuan had met three Australians in a friendship sense, and all were lovely. "Yes they're nice."

"Chinese guys?"

"I love Chinese guys! If they want to dance, and later ask, always yes."

Peng shook his head. "You're hopeless."

Nuan giggled at her story. Then she finished her coffee. She stood. "Zài jiàn."

"Zài jiàn party girl."

Nuan headed outside while sensing Hu following her. She went home, unlocked their door, to hear footsteps behind. She waited.

"That was more than an exchange of money for E," Hu said.

"Peng's got himself a girlfriend; a pretty girl from a massage parlour. So we talked and I spun him a story about 4,000 a night for guys I dance with if they ask for it, and found out he's triad." Nuan thought. "I'll ring Jia."

Nuan put her bag on the counter before taking a stool. She scrolled her contacts to ring.

"Wéi Lo," Jia greeted.

"Wéi Jia. I won't keep you but it's simple anyway. Peng found himself a girlfriend from a massage parlour, I didn't ask how, but we had a talk about it and I found out he's definitely triad. He won't say which gang, of course."

"We know about his girlfriend," Jia said. "We tailed him on Saturday."

"What's she like?"

"Kind of cute, actually."

Cute was good.

"He visited someone in Yue Xiu so we're hacking and checking," Jia said. "To know Peng's triad is great, because his Yue Xiu contact must be triad."

"Peng's just a 49er, although he's got some go in him. Obviously we're aiming to dismantle his gang, but if we didn't I'm sure Peng would go places. I talked with him about girls, and bang, cute girlfriend."

"So you're behind his girlfriend?"

"Yeah."

"Your relationship with Peng might come in handy," Jia said. "I'll let Superintendent Ma know, and I'm sure he'll keep this in the back of his mind. Have you thought of an undercover future?"

"Absolutely not!" Nuan exclaimed. "Living lies and deceit is too draining!"

"I understand. Well, you've got Hu, and you've got me to help you as much as I can."

"If I'm undercover for a while, I'll take a day off every now and then to recover. If the opportunity comes and I can find which gang, I'll let you know. Zài jiàn."

Nuan ended the call.

"How did you come up with 4,000 a night?" Hu asked.

"When we patrolled in Beijing, I found the price at a massage parlour was 200, plus 200 extra for full service. So for a Westerner, what would an English-speaking Chinese girl, dressed up to party, be worth for all night? Ten times half an hour in a back lane massage parlour?"

"Where did you get the idea?"

"I really don't know, but fuck it worked! Now he thinks we're kindred sprits living on the wrong side. Retailing E is one thing, but when you add in prostitution that makes me more....."

"Of a criminal."

"Peng's seen me dancing with Western guys so it's believable for him."

Hu shook his head while Nuan imagined men paying her 4,000 just for her looks, her body, her personality; what she could do with them sexually. In a night, just for sex, she could almost a week's wages. That fantasy was hot, so hot.

Chapter Fifteen

Jia heard the laser printer wake from sleep, and turned to see the page slide out. A picture of Mo Feng from his ID record; aged 50 with a record of triad-type crimes, and on the same page, his wife Lu Tu aged 48.. Jia took it to stick on the whiteboard with a magnet.

"I believe that's our suspect, Mo Feng, and his wife, Lu Tu," Jia said to Superintendent Ma standing alongside. "Another thing; Nuan, sorry, Sergeant Shui has confirmed Li Peng is triad. More that she's building a close relationship with Li. Li Peng has a girlfriend who we saw on Saturday, and somehow Sergeant Shui was involved with that. She said she talked with Li Peng about girls and he moved fast to get a girlfriend."

Superintendent Ma nodded his head slowly. "Sergeant Shui could have a long-term future in undercover policing," he said.

Jia wondered how to protect Nuan. "Sergeant Shui is a talented police officer at whichever task she's involved with," she said. "I would hate for Office 1.10 to lose her to full-time undercover work."

"That's true. But for now, I'll leave her there."

Jia knew Nuan was expecting that.

"What's next, Sergeant Xiong?" Superintendent Ma asked.

"I'll hack the security cameras for 70, Zongshan Fifth Road. We'll track Mo Feng in and out, and when he's out we'll send a maintenance team around to fix his airconditioning."

"You'll bug his apartment?"

"Yes."

"How will you get in?"

"A summons to get a master security card from the property managers."

"Will they tip-off Mo?"

"China Real Estate Group is a large corporation with hundreds of apartment buildings under management. A tip-off from a corporation like that would be unlikely. Besides, it's a master card for all apartments in this building, not his specifically."

"Good point. I'll do the summons and you continue your hacking."

"Yes, Superintendent Ma."

Jia sat while thinking: *you could have said good work or something.*

"What is it?" Huang asked.

"Let's hack their security cameras."

"Let's."

Huang pulled his chair around while Jia browsed. Eventually she found the security guard screen with three images.

"That one there," she said while pointing. "That's the entrance foyer from what we saw. This one with the boom gate is the carpark entrance. I don't know this one, but it's concrete-looking so that might be the carpark lift foyer. If it is we're in luck."

"I'll catch a train to Yue Xiu. When I get there I'll go to the carpark lift foyer."

"Ring me when you get there so I can confirm or otherwise."

"I will."

Jia used the Office 1.10 user id and password to log into Motor Registry. A quick search, and with the details on her screen, she went to the whiteboard to write beside the pictures of Mo Feng and Lu Tu.

'Lexus NX SUV; registration 粤A 686534K, blue.'

"Mo Feng's car?" Superintendent Ma asked.

"Yes."

He walked away while Jia returned to her laptop to open the security camera surveillance screen. With her smartphone open at Mo Feng's image, she selected three days ago for the suspected carpark lift foyer camera, and ran it at high speed. In and out, in and out in and out in and out; on and on and on and on – stop! Great!

"Superintendent Ma!" Jia called.

He came across.

"I believe this is a camera in the carpark lift foyer of 70, Zongshan Fifth Road. That's Mo Feng holding hands with his wife Lu Tu. If that's the carpark camera, they went out together in his car. If so, on that day at that time their apartment was unoccupied."

"Very good Sergeant Xiong."

"Constable Zuo is on his way to Yue Xiu to confirm that's the carpark camera."

Superintendent Ma brought his chair around. "If that's the case, we can see if they have regular times they go out, or simply wait until they go out."

"We'll have a master security card for the building including the carpark, so we can park a van, I think, and wait."

"I'll organise a van now. Well done!"

At last recognition!

Jia returned to the security cameras to browse for the past week, to catch Mo Feng and Lu Tu, singly or together, to find a pattern. Even though she was concentrating, Jia remembered a conversation with Huang about Office 1.10. He was so right, their jobs were fantastic. Then her phone rang.

"Wéi Huang," Jia answered. "Are you there?"

"I am."

"Just a moment."

Jia put the phone on the desk, pressed speaker, and then used the mouse to get to the right camera. *Great!*

"I see you. You can come back now."

"Alright."

Superintendent Ma rolled his chair around again. "You were right?"

"Yes I was. I've been through the past week's files on that camera to see Mo Feng and his wife go out at least every second day. So we have the chance to bug his apartment totally incognito."

"Then what? Is he going to talk business at home?"

Jia had that worked out. "Triad say thinks like merchandise and shipment, so if we hear him on the phone using those words, we've got him. More specifically, we followed Li Peng on Saturday where he went straight to his boss. If we hear Li Peng in that apartment, then for sure Mo Feng is our man."

"Of course. The next step with this is to buy bulk methamphetamine, and chase that up their leadership pyramid. Normally this sort of deal would be done by men, but given this has been your case, and given these days it's possible for a woman to be involved with such a deal, I would like you there when we do this. You could be our finance person, but you would need the right look for that. Do you have a suit?"

"No I don't."

"Get some money from Commissioner Shui's personal assistant."

"I'll do that."

Jia knew the look she needed. A black jacket, white blouse, black, knee-length skirt, black pantyhose, and black leather shoes with chunky heels. Office manager look.

Superintendent Ma moved closer. "Sergeant Xiong, I've been impressed with your work these past weeks," he said. "Our last case was more Sergeant Shui, but this is your case, even being Sergeant Shui's handler. I have nothing but praise for your efforts, while Commissioner Shui is aware of how this is going."

Jia was quite shocked. "We've a long way to go and I'll keep doing my best," she said.

"I'm sure you will. I've organised the summons, the van and the bugs. I'll put Sergeant Suo and Constable Tang in the carpark, in overalls, with the bugs and a ladder. There they will wait for you to tell them when Mo Feng and his wife leave for their car."

"Will they be SIM-card based bugs?"

"Yes they will. We'll monitor his apartment from here."

Superintendent Ma went to his table, while Jia got up to roll her chair to Shen; Sergeant Suo."

"You've been busy," Shen said as Jia sat alongside.

"You're doing...?" Jia asked.

"Working with Liko and Bo to piece together the 18K and Big Circle triad groups, while you're attacking this from the opposite end."

"I understand. We're going to be bugging a suspected triad Red Pole, and you'll be doing this because we need airconditioning maintenance men, even though I expect the apartment to be unoccupied while you're there. While it might be tempting to poke here and there, it's important to get in, install the bugs, and get out. If something's moved, even a centimetre, that might ring alarm bells. The bugs you install will tell us all we need to know."

"I understand."

"That bad news is you and Bo might be in a van in a carpark for a couple of days, waiting for the suspect and his wife to go out together."

Shen laughed. "Thank you for that. I'll bring my laptop and connect to 4G. That'll keep me busy while I'm waiting."

"I'm sorry."

"You don't look like an airconditioning maintenance man, so I understand."

Jia shrugged her shoulders, before getting up to roll her chair back to her table. There were many things women could do, even drug deals, but not faking airconditioning maintenance.

The door clicked for Huang to come in. He sat beside Jia who briefed him.

"Assuming this all fits together," Huang said, "the most likely outcome is Superintendent Ma and you will be visiting Mo Feng to arrange a meeting with his superior, who is likely a Deputy Mountain Master. Mo Feng's apartment is bugged, you'll be wearing transmitters to back that up, and the rest of us with uniformed officers will be nearby as backup. Right?"

There were three people in this world Jia would trust with her life: Shui Nuan, Zhang Hu and Zuo Huang. "I want you to monitor our transmitters during this meeting to make that call. I'll speak with Superintendent Ma, and if necessary Commissioner Shui, although I don't think it'll come to that." Jia leaned close so nobody would overhear. "You and I when we're not working are you and I, but at work I can't find the right words. All I can say is you're great with everything." Jia looked up at the clock, just past five. "That's time for today. Are you interested in Fujian-style spring rolls for dinner?"

"Only if it's not too much trouble."

"You can help me cook, as always, and you know I find cooking relaxing after a busy day."

"I know."

She stood. "Zài jiàn everyone."

"Zài jiàn everyone," Huang echoed.

They went outside to where Commissioner Shui waited at the lift. Jia saluted, as did Huang, which Commissioner Shui returned. The lift opened and they all stepped inside.

"Sergeant Xiong and Constable Zuo; I've heard good things about you two. Office 1.10 is important to me, so I thank you both."

"Thank you, Commissioner Shui," Jia said.

"Thank you, Commissioner Shui," Huang echoed.

Commissioner Shui half-smiled which confused Jia. "Is Sergeant Shui well?" he asked.

"Working undercover is stressful," Jia said. "I'm supporting Sergeant Shui as much as I can."

"I heard that too. In a personal way I thank you for that."

Jia nodded her head as they reached the ground floor. The door opened where Commissioner Shui saluted again, which Jia returned, before she and Huang followed him across the foyer.

Chapter Sixteen

Mai slipped out of bed to dress before preparing breakfast. Yuanfu slipped out to dress too, unusually.

"Cook, don't eat, don't drink," he said.

"Why?" Mai asked.

"Don't eat, don't drink."

Mai didn't understand, but if she wasn't to eat then she wasn't to eat. First as always she soaked the rice in water, and while that was happening she set the table. After a time soaking, Mai set to cooking congee with a little oil which made it smooth and soft. Mai was never that hungry in the morning so she didn't mind not eating but she couldn't understand why. Mai was terribly thirsty as she watched them drinking the tea she brewed. After eating Mai expected Yuanfu to go to work with Gong Gong, but Yuanfu took Mai to the square where that truck waited. Now she had a terrible feeling.

"No," Mai said. "No, no, no."

Yuanfu looked firm while Mai wished she had the words.

"Sib-tsoob txhua hnub," she said. *Sexual intercourse every day.* She knew some of the words in Chinese. "You, me, every day. Good! Yes, good."

Every day or not, good or not, wasn't going to change things, as Yuanfu opened the door to push Mai to the step. Mai climbed in, Yuanfu climbed beside, for the driver to head off. Soon they were roaring along that road Mai walked along one night. Then it seemed so far but now it wasn't far enough. Mai wished she would never get to that town.

In the town just past the police station, the driver turned left to stop at a house. There Mai was taken inside, and then to another room while Yuanfu was left behind. A man in a white jacket, a doctor surely, told Mai to lie on a funny, curved bed. He brought a small television set on a trolley, lifted Mai's t-shirt, smeared cold goo on her now swelling stomach, it being quite a few weeks now, about 12 weeks or even more than 12, before running a torch connected by a lead to the small television across her stomach. Mai was mesmerised by the black and white picture on the screen. *Was that really inside her?*

The doctor frowned before going to the other room. He came back to give Mai a couple of tablets but she shook her head. Yuanfu entered the room to forcefully open Mai's mouth for the doctor to put the tablets in her mouth, and then Yuanfu massaged her jaw until she chewed and swallowed. *Was that it?*

The doctor held up two fingers and said, "Two."

Mai understood: in two hours. She nodded her head while terror overtook helplessness. She lay there for what seemed like all day, until the doctor wheeled the trolley with the television away to bring another trolley with two large, steel cylinders in its place. He undid her jeans and pulled them off, and her panties, before a rubber mask attached by hoses to these cylinders was strapped around Mai's head. She heard hissing and after a time, felt calm and floating. She felt like she was floating even when the doctor stuck things into her vagina, aborting her. It didn't take long but Mai was never going to forgive Yuanfu for that. More, he would never touch her again. If he didn't fuck her then she would never have to go through that again.

The doctor stood and spoke in Chinese. Mai picked up two words, two weeks, which meant no fucking for two weeks. Well, as far as Mai was concerned it was no fucking ever again. They could beat her to death but she wasn't going to. How could she let a man she hated inside her body, to do that again or worse, to give birth and have her son sold? No, never would he touch her again.

Chapter Seventeen

Jia felt her concentration wandering and was about to call Huang to take over, when she spotted movement on her screen. A couple emerging from the lifts, hand in hand in a familiar way. Jia didn't like that for herself; perhaps holding hands signified a man holding onto his woman as his possession, or even marking his territory to show other men. Outside of work, Huang had never held her hand. Maybe confident men didn't need to hold onto their possession or show other men. Maybe confident men knew their partner was there because she wanted to be. Jia focussed: that couple were Mo Feng holding hands with his wife Lu Tu.

Jia pressed the PTT lying on her desk. "Shen; I see suspect and wife heading from the lift. Get ready and I'll tell you when their car leaves."

"Alright Jia."

Jia switched to the carpark camera at the gate, where soon after she spotted the Lexus SUV drifting up, waiting for the gate to raise, and heading off.

"Shen, you're free to go."

"On our way."

In a large apartment building, two men in overalls carrying a ladder was about as good a cover as anyone could imagine. She pictured them greeting residents all the way to floor 22 where they would use their card to enter. There, based on the floorplan on the developer's website, they would bug the living room, the main bedroom for what that was worth, and the second bedroom. Jia swapped over to the second laptop connected to the sim card bugs.

"This is the living room," she heard in Shen's voice on that laptop's speaker.

Jia pressed the PTT. "Loud and clear, Shen."

"This is the main bedroom."

"Loud and clear."

"This is the second bedroom."

"Loud and clear."

"On our way," he said to the bug.

Ha – too easy!

Soon after in the carpark camera, she saw their Volkswagen van heading out. Done! Jia was going to take Bo from Liko to monitor the bugs, which were recording all day, every day. What a job. She needed a break so headed to the tearoom. More she needed coffee, even terrible coffee, so she dropped a two yuan coin in the slot for milk coffee, although it was the strangest milk she'd ever come across. Huang came to buy coffee too.

"All good?" he asked.

"Yeah," Jia said. "Just weary."

He got up close and whispered in her ear. "I love you."

Jia couldn't help but smile and oddly her weariness instantly disappeared. She looked around an empty room. "I love you too."

Jia finished her coffee to throw the cup in the bin.

* * *

Bo was at his computer with his headset on, giggling. Jia was annoyed by that stupid noise, and couldn't understand why surveillance would be funny anyway. She went to Bo.

"Amusing?" she asked sarcastically.

Bo turned his head with his mouth open. Jia reached for the headset to slip it on. She heard a bed creaking regularly and evenly, creak – creak – creak and in harmony a woman's moan, uh – uh – uh. Huang came alongside so Jia handed him the headset. Huang listened while frowning. *How dare Tang Bo behave like that!* Jia felt flushed, her heart raced, and she realised her hands were clenched into fists.

"I'm very disappointed in you, Constable Tang," Jia said firmly, but as calmly as she could manage. "We're investigating a suspected high-level criminal, and to do that we have to invade their private space. But this is for a serious, criminal investigation."

Huang handed the headset back while Jia stormed from the room. She dropped a coin in the slot of the coffee vending machine, pressed a button; then took the bitter-tasting milk coffee. She sipped as Huang entered the room. He bought a milk coffee too.

126

"Are you alright?" he asked.

"I'm fine," Jia said. "No, I'm angry."

"You handled that well."

Jia watched as he sipped his drink.

"I've leaned a lot from you, especially since we've been partners," Huang said. "On this case over these past weeks, you've been fantastic. You've carried this case." He moved closer. "You're the best detective in this building," he said quietly.

Jia felt her rage dissipate. She was the best detective like she was perfectly proportioned. But she was proud of filing the gap with two members of their team undercover, and she was proud of her contributions to this case. And her figure? She was alright.

"When we next have a weekend day free, Saturday or Sunday, would you like to meet my family?" Huang asked.

There was an implication in that, but it was the right time for it. "Yes, I would like to meet your family," Jia said.

"Would you like to meet my family as my girlfriend?"

Girlfriend implied marriage in the future, but plans of marriage, even after a few weeks together; it was the right time for that too. Jia knew she would never find a better man than Zuo Huang: smart, independent, didn't want to run her life, and he loved her. More that she loved him: a subtle brightness, a smile she couldn't quite wipe off her face, and light-hearted in a way she'd never experienced before.

"Yes I would to like to meet your family as your girlfriend," Jia said. When we next have a weekend free, would you like to catch the train to Fuzhou to meet my family as my boyfriend?"

"Yes; very much."

To present her boyfriend to her family implied marriage and children. Jia knew Nuan wanted one child after she'd better established her career, while with one child she could continue her career after a few months leave. Like most things, Nuan was right with that concept.

Jia studied her empty cup. "Boyfriend and girlfriend implies things for us, but we have time for these things."

Jia looked up to catch Huang's eyes glance at her. "Things at the right time," he said.

"My parents don't have a computer so I'll write them an old-fashioned letter. I want to set expectations. I studied for four years, I've only been working for a few months, and I'm only 23. Each step will happen when it's the right time, and I want to make sure they know that."

"I'm comfortable with that."

"You should move your things into my apartment, which will be our apartment."

"I will."

Jia tossed her empty cup in the general direction of the bin. "Let's get back to work."

* * *

Huang lay between Jia's legs while he kissed her; then suckled her nipples. He moved so she reached to guide him, and gasped as he filled her. He propped high with arms stretched, and slow and deep for one delicious moment, then hard and deep. Hard, regular and deep with their bed mirroring the rhythm of his fucking: creak – creak – creak. Jia closed her eyes, overwhelmed by his masculine power. His strength, his drive, his energy his.... She heard herself moan, uh. She was feminine, woman, and he was fucking her. Uh – uh – uh – uh; as he fucked her hard, regular and deep. Man fucking woman, as was meant to be.

Chapter Eighteen

Mai sat on the stone wall by the lake with Na and Hu.

"You're quiet Mai," Na said.

"Yuanfu gave me an abortion about two weeks ago, we then we had to wait for two weeks."

"Oh. How do you feel?"

"I'm angry! A baby isn't a baby until it's born, but he killed any chance of that happening. I hate him for that and I won't have this happen again. I hate him and I'm not going to let him touch me."

"How?"

"I'll fight him. I'll scream the house down! I'll scream the village down!"

"That's dangerous Mai."

"I don't care. How can I let a man I hate do that to me? I just can't." Mai looked at the water. "I'll die first."

"You're too young to die, Mai."

"What life is this?"

"If next you have a son they'll sell it, that's bad, but after that you can have another son and they'll keep it. Then you'll have your child. Even more, another son after that. Then you'll feel better."

"But I hate him so much I won't let him touch me, let alone have his children!"

Hu touched Mai's arm. "I'm sorry for what you went through."

"They're going to sell your son, Hu. You know this."

Hu's belly was well swollen. She stared at the water. "I know."

"Do you let him touch you?"

"It is what it is."

"Not for me!"

"Be careful Mai."

Every day that passed made Mai angrier. Every breakfast reminded her of that morning she couldn't have breakfast. Every day she came to the square to see Na and Hu reminded her of that truck waiting. Every time she went to bed reminded her of the many times Yuanfu fucked her, only to abort any chance of having a child.

"How could a father do that? Mai exclaimed. What a monster! Neither of you have gone through this but I have!"

"Mai is right," Na said. "We can say be careful but we don't know what it's like. These men are monsters to buy women, sell sons and abort daughters. Every single one of these men is a monster."

"I should get home," Mai said. "I don't know if it's tonight or tomorrow night or when, but there's no point in making bad things worse."

"Good luck Mai," Na said.

"Thank you both. You've helped me so much I wish I could repay you."

"Every day together is thanks," Na said. "Once we were two but now we're three, and three friends are better than two."

Mai smiled a bit. At least she was worth something. She went home where Po Po told Mai to cook rice with broccoli and cabbage, which she did. Later they ate, Gong Gong and Yuanfu with glasses of beer while Po Po and Mai had cups of tea. Later still the family watched television, while Mai washed and dried the plates and everything she used for cooking, before joining them. Later still they all went to their rooms. There Mai removed her t-shirt and jeans before taking her nightgown from her chest, only Yuanfu grabbed her arm.

Mai shook her head. "No!" she said firmly in Chinese.

"We'll make love," Yuanfu said.

"No!"

"Yes!"

"No!"

He slapped her so she slapped him. Mai had been in this place before but this time she knew what to do. He punched her so she punched him. She punched him and punched him and punched him, until he stopped to remove his own t-shirt. Mai watched and waited until he removed his jeans and underpants, his penis already erect. He pushed her towards

132

the bed but she pushed him back, so he pushed her harder and she pushed him.

"No, no, no!" Mai shouted. "No, no!"

Yuanfu pushed Mai extra hard who fell backwards on the bed, where she didn't want to be. He climbed onto the bed so she kicked his face. He swore.

"Ka tsaug, taug aws, txiag koj niam! Ka tsaug, ka tsaug!" she swore at the top of her voice, so loud that her throat hurt. Taug aws, taug aws!"

By this time Yuanfu was on top of Mai holding her shoulders, so close. So she kicked him there. He groaned and fell to one side while she climbed off the bed to stand, arms crossed.

"Kav, ywm hlab!" she scoffed. *Weak cock!*

Yuanfu jumped of the bed and grabbed Mai's throat to push her against the wall with his hands tight. Mai fought and fought and fought to get him off her.

The door burst open and Po Po shouted first at Yuanfu and then at Mai. Yuanfu let Mai's throat go and she bent over gasping for breath.

"No!" Mai said. "No, no, no!"

Mai stood straight with her arms crossed while Po Po glared at her. Then Po Po spoke to Yuanfu while pointing in the general direction of the front door. Mai knew what that meant; Po Po was getting rid of her. Good. No place they sent her could be as bad as that house. At least Mai got what she wanted. After what Yuanfu did, never again would he fuck her.

* * *

Mai slept on the floor of their room, fully clothed, to be as far from Yuanfu as was possible. When she woke she was surprised he wasn't there. Mai went to the kitchen to make tea. She was surprised Po Po didn't say something but then saw Gong Gong's dark looks towards his wife. At least when she was going, he, the only decent one in that family, finally stood up for her.

Yuanfu came through the front door to grab for Mai, who told him "No." Instead she took a hessian bag to pack her few belongings, before Yuanfu led her to where that truck waited in the square. The driver of the truck, a man in his 40s or 50s with a couple of missing teeth, smiled at Mai who wondered. Could she offer him something to get out of her misery? Could she fuck him in exchange for taking her to a police station not at that town but the city where the bus stopped? But she didn't know the right words and he probably wouldn't do it anyway, given he was a friend of that horrible family. Fuck her yes, but not the rest.

Soon they were on their way through the town, through the city even, then onto a busy road with many lanes tracking the route Mai took by bus all that time ago, all the way to the chaos of Guangzhou. Along Guangzhou roads packed with cars, footpaths packed with pedestrians, sirens wailing, car horns blaring; din and noise beyond reason. And still he drove past tall, tall buildings to an older place. There he went down a ramp to park his truck amongst many other cars underground. He took Mai up a staircase to a crowded footpath and a little way further along to a pair of glass doors propped open. Inside they climbed concrete stairs to floor three where he knocked on door 303. A big and bulky young man wearing nice clothes, better than jeans and a t-shirt, opened the door. Mai was led inside to a room with many women. The man with the truck left while another young man, also big and bulky and wearing nice clothes, entered the room. Mai was led to sit on a couch, with Vietnamese women on that couch, on another couch, and on two armchairs. In the background lurked an old, lined, Chinese woman, watching silently.

"Mai," she said.

"Sua," one said.

"Dawb," one said.

"Kawm," one said.

"Hmong?" Mai asked.

"Yes," Sua said in Hmong before gesturing to the other women. "Kinh."

There was animosity between Hmong and Kinh but given they were in a bad situation in a far away place, there was no place for animosity there.

"We're all Vietnamese," Mai said in Hmong.

"Mai," she said before pointing.

"Sen," the first Kinh said.

"Tien."

"Hoa."

"Lan."

Mai pressed the palms of her hands together and bowed her head to the Kinh in greetings. In turn they all did the same. Now Mai had eight friends in that apartment. Why she was there she had no idea, but at least she had friends there.

Chapter Nineteen

Nuan stood at her usual place beyond the end of the bar in Xi Gong with a packet in her hand, just in case. She wore her new outfit: a gold-coloured silk blouse, a short, white skirt, and knee-high, black, stiletto boots. Seven nights a week at that nightclub needed a few outfits. A young woman in a patterned, black minidress, a fedora hat and black stilettos came by to slip two notes into Nuan's hand, who slipped a packet into the young woman's hand. Nuan didn't like dealing drugs like that, but she had to and it was only ecstasy. Nuan reached into her cross-shoulder bag for another packet, when she sensed someone close.

"Party girl!" he shouted in her ear.

"Wanshàng hao Peng," she shouted back. *Good evening.*

"Good business?"

"Your stuff is good, you know."

"You've tried it?"

"Are you that naive?"

"Can we talk?"

Nuan grabbed her gin and tonic resting on the end of the bar, to follow Peng outside to the deck. He sat and she sat opposite.

"Once we talked and you said you were picky and it took love, and love was a man with Yin who matched your Yang. Yet you dance with guys and then you fuck them for money."

Nuan sipped her drink while thinking, and there was only one answer for that. "If men want me for free, I need a relationship based on love. But if men want to just fuck me, then it's 4,000."

Peng reached behind his slacks, unusual for Peng not to be wearing jeans, and pulled out a bundle of notes. He counted four and placed them on the table under the ashtray. Fuck!

"You have to wear a condom," Nuan said while hoping that would put him off.

"Fine."

Nuan breathed deep while looking for other excuses. "I'm sure you live too close to my home."

"I have a place near here."

Nuan knew something from her Beijing patrol days. "No hotels. They monitor girls like me."

"I have an apartment."

Nuan was totally fucked! She picked up the money and put it in her bag. When she fell pregnant with Hu and had an abortion, they fitted an IUD which was good, but at the same time they showed her how to use condoms, fortunately. Otherwise she didn't have a clue.

"Wait here. I need to go to the ladies; I won't be a minute."

"I'm not going anywhere, party girl."

Nuan eased through the club to join a short queue. There inside she dropped a two yuan coin in the vending machine

to get a little, plastic packet. Then she realised – all night.
She bought two more to put into her bag. Back to the
balcony where she picked up her drink to finish it. Peng
stood.

"That's a great outfit!" Peng exclaimed.

"Thank you."

He headed off so Nuan decided to do the right thing and
slip her hand inside his arm, like she'd seen Meilin with her
one-time triad gangster boyfriend. Nuan was tall, as tall as
Peng, and now she was seriously taller.

"You speak good English yet you deal drugs and fuck for
money."

Nuan decided to borrow part of Mother's life to mix with
her own background. "I have a degree in economics where I
learned English, but I earn as much in one night doing this as
a week working as an economist."

"You live in Renhe."

Nuan thought. "I'm saving to travel and I'm saving to buy
my own apartment, so I don't want to waste my money
renting an expensive apartment." Nuan thought more.
"When I reach my goals I'll go back to economics."

"I've never met anyone like you."

Nuan didn't doubt that. The real Nuan was outside his
normal sphere, but the undercover Nuan was way out there!
She didn't want to fuck him, but short of blowing her cover,

which could even be dangerous, there was no way out of it. At least she had the upper hand.

"I'm different to 200 plus 200 for half an hour in a massage parlour," Nuan said. "Go with what I say to get your money's worth. Alright?"

"Alright."

"This is it," Peng said.

'This' was a modern, multi-storey luxury apartment building in that district of Yide, which no doubt had serviced apartments for short-term rental. Peng had this all planned, which in a way was sweet. As they entered the foyer, Nuan decided to shower together to start, then hug him, kiss him, give him a blowjob, then while he was on his back, roll on the condom and fuck him cowgirl. She suspected he had stamina, so his next turn would be doggy which would do him for the night. Sleep naked, given she didn't have anything in her bag beyond her essentials and three condoms, fuck again in the morning, and piss off home.

He pressed the button for the lift.

"I'm looking forward to his," Peng said.

Now that she'd gotten over the shock, Nuan was, in a strange way, looking forward to it too. The lift arrived where Nuan, with her hand still inside Peng's arm, stepped inside.

* * *

Nuan sat on the edge of the rumpled bed pulling her left boot on, when she heard the water in the shower stop. She zipped

140

it before pulling on her right boot, as the bathroom door opened and Peng entered the room, rubbing his hair with a towel while dripping water on the carpet.

Nuan was overcome with curiosity. "How was it?" she asked before zipping her right boot.

"I've wanted to get you naked since I first met you."

"No not that. How was it for you? Have you ever done this with a high-class girl before?"

"Yes I have and she wasn't as good as you. Nowhere near as good."

Nuan was pleased. "I like to give my clients value for money." She stood to slip on her cross-shoulder bag.

"Are you going home to Renhe?" Peng asked.

"I'm going to find a cafe for breakfast."

"You can head off for breakfast as if nothing happened?"

"It was just sex."

"Good sex?"

Actually it was. "Yes it was good sex. Your cute girlfriend is a lucky girl."

"You've seen her?"

"I've been told she's cute."

"Cute. I like that."

"Cute is good."

"If she's cute, what are you?"

"Expensive," Nuan said, and giggled. "Zài jiàn."

"Zài jiàn party girl."

Nuan's stiletto heels were noisy on a granite-tiled corridor as she strode to the lifts. Dressed that way implied one thing, which didn't bother her at all. She pressed the 'down' button, and moments later, the lift appeared. She entered where an older Western couple had a couple of large suitcases on wheels.

"Good morning," Nuan greeted in English.

"Good morning," they both replied.

They reached the ground floor, where Nuan strode across more granite tiles with her stilettos still noisy. Outside to take stock on a cool, sunny and rather lovely morning. A little way along she saw office workers with cups of takeaway coffee, so Nuan headed in that direction to see a cafe at the ground floor of the next building, with the inevitable blackboard of specials. She went inside to a queue of takeaways and nobody at the many tables. She took a chair where a young woman brought a jug of filtered water, a glass and a menu. Nuan reached into her bag for her phone, to scroll her contacts for Hu. She opened a text message.

'All good. Will be home in a few hours.' Send.

Nuan poured a glass of water and sipped, before scrolling to her next contact. She pressed 'call'.

"Wéi Lo," Jia greeted.

"Wéi Jia. This is a story, so listen. A while ago I made up a story for Peng about freelance prostitution at 4,000 a night, to find out if he was triad. That's believable for the role I'm playing. So Peng came to in Xi Gong yesterday evening with 4,000 yuan. I tried to get out of it, but he had it all planned so I went through with it."

"Are you alright? No. Wait a moment." Nuan heard a door open then a while later. "Are you there?" Jia asked.

"Yes I'm still here."

"I'm somewhere private. Is there anything you want to tell me about last night?"

"Peng was alright and I'm fine."

"Whatever you do, don't tell Dewai. He'll never understand."

Nuan knew that. "He's not a detective, like you and me."

"Not only that but there's still this thing about men being studs and women being sluts. Even if he was a detective, he wouldn't be able to get his head around sex for the sake of sex."

"You do?"

"Yes I do. When you were in a relationship with Hu at university, I didn't have time for a full-time boyfriend, study, assignments and passing, but that didn't mean I was celibate. If I liked a guy and it seemed right...."

What a surprise!

"So if you're good, I'm good," Jia said, "but if ever you need to talk, even months or years in the future, I'll be available."

"I'll keep that in mind. Now, the important thing. While Peng was snoring I went through his contacts and I have mobile numbers for his 426 and the 438."

"You've just broken this case!" Jia exclaimed.

"I know."

"I'll get a pen and pad." A few moments later. "I'm ready."

"The 426 is 155 4825 7731, and the 435 is 155 0198 3361."

"That's great Nuan. Are you good?"

"I'm good. Is there anything else you need to know?"

"I'll start on those numbers now. Remember if anything comes up or you need help, call me."

"I will. Zài jiàn."

"Zài jiàn."

Nuan ended the call. The waitress came, so Nuan quickly scanned the menu.

"A flat white and poached eggs on toast."

The waitress took the menu and stomped away, while Nuan imagined what she was thinking. Only a slut or a whore would still be in her nightclub outfit, mid-morning having breakfast.

* * *

Jia tore the top page off before handing the pad and pen to Lai Chun; Commissioner Shui's personal assistant. Then she was aware of someone. She turned and then saluted, which Commissioner Shui responded casually.

"I was on a call to Sergeant Shui as her handler, but I didn't want our office to overhear."

"Is she alright?"

"She's good."

"Come into my office."

Jia entered for Commissioner Shui to close his big door. He went to the big table to sit, and gestured for Jia to sit alongside.

"I have something," Jia said as he handed the page across.

She watched his eyes rise. "Nuan found this?"

"Yes she did."

"Office 1.10 started as my idea, including women detectives, while other things came from Nuan. I wanted women who typically pause and think, to balance men who are more likely to rush into things. Superintendent Ma told me he's letting you mostly run on your own, because he's more than happy with the way you're handling things."

Jia already knew that, but she was pleased to hear it again.

"Where do you plan to go from here?" Commissioner Shui then asked.

Jia knew. "We'll trace and monitor those numbers to start. The original scenario of buying ice in bulk to sell to island nations; still stands. Small boats can tranship ice from a mothership, land at beaches on those islands, then tranship ice to four-wheel-drives. Ice would be everywhere in no time. Police corruption is worse than here, while the standard technique to get a new market established is to hand out free ice where potential customers hang out, like schools or where the unemployed congregate, to get customers addicted. Superintendent Ma will arrange a meeting with Mo Feng, now using the number we have for him, get their 438 into the same meeting, and we'll record it. Then we'll monitor their phones while they convict themselves."

"You know more about this than Superintendent Ma, yet he's going to run this meeting with triad."

Jia thought. "I'll write a script for Superintendent Ma to memorise. I'll be at this meeting, so if they throw questions at us I can answer them."

"Anything else?"

"Based on the Axe Gang case I think we should order 1,000 kilograms, and as new customers we'll pay a deposit of 10% in US dollars. Is that alright?"

"The scenario is you're the finance person, so you'll attend this meeting with an attache case of cash. Don't worry about the deposit; when they're arrested we freeze all their assets, and when they're convicted we seize and sell their assets as proceeds of crime. Now, what about the rest of the leadership of this gang?"

Jia had thought about that. "With the Axe Gang case, Sergeant Shui arranged for her friend, Yun Meilin, and Yun Meillin's friend Jia Wen, to testify in exchange for protection." She leaned closer to Commissioner Shui. "The standard interrogation technique is to lock the suspect in an interrogation chair which is quite confronting. What I propose is a variation on what Sergeant Shui did, which is to get the wives, one at a time, in a small room one-on-one, and have an off-the-record discussion that they're either going to be executed, or if they're lucky, get 30 years, while their husbands will definitely be executed. But if they give us the other members of the leadership team, we'll give them new IDs, Shanghai residency, and because they're older than Yun Meilin and Jia Wen, a furnished apartment. The main difference with Yun Meilin and Jia Wen is these women losing contact with their children, so these women will have to give their details to their immediate family while hoping triad don't find out."

"That's worth trying. The worst that can happen is they refuse."

"I believe as mothers, the alternatives of execution, or 30 years in prison, maybe far away with irregular visits only, against new lives and normal relationships with their children, and grandchildren in time, will be hard to resist."

Commissioner Shui nodded his head slowly. "I see the logic in that."

"These one-on-one discussions will have to be tough."

"Can you be tough, Sergeant Xiong?"

"Maybe as a woman who will have her own child in time, I bring something to this scenario compared to a male."

"Your proposed discussion rather than interrogation breaks normal procedures, so we'll keep it off-record." Commissioner Shui stood. "I'll let you get back to work."

Jia stood to salute, then left his office. To Office 1.10 where she gave the sheet of paper to Superintendent Ma.

"I'll arrange traces on those numbers now, and for Constable Tang and Constable Zuo to monitor their calls."

Superintendent Ma nodded his head.

"Commissioner Shui agreed for you to call Mo Feng on this number to organise a meeting to buy 1,000 kilograms of ice for the first month, with the intention to buy more in subsequent months, with Mo Feng's manager for want of a better word, in attendance, given these quantities. For our first order we'll pay 10% deposit in US dollars. I'll write a script for this meeting so everything is clear for both of us. Is that alright?"

"This is Commissioner Shui's original idea, now refined with what we've subsequently discovered.

"That's right." Jia thought. "Do you want me to write a script for your telephone call?"

"We need to be precise on this, so that's an excellent idea."

"Can I have that page, please?"

Superintendent Ma handed it back. Jia setup the traces, then quickly prepared a roster to monitor those triad numbers, where Bo would mostly work evenings and weekends. Jia wanted Huang working regular hours so he could help with other tasks. Then she set to writing the telephone call script based upon what they uncovered with the Axe Gang case. A bare bones version of how their purchase and shipment would most likely play out. Once Superintendent Ma sketched that to Mo Feng, who would totally believe her fabricated scenario given it was based on a real case; their meeting would follow to confirm that call.

* * *

Nuan climbed the stairs to unlock the door to their shared apartment.

"Ni hao Hu," she greeted.

"Ni hao Nuan," he responded.

"Before you say anything, I texted you last night and again this morning, so you wouldn't worry."

"What were you up to?"

Nuan contemplated Hu while thinking Jia's observation was right. Even a male detective wouldn't accept her behaviour. Studs and sluts. "I found the contact numbers for the 426 and the 438," she said. "I rang Jia and she's working with those now."

"They'll be able to track them and monitor them," Hu said.

"For sure this is a big breakthrough."

Nuan went to her room to change to jeans and a t-shirt, before powering up her personal phone. She texted Dewai – 'want to meet sometime today?'

'when?'

'now?'

'yes.'

Nuan pulled on a pair of ankle-high boots, before grabbing her bag now with two phones.

"I'm visiting my boyfriend for a few hours," she said to Hu. "If you need me, call."

Nuan headed to Renhe Metro Station, and not so long after was home. She opened her door sensing Dewai. Indeed he was home waiting, so she moved close and rested her head against his shoulder. He wrapped his arms around her.

"I love you," Nuan murmured.

"I love you too."

Nuan was there for a reason. "I have to play a role, and I have do things that aren't really me," she said. She looked up at his face momentarily. "I want to be the real me, with you, for a few hours."

"You can have me for as long as you want."

Nuan knew she had him for as long as she wanted. Fucking Peng was just fucking, while making love with the man who loved her was the same basic act but an entirely different thing. Nuan eased away, took his hand, and led him past the table to their bedroom. There she started on the buttons of his shirt while sensing their dynamic.

Chapter Twenty

Liko's mobile rang from an unknown contact. He hesitated but knew he had no choice but to answer.

"Wéi," Liko greeted.

"Second chance. What is Office 1.10 up to?"

Liko knew he had no choice on this either. "Other members of Office 1.10 are investigating an unknown gang manufacturing methamphetamine in Guangdong Province."

"You have to do better than that."

"Honestly, that's all there is! Maybe pieces will fall into place or maybe not, but at the moment others, not me, are trying to trace one gang of which they don't know the name, or location, or anything much."

"To settle your debt and to protect your family, you have to come up with more."

Liko thought. "I have your number from this call, so I'll call you when there's something definite.

"Do that."

The call ended.

* * *

The nine Vietnamese women were taken downstairs to the busy street of shops, where the two men and the old woman, Pang Fan, then led them just along into a small arcade of shops, then down a staircase to a basement of shops where only one shop had lights on. Only one shop was open. They were led inside to a large space with rails for curtains hanging from the ceiling, all curtains pulled back to reveal 12 narrow beds with long legs of a type Mai had never seen before. By the murmurs of the other women they were equally befuddled.

The two men and Pang Fan spoke briefly before one of the men took his shirt off to lie on a table, face-down.

Pang looked at the Vietnamese. "Wushí," while holding a note with '50' on it. "Yibai," while holding a second note with 50 together with the first, to make 100. Then she gestured so Mai first, then the others, repeated those words. Then she said, "Chui gong wushi, cào yibai," and again asked all to repeat that.

Pang then rubbed the man's shoulders and back, before getting him to roll over. Then she went to a soap bottle on the cabinet beside the bed, to spray some soap on her hands before taking a realistic rubber penis, only bigger than Yuanfu's penis, and placing it above the man's penis still inside his trousers. Then Pang stroked the penis, slow at first and then quite vigorously while Mai realised where that would end, with the stuff from the bottle making Pang's hands quite slippery before she stopped.

"Chui gong," Pang said before taking that erect penis, still over the man's penis, in her mouth and then sucking while bobbing her head. How awful! She sucked and sucked while pointing at her cheeks clearly sucking. Mai realised where that would end too, but never did she want to do that. Then Pang stopped, took a tissue from a box also on top of the cabinet and spat into it before throwing it into a plastic rubbish bin in front of the cabinet.

"Cào," the woman said, before taking a packet from her pocket and tearing the top. It was an odd thing until she rolled it over that rubber penis like a glove. Once more she squirted not soap but lubrication on her fingers than rubbed that onto the penis, before gesturing it at her vagina. Mai understood. Chui gong meant sucking before spitting, for 50 or wushí, while cao meant fucking with one of those things on a man's penis, with lubrication, for 100 or yibai. But that was horrible. Pang unrolled the rubber thing and threw it in the plastic rubbish bin.

Pang then gestured for Mai, who squirted slippery lubrication on her hands before rubbing the penis, which Pang once more held over the man's penis, while Pang said, "good." Then chui gong which tasted quite horrible but Mai guessed the real thing wouldn't taste as bad. Pang poked Mai's cheeks to suck harder, and then said, "Good." Finally, Mai took a packet from the top drawer of the cabinet, tore the top, and unrolled it down the rubber penis with some help from Pang. Again Mai was told, "Good." Mai rolled the rubber thing off before throwing it in the bin.

In turn each woman was given a practice with the man and the rubber penis held in place, eventually to Pang's satisfaction. The man was then allowed to replace his shirt.

Pang reached into a shelf below the drawer of the cabinet to take out black underwear. She gave one set to each woman and it was clear they were expected to change. So change Mai did, as did the others, to now wear a tiny black bikini.

Mai wanted to say something but knew she would get into trouble, so she kept it to herself. Men would come to see women wearing tiny black bikinis, who would massage them and then rub them to come, or offer chui gong for wushí, which was sucking until they came, or cào for yibai, which was first one of those things onto a man's penis followed by lubrication followed by fucking until they came. If anything Mai preferred to be fucked, especially with a plastic sleeve in the way, than to have men come in her mouth like that, even if she could spit into a tissue. All of that made Mai's stomach churn, but the alternative was all day, every day with Po Po. What was worse, strangers for however long they took, or all day with Po Po? Mai wondered as Pang now drew grey curtains along those tracks around each narrow bed to form tiny cubicles with just enough room. How could Mai and a man be separated from other couples only by curtains? That was as revolting as any of the acts they were expected to perform. Mai sighed deeply. From those moments when she was silly and childish with that boy Long, really she had been silly with a crook who got paid for stealing her, Mai's life had been endless misery. The only good things were her friends in Fusi and her colleagues here. Now they had something to make them even closer, sharing the same misery.

Chapter Twenty One

Jia contemplated the transmitter. She needed help but fortunately help was in hand.

"Huang," she said. "Grab your laptop and headset and come with me."

They walked to the corridor with the mens and ladies, where Jia told Huang to wait. She went inside the ladies to emptiness. She beckoned Huang in.

The stalls were too small, but that didn't matter. Jia unzipped her skirt and dropped it to the floor, then stood with her legs somewhat apart.

"Can you wrap that velcro band around the pantyhose on my upper thigh, as high as possible, and put the transmitter in the pocket of the band while facing inside, antenna down through the hole, and switch it on. The switch is on top."

Huang knelt to do that. Jia pulled on her skirt and zipped it.

"Is that alright?" she asked.

"That's outrageously hot, actually."

"Is it?" Jia asked, somewhat surprised.

"Absolutely!"

Odd, but that wasn't what she wanted to know. "Is my zip square and straight at the middle of my back?"

"Here."

He moved it.

"Better," he said. "Still looks totally hot."

"Go outside and plug in your headset. I'll talk and you can check."

"Right."

Jia counted: "yi, èr, san, sì, wu, liù, qi, ba, jiu, shí." She poked her head out of the door.

"That was good," Huang said.

"Let's go," Jia said.

"Nervous?"

"Are you serious?"

"I could say things like we'll be there listening, but that won't help you feel better until this is over."

"Right."

Superintendent Ma wore a charcoal-grey man's suit with a white shirt and a blue tie, while the male officers: Liko, Shen, Bo and Huang, all wore body armour and had pistols and batons. They headed downstairs to the basement parking area where there was a white Nissan Sylphy, and a white Volkswagen Caddy van with an additional 10 armed officers, as well as four laptops monitoring triad phones and the two transmitters. Jia got behind the wheel of the Nissan, adjusted her seat for comfort, before pulling out for their drive to Xiulu. In the boot of the Sylphy was a leather attache case with the agreed deposit. Jia checked her mirror for the Volkswagen following, which it was. Their destination was a private dining room in the Guangzhou Restaurant. When she discovered that, Jia refined her script to include business etiquette. Business lunches were to get to know you with a meeting to follow.

The Guangzhou Restaurant on busy Wanchang South Road was big and bright in ochre and red, of three storeys with an imitation pagoda-type roof. Jia parked about 50 metres further along while worried their van would have to find space wherever it fitted, and maybe would have to park again if they moved to another location for their meeting. No mind: with attache case in her hand she walked side-by-side with Inspector Ma, now Chang Yi while Jia was Wu Na, between ochre columns and up a couple of steps, at a modern building trying a little too hard to look traditional.

Inside was a totally massive, ear-shatteringly busy dining room in shades of brown with brown carpet, dominated by a huge, domed-type light fitting in the ceiling. Horribly busy, especially compared to friendly little restaurants in Renhe with great food. Jia wouldn't have eaten there if it was the last restaurant in the city. At a rostrum, Superintendent Ma or Chang Yi, asked the waiter for the room booked by Mo Feng. The waiter led the way to a small room of dull yellow walls, brown carpet, and three triad: two older men and a younger woman, maybe in her 30s, dressed the carbon-copy of Jia right down to black pantyhose and black leather shoes with chunky heels. Chang Yi was introduced to Qiao He, clearly the Deputy Mountain Master or 438, Mo Feng the Red

Pole or 426, and the woman, Chen Ru. With each greeting he shook hands while bowing, as did Jia or Wu Na, carrying the attache case in her left hand.

In reality Qiao He called himself 'manager', Mo Feng 'assistant manager' and the woman, Chen Ru, was 'finance manager', which made her the White Paper Fan or 415. Jia's equivalent in her undercover role. As was custom, the most senior, Qiao He, sat first, followed by his two subordinates and their guests. Qiao He then stood.

"To our new business partners, may today be the beginning of a relationship profitable to both. Ganbei."

Jia stood with the rest, to drain her small cup of fiery baijiu.

Now it was the turn of Superintendent Ma.

"Let today be the start of a new and prosperous relationship. Ganbei."

Jia had already filled her cup, so once more she stood and drank, before sitting as they all did.

"Don't you find it amusing that finance, numbers and money, draws beautiful women?" Qiao He asked. "I feel like I'm working in the wrong area!"

They laughed so Jia laughed too. She understood his sentiment, and in fact finance and economics were primarily feminine occupations these days, which as a woman made her proud. Jia wondered.

"I'm sure Chen Ru will agree with me that the women of China have found their niche in the engine-room of Chinese business."

"Indeed we have!" Chen exclaimed with a bright smile.

Jia's actual niche was somewhere different, where men outnumbered women more than five to one.

The door opened for waiters to bring their banquet. This part didn't need to be scripted: the host, Qiao He, served first, followed by everyone serving rice and a small portion of the dish opposite. During their meal the platter was rotated to share out their dishes. The food was good but no better than Jia's favourite Cantonese restaurant.

"Nice food?" Qiao He asked.

"Great food," Superintendent Ma said.

"Very nice," Jia agreed.

So it went on, with talk about nothing much and even Jia's past, Fuzhou and Beijing, and how much she loved Guangzhou, which she honestly did. They eventually demolished most of the banquet, leaving the dishes on the rotating platter somewhat bare.

Qiao He stood. "We have an office near here if you would like to accompany us. There we can discuss the finer points of this matter."

Near here probably meant walking distance, which was a problem, unless someone in the van was switched on enough to intercept them at the door and tail to their destination.

This was one of those times when Jia wished Nuan was in the van, and she doing the banquet, or the other way around. She hoped Huang would twig what he had to do, as they followed Qiao He through the chaotic main dining room of Guangzhou Restaurant to the relative peace and calm of a busy street at lunchtime. There Qiao He led the way while Jia hung to the rear while discreetly looking around to spot Huang, body armour now discarded, just metres away. Impressive. She put her head down to hide her smile, as she followed the men with Chen Ru by her side.

"I liked your comment," Chen said.

Jia wasn't a finance person but she had a university degree in one of the toughest courses in China. "You and I show that women can do anything that men can do."

"If only men in charge would see it that way."

Jia nodded her head in agreement. The 'men in charge' was the politburo of the Communist Party of China: almost all men with only a few women, virtually token women. "You and I both have degrees, yet we know we'll only go so far."

"That's true."

If there was a woman who in the future could be Police Commissioner of Guangzhou, that woman was Shui Nuan following in her father's footsteps. But for sure that would never happen. Instead, a lesser man will fill that role in time.

"Our role is to show these men our abilities at what we do now, to chip away at old beliefs and stereotypes," Chen then said.

"I agree," Jia said, even though Chen was triad. "You have done well for yourself though."

"A younger woman in my role is unusual."

Qiao He entered a building of small businesses: the directory showed lawyers, accountants and specialist doctors. They took a lift to the third floor, passed an empty reception desk to a simple meeting room dominated by a large table with many black leather chairs. Qiao He beckoned all to sit, with Qiao He at the head of the table, triad on one side and police opposite. Jia put the attache case on the table in front of her.

"You discussed this with my assistant manager, but I would like to hear your details again," Qiao He said.

Superintendent Ma recited the script while Jia listened intently.

"You say daughter ships will tranship merchandise from our mothership?" Qiao He asked.

That wasn't quite right. "We plan for one daughter ship to intercept your mothership, and then we'll tranship the merchandise to a number of smaller craft for each destination," Jia said.

"Ah yes."

"Is this method of acquiring our merchandise, feasible for you?" Jia asked.

"Yes it is."

"Now the merchandise...."

"The highest quality."

"I wouldn't expect anything less. Sources of the ingredients?"

"High quality ingredients from chemical factories in this province, sourced as legitimate product."

"Manufacture?"

"Small-scale manufacturing operations supervised by our staff."

That meant manufacture in villages covered by corrupt police officers and corrupt cadres. "Shipment?" Jia asked.

"From order to shipment is one month, with product leaving Nansha Port on one of three vessels."

"Regular Nansha Port to Australia vessels?"

"Yes they are. The route these vessels take will suit your operation."

"That's correct. Now prices?" Jia asked.

"Ah, your finance role. Chen Ru?"

Chen took out a leather-bound, A5 folder from her bag, and unfolded it while putting on black-framed glasses. She looked at her folder and looked up.

"Our normal price is US dollar 150,000 per kilogram, plus shipping costs of 100,000 US dollars per shipment. For your quantity we can do 140,000 per kilogram, plus shipping."

"As we achieve greater penetration into our markets, I expect our ordered quantities to steadily increase," Jia said.

Chen glanced down. "At 1,500 kilograms a month, we'll revise our prices down by 10%, and at 2,000 kilograms a month, a further 10%. Is this satisfactory?"

"Yes it is. Our first order is 1,000 kilograms."

"That will come to US dollar 140,000,000, plus shipping. You're prepared to pay a 10% deposit?"

Jia flicked the gold-plated clasps of the attache case, which clacked loudly in the quiet room, to lift the lid on US $1,410,000, in new 100-dollar notes. Jia slid the case to Chen Ru directly opposite.

"One million, four-hundred and ten thousand US dollars," Jia said, "as deposit on 1,000 kilograms of processed methamphetamine, plus shipping costs, to be shipped by the first of December, and subsequently transhipped to our vessel according to the sailing schedule of your contracted vessel, of which we will be notified one week in advance. The balance will be paid to your agreed representative when we're notified the product has cleared port. Each week, you'll provide progress reports on production, with shipping details to be confirmed in your last weekly progress report."

Chen Ru checked her folder. "Agreed."

Jia barely believed it! The little transmitter on her thigh caught all that!

Qiao He stood. "I believe this is our meeting concluded," he said.

All stood, where Superintendent Ma and Jia shook each hand in turn, while bowing, and triad bowed too. Jia, now unburdened of the attache case, followed Superintendent Ma to the lift, down, and to the street. There she strode with him to their car, to press the remote before climbing behind the wheel. She put her hands on the wheel to realise they were shaking.

"Intense but unbelievable," she said.

"A good description, Sergeant Xiong."

"Can you believe this happens, all the time? So much money."

"That's up for other law enforcement agencies to deal with. We're only interested in the Chinese methamphetamine problem."

"Can we actually achieve anything? The chemicals to make that quantity are worth hundreds of thousands in US dollar terms. We took out one gang with the assistance of Australian police, we'll take out this gang, but as we take down each gang, surely another fills the vacuum?"

"When you were talking those numbers, I thought exactly that. We can't say we don't have a say because we have a direct line to the commissioner. We'll see this case through, wipe out this triad gang even though we still don't know which gang they actually are; then I'll have that conversation."

Jia started the car to drive to the Guangzhou Public Security Bureau. Soon they were all in Office 1.10. There was an air of intense energy, a buzz of adrenaline. They heard the lock release where Commissioner Shui entered.

"Did it go well?" he asked.

"Your idea worked," Superintendent Ma said.

He nodded his head while Jia had an idea, now that she knew Commissioner Shui better.

"Commissioner Shui," she said, while standing by a laptop. He came to where she handed him the headset. With the mouse she slid the slider to the beginning of the meeting, and pressed 'play'. She watched him frown. Then he put the headset down.

"Do we have details on this new actor: Chen Ru?"

"I'll check for her now," Jia said. "I can't imagine a criminal record, but she has university qualifications probably in finance."

"You have the address for Mo Feng. How about Qiao He?"

"Through monitoring his phone we've located his residential address. We've hacked security cameras in his building."

"As well as the two men we know, I would like to take down Chen Ru. This only leaves the other Red Poles who would manage their gambling and prostitution. Do you ideas on how best to take into custody these three actors we know?"

"I'll think aloud," Jia said. "In a month's time a ship will leave Nansha Port carrying 1,000 kilograms of ice, of which we'll be notified in advance. At that time we'll have the locations of Mo Feng and Qiao He from their mobiles and security cameras, so we'll get them from that. Our coast guard will intercept their ship to uncover the methamphetamine as evidence. If Chen Ru is the recipient of the balance of the cash, we'll get her when that happens."

"Some good thoughts there," Commissioner Shui said with his finger resting on his chin. "In advance we'll confirm place, time and method of payment, when they contact us with their weekly progress report."

"But we don't know if Chen Ru is the person to receive the actual balance of cash," Jia said.

"If she's not the person to receive the cash, we'll have to know her location like the other two, keep her under surveillance, and then we can take her into custody. Knowing she has a university degree is a head start on that. Alright Office 1.10," Commissioner Shui said. "That's your next task."

He headed from the room.

"Alright everyone," Superintendent Ma said. Sergeant Suo and Constable Tang; you monitor the phones for Qiao He and Mo Feng. Listen to every call made since our meeting. Sergeant Xiong and Constable Zuo; you start on locating Chen Ru."

Jia sat at her laptop. Huang sat at his laptop to her right.

"I saw you following us," Jia said. "I don't have to say well done, but well done."

"Thank you. Now we browse universities?"

Jia thought that was too random, and wouldn't tell them more than her address from when she studied perhaps many years ago. "We'll find her ID record first, which will give us her date of birth. Then we'll check for finance or accounting professional associations to see if we can locate her that way."

Huang typed quite furiously for a moment.

"There she is," he said. "Date of birth: tenth of October, 1988."

"Let's search for accounting associations to see where that takes us."

Jia turned to type into her favourite search engine, and in parallel Huang typed too. To find that one woman in Guangzhou was like searching for a needle in a haystack, but not impossible. This would take time but they had a month to find her.

"Superintendent," Suo Shen called. "Mo Feng made this call."

Shen put his computer on loudspeaker, where the office heard him call an unnamed associate, confirming 1,000 kilograms of merchandise ready to be shipped in three weeks, then call ended.

Jia, standing behind, knew the shorthand. Merchandise was their methamphetamine order, while three weeks gave this gang time to get the methamphetamine from the place of production, usually a village or a small town, to the mothership at Nansha Port.

"The recipient of that call?" Superintendent Ma asked, but got a blank look from Shen, who didn't have the technical skills.

"May I?" Jia asked.

"Please, Sergeant Xiong," Superintendent Ma said impatiently.

Jia navigated menu – track and trace. "The recipient number is 159 8870 9821. This is a newly issued China Mobile number. She went to menu – location. "The recipient was connected to a tower at the town of Baitang." Jia went to menu – map. "There." Jia went to menu – address. "He was at street number 598 on 447 Country Road in the town of Baitang." Jia went to menu – satellite. "There." She zoomed it. "I'll trace all future calls to and from that number." Jia overlaid menu – track and trace while Superintendent Ma peered over her shoulder.

"This new actor will be a 49er," Jia said. "Based on what we learned with the Axe Gang case, this town, or a village nearby, will be where this gang makes methamphetamine, while this 49er will be the liaison to local police and cadres."

"How big is Baitang?" Superintendent Ma asked.

Jia zoomed the image outwards. "Bigger than a village but not that big. You can see it here."

Superintendent Ma looked around. "Sergeant Kam; you're not doing anything critical. You can monitor calls from this 49er, and track his movements. Sergeant Xiong; you and Constable Huang get a car, if possible find a car in need of a clean, and go for a drive to Baitang."

"The only way methamphetamine production can happen in a town this size, is with local police and cadres being involved," Jia said. "How about we put the police superintendent and the mayor under surveillance to see where that takes us?"

"Make sure you're not caught!"

That would blow the case and all of Nuan's hard work. "A dirty car is a good idea, and we'll dress casually to match. I'll get Lai Chun to make bookings for us for the next two nights. Cameras, radios and weapons."

"You know what to do, but be careful!"

Soon they were in a car heading east to Baitang, having grabbed their basics from Jia's apartment on the way out of Guangzhou.

"You remember our last case when we went to Guangning County for surveillance," Jia said. "That went pear-shaped but Nuan took advantage of that surveillance in other ways. Later she went there with her boyfriend for a weekend away."

"That's an idea!" Huang exclaimed.

"When this rush is over I'll find out where she stayed, and I know she rented a car." Jia caught the flash of Huang's smile.

"You've met her boyfriend; what's he like?" Huang asked.

"He's about your age and he's calm and measured. Nuan is a bit out-there, always two steps ahead of the rest of us, so I think he grounds her while she spurs him on."

"And us?"

"Is our age difference an advantage? Do you suit me better than a guy my age?"

"Do you think so?"

"Yes."

"Anything else?"

"I'm not out-there like Nuan and you're not measured like her boyfriend, so we match each other in the middle, I think. We're on the same wavelength. Really, it doesn't matter. Us together has always felt right for me. I'm not going to over-think it; it just feels right. And you?"

"From our first date it felt – right like you said. Since then and even here in this car, it feels right."

Jia's university course was tough. She needed an EER of 580 to qualify, as good as the most sought-after courses in Beijing. She got 610. Then there were 12 disciplines: law, public order, criminal investigation, criminology, police administration, international police and law enforcement, forensic science and technology, policing information engineering, cyber defence, counterterrorism, police command techniques, and traffic management engineering, and other skills like firearms training and hand-to-hand combat. More than learning facts, Jia learned to learn. She entered university aged 18, but graduated feeling older than 22. As they sped along country roads, Jia thought it took luck they fell together that evening because for sure they fitted together, with Huang being mature and street-smart from his working experiences. Eventually they arrived at Baitang, a decent-sized and reasonably prosperous-looking town on the Pearl River Delta. Huang drove to the town's administration centre where Jia readied her camera. There they would wait, while on her phone she had pictures of the police superintendent and the mayor from their ID records, so she knew who to be looking out for.

"Jia," Huang said.

"I see it."

A new red, Nissan Qashqai SUV pulled in. The major climbed out to go inside the building as Jia ran off a few shots.

"Corruption," Huang said.

All the hallmarks. "Let's check where he lives."

Jia put his address in the GPS. Five minutes later, Huang parked opposite in the shade of a tree while Jia ran off shots of a new, single-storey house hiding behind a grey-painted brick wall, on a large block of land nestling against parkland.

"Police superintendent now," Jia said as she entered his address. Drive time, three minutes in the expensive end of town. A large, two-storey house behind a low brick wall, showing an over-abundance of columns and porches and a well-manicured garden. More pictures.

Jia typed the address of the public security bureau into the GPS, again three minutes.

Two waterways joined near the centre of town, which had stores, restaurants and shopping malls. The public security bureau was a simple, two-storey brick building with the carpark to the rear protected by a lockable gate, so Jia left the camera behind to walk to that wire gate. Amongst a motley assortment of police vehicles identifiable by white with blue flashes, was a black Nissan X-Trail SUV, new and relatively expensive for a police superintendent. She took a mental note of the registration, where, back in the car she used her laptop to connect to 4G. That registration belonged to Fang Sheng-li, or the police superintendent as Jia expected.

"More corruption," she said. "Expensive house and a new SUV." She rubbed her temples for inspiration. The address of that telephone call. She put that in the GPS.

"There, Huang."

They arrived at a house neither ostentatious or shabby.

"This is where our 49er was called. We'll base our surveillance here."

Jia reclined her seat to be more comfortable, and with the camera on her lap, she waited.

"Is he even here?" Huang asked.

"His mobile's connected to the tower here," Jia said, then thought. "When this case is over and we have some free time, I'll teach you this technology. That will help our team, and that'll help you personally."

"Two things on the agenda after this case is over: lessons in mobile tracking and tracing and a weekend away."

Jia looked forward to their weekend away together. Even this business trip wasn't going to be so bad. They would find somewhere nice to eat and they had a shared room for later.

"A car's coming," Huang said.

A blue Havel H6, a popular medium-sized SUV, approached and parked. Jia took a few pictures, and of the young man in a blue button-up shirt with long sleeves, over jeans and white runners, as he headed inside.

She put her camera down to pick up her laptop and wake it from hibernation. Then, a call – to the 426! She slipped her headset on to catch the end, so rewound to listen to the call: production on target for three weeks. Jia sighed. He was their man but her pictures, side-on from a distance, were useless for facial recognition, while production could be anywhere in that town, or even in a village nearby.

"That's our 49er. He rang the Red Pole confirming production on target." Jia checked her watch. "It's four and unlikely he'll return to the source of production today, or even in the next few days, although we don't know. I say that's it for surveillance for today, so we'll check in to our hotel, and return here tomorrow morning."

Huang started the car and pulled away for the drive to their hotel about 20 minutes away in Huazhou. It was a budget hotel, but as long as it was clean and the bed was comfortable, Jia didn't mind.

"Let me think out loud," Jia said as Huang sped along a road bordered by lush, green rice paddies. "Production of the methamphetamine could be in Baitang, but it could be in a village nearby. When, or if, we can find production, we leave it be so not to raise suspicions. When this goes down we send in the People's Armed Police Force to arrest the mayor, the police superintendent and this guy, and the people making this stuff, because even if they clean up there will be traces of ingredients there."

"Sounds right to me," Huang said.

"So we keep following this 49er around until he gives us the location where they're making this stuff."

"If we become his shadow, that could reveal us."

"We'll have to follow him at a distance. Actually I can ring him, I only need him on call for a second, and I'll have his location. I'll find the police superintendents number and spoof that for the call."

"Pardon?"

"I'll use the police superintendent's number to call that 49er so he won't be suspicious."

While they sped along the road, Jia rang Superintendant Ma where she asked him to text to her the police superintendent's number from the directory. Then she used 4G to log in and start her report in their case file system. At the hotel she would upload her pictures to the same system. She looked up from her computer to see a bigger town: Huazhou. They parked outside a low-set brick building fronting a carpark, where Jia went to reception for their key. Shortly after they were in a room, somewhat musty, finished in green-coloured plaster walls with timber slatted trim; all a bit water-stained. A bed, two tables, a cheap wardrobe and a chair with green fabric. Huang pressed on the bed: creak. He pressed several times: creak, creak, creak; creak.

"Please!" Jia exclaimed.

"We'll keep our neighbours awake," he said.

He was right about that.

"I'm no longer Sergeant Xiong so this is a discussion of equals. Not many have checked into this hotel from what I saw of the keys at reception, so we can shower now to freshen up, and then before this place fills up?"

"Good idea."

"You shower first. I'm a bit obsessive which you're going to have to get used to. I'll upload my pictures from today and then I can relax."

Jia sat on the bed with a big creak, while Huang undressed. She wanted to get her work done and her mind clear. She moved, creak; creak. Later lots of creaking, or perhaps the chair or one of the tables.

Chapter Twenty Two

Once more they parked close to number 598 on 447 Country Road, but not too close. They got up at seven, and after breakfast and getting ready it was just past eight. Nothing stirred. Once more Jia reclined her seat to be comfortable waiting. Waiting, waiting; waiting.

"There he is." Huang said.

Jia focussed and took two pictures while Huang started the engine of their Nissan. The 49er, whoever he was, got into his Havel to head along 447 Country Road before veering right

"Remember, keep a distance," Jia said. "I'm going to locate him electronically."

"He's just a speck."

Jia looked up from her laptop, and so he was. They were now on the road heading to a number of villages quite close to each other. Approaching Fukeng which Jia didn't think was the place. Too close to Baitang.

"Keep going Huang," she said.

"Alright."

They slowed for the small village before emerging out the other side.

"I've lost him," Huang said. "His car's too dark against the bitumen."

"Just along is Licoapa Village. Stop there."

They entered another village of 40 or 50 houses scattered around the main road and surrounded by rice paddies. Huang parked.

"Now we wait," Jia said. She had an idea of what was happening. In fact she was impatient to know if she was right, but she had to be patient. Waiting, waiting, waiting; now close to ten.

"I'm calling him."

Jia slipped her headset on, keyed the mobile number from the text message, and called. It rang five times before he answered 'wéi'. Jia ended the call. *There!*

"He's in Shalongba," Jia said. "There are four villages close to each other; like one big village with more than 100 houses." Jia frowned as she studied the satellite image. "Closer to 200 houses."

"They're making methamphetamine there?" Huang asked.

"Time will tell," Jia said. "Back to his place."

Twenty minutes later, Huang parked at Baitang.

"Too much coffee!" Jia exclaimed. "I need a pee."

"You pee and I'll watch."

"You could have expressed that better."

Huang laughed while Jia got out to search for somewhere private. In the end she hid behind a tree near the river. Back to the car.

"My turn to pee."

"I'll get behind the wheel. Just along there you'll find some trees."

"Thanks."

Jia stayed behind the wheel when Huang got into the front passenger seat so they didn't look suspicious or idiotic. Later Huang bought some Cantonese with two bottles of water. Time ticking on; ticking on.

"That's him!" Huang exclaimed.

Jia checked her watch – four again, before taking a couple of pictures of the young man, unfortunately still from a distance, but that didn't matter. Jia waited until he entered his little brick house and closed the door.

"This is the same time as yesterday," Jia said. "Probably he's heading off at nine each morning to Shalongba to supervise production, and coming home each afternoon at four."

"That makes sense."

"So when this goes down, we'll send the People's Armed Police Force to Shalongba and surrounding villages to arrest the villagers and search for any methamphetamine or ingredients, and armed police here to arrest the mayor, the police superintendent and this guy." She caught Huang's eyes for a moment. "Our job here is finished, although it's too late to drive to Guangzhou. Let's go back to our room to deal with that creaky bed."

Jia started the car to pull out to drive to Huazhou. Like yesterday she would write her report in the case file system, upload her pictures, and then her mind would be free.

Chapter Twenty Three

Nuan contemplated the kettle on their bench and that tin of instant coffee. Her coffee machine and her nice coffee were at her real home. No she couldn't.

"I'm going out to get a decent coffee," she said to Hu.

"Alright."

Nuan skipped down the stairs to get a shock: Peng and a young woman, quite small and slender, climbing. Nuan stopped at a landing.

"Ni hao Lo, Peng greeted, which was unusual. He'd taken to calling her party girl. "This is my girlfriend Binbin."

"Ni hao Peng and Binbin," Nuan greeted while thinking cute was an apt description. She would never turn a man's head but she was alright.

"Ni hao," Binbin greeted.

"There's something important we need to discuss with you," Peng said, "and get your help if you can."

'We' was unusual. "I'm heading out for coffee if you want to join me."

Nuan led the way to Als Gong Cha where she ordered and paid for three flat whites. They took a table.

"So how can I help you?" Nuan asked, as the waitress brought a tray with three cups.

"This is something Binbin discovered," Peng said, but Nuan noticed Binbin was looking down at the table.

"Does she know about me?" Nuan whispered in Peng's ear.

"Not beyond you being one of my dealers."

Nuan guessed what Binbin's problem was. Nuan took a cup to sip while framing the right words. "Binbin, you and I have something in common, beyond knowing Peng. You know I deal E, but I do other things. Men pay me for sex, all night and the next morning. That's different to you but really it's the same."

Binbin looked up with her little, dark eyes quite wide.

"Sex can be sold but there's something else," Binbin said. "We're losing business and there are rumours of a secret massage parlour with the same services for cheaper, using women stolen from Vietnam and other places."

Sex slavery. "So you came to see me?" Nuan asked.

"You're smart and you're someone I trust," Peng said.

"Ah, I see." Binbin was breaking the law, where from time to time massage parlours were raided and workers were sent away for up to two years to be 're-educated' in detention centres. A smart, trustworthy friend, rather than the police, made sense. "Do you know where this place is?"

"No I don't," Binbin said.

Another option. "Do you know a customer you have lost? His name, where he lives?"

"We don't visit men at home but I do know where some men live. Renhe is small that way."

"Let's finish our coffees, and visit a former customer to find what he can tell us."

"You don't mind?"

"That we're trying to rescue sex slaves? Of course not!"

Nuan finished her coffee, to follow Peng and Binbin into the Saturday morning crowds of Renhe. On and on to another apartment building.

"I know he lives on the ground floor."

"Let's check every ground floor door," Nuan said while she reached into her bag for her stash of notes. She counted out five, which was a starting point.

Binbin knocked, where a younger man answered.

"Sorry," Binbin said.

Nuan got closer when Binbin knocked at the next door. A middle-aged man, or older with lines and wrinkles, answered.

"You!" he gasped, just as Nuan muscled Binbin out of the way to stick her boot in the gap. She winced with pain as he slammed the door against her foot.

"Five-hundred yuan!" Nuan shouted.

The door opened a little further.

"What for?" he asked.

"A talk. Five hundred more for information."

The door opened wide, so Nuan led the way inside to stale sweat and tobacco smoke. What a dirty, untidy, shambles. Nuan handed over the bundle of notes.

"There are rumours of a new massage parlour, with cheaper prices and Vietnamese women," Nuan said. "If you tell me the name and where it is, that's five-hundred more."

"I only go there because it's cheaper."

Nuan understood. "How much cheaper?"

"One-hundred, plus one-hundred for full service."

"Alright. I'll give you 1,000; that makes up the difference at Feifan Massage for a few sessions."

He nodded his head.

"Name and address?" Nuan asked.

"Happy Massage in the basement of Miss Saigon Restaurant."

"Do you know where that is?" Nuan asked.

Binbin nodded her head.

Nuan reached into her bag to count out ten notes. She placed them in his yellow, tobacco stained hands. He smiled showing yellow teeth with a few missing.

"We'll go," Nuan said, to lead the way outside, while thinking. Logically Peng was her man to do this investigation, and Peng wasn't faithful anyway. But Nuan didn't want to encourage that in front of his girlfriend, although there was another way.

"Peng, as a man you can investigate for us. Pay for a massage, but when she reaches for you cock, get all horrified and run away. Is that alright?"

"That's a good idea," Binbin said.

Nuan thought so too. "Peng, while you're there, check everything. See if the women are happy to be there, or are cowering and frightened. Check they understand Mandarin or not. Get an idea of how many workers as best you can. Waste your time before they take you to a table or whatever they do, to learn as much about this place as you can."

"Then what?"

Nuan wondered what to say. "I know someone in the police. With what you learn I can make things happen, but you must keep this secret to protect these women. The police will rescue them and take them home, if that's Vietnam or wherever, but if the people who run this shop find out, I'm sure they'll take these women somewhere else."

"The people who run this shop could be bribing police," Binbin said.

That was possible if not probable. "My friend is a detective where they don't take bribes." Nuan looked to Peng. "Are you good with this?"

"Yes," he said.

"Now?"

"Yes."

They headed off with Binbin leading the way.

"I told you she was smart," Peng said, which didn't puff-up Nuan's ego. This was a simple crime where she was doing her real job. They reached Miss Saigon Restaurant.

"Are you good with this, Peng?" Nuan asked.

"I am."

He went inside. Nuan looked around to spot a clothing shop.

"You and I will go there to look at clothes, and keep an eye open for Peng when he emerges."

Nuan crossed the street with Binbin while thinking her day had taken an unusual turn. They reached the shop to play around with jeans, where Nuan had an idea.

"What size are you?"

"160."

Tiny-sized. Nuan went to women's jeans where she found a pair of regular size 160, and size 160 in a skinny style which she thought would suit better. She took both to the change rooms, to hand the regulars across.

"Try these on," Nuan said.

It didn't take long for Binbin to emerge.

"See in the mirror?" Nuan asked.

"Yes."

Nuan gave the skinny ones to Binbin.

"Try these," she said.

Once more it didn't take long for Binbin to change.

"What do you think?" Nuan asked.

"They look great!"

"You're a pocket rocket!" Nuan exclaimed. There wasn't a lot to her, but she showed all the right curves in those jeans.

"I'm buying these, they look like you. We don't have time but next time I'll buy boots like you."

"Do that."

While Binbin was at the register, Nuan glanced out of the window to spot Peng looking lost.

They headed across the street with Binbin now holding a paper bag.

"When I was in school, a friend and I used to do that all the time," Nuan said.

"That was fun!"

Nuan liked Binbin, once they broke their initial awkwardness. Nuan wished she could promise to do that again when they had more time, but she couldn't promise what she might not be able to deliver.

"What were you doing?" Peng asked grumpily.

"Women's favourite sport – shopping." Nuan giggled. "Now seriously, what was it like?"

"Terrible. Maybe 10 or 15 women. They know a little Mandarin but just prices for the extras. Young...."

"How young?" Nuan asked.

"Not children but too young to be doing that. Something's wrong there."

"Mamasan?"

"Chinese."

"So a Chinese gang has trafficked these young women across the border, and they've ended up here. Unlike Binbin

188

or me, they don't make a single yuan for what they're forced to do."

Binbin looked shocked at that.

"Leave this with me and I'll make something happen," Nuan said. "Remember, not a word, no matter how long this takes, although I'll try to make this happen quickly. I'll leave you now to make a phone call."

"Thank you Lo," Binbin offered.

Nuan strode off, quite clear with what needed to be done. Clearly Binbin would benefit financially from the sex slaves being closed down, but to rescue these young women was far more important. Nuan wondered how big of a problem sex slavery was. She decided to look into that when she had time.

She reached home to power up her personal phone, scrolled her contacts, found 'Father' and rang.

"Nuan!" was the not unexpected answer.

"Wéi Father."

"How are you?"

"I'm good. Can I see you about something?"

"Yes of course. Now?"

"I'll be there in about an hour."

She ended the call.

"I'm going out Hu."

"Alright."

Nuan headed off to catch the metro to the apartment where she once lived. That part of her seemed a lifetime ago even if it wasn't.

* * *

That apartment building never changed. Nuan pressed the buzzer for it to be answered by her mother who hugged her tightly. Nuan knew Mother knew everything. They hugged for a while before Nuan hugged Father.

"Come in, Father beckoned.

Nuan entered their living room always with that brown leather lounge suite. Father liked to pay more for quality that lasted.

"Do you want something to drink?" Mother asked.

"Just a glass of hot water please."

"Are you sure?"

"I'm coffee-ed out!"

Nuan sat on the couch, where Father sat beside her. Mother brought the glass before sitting in one armchair.

"I haven't had a chance to speak with Jia – Sergeant Xiong," Nuan said. "I expect with what I discovered they'll be able to make good progress."

"Yes they have," Father said. "This is Superintendent Ma's call, but I don't see a real need for you or Constable Zhang to remain undercover."

Nuan nodded her head. "My undercover contact is a drug-dealer named Peng. Peng has a girlfriend named Binbin who works in a massage parlour. Through Peng and Binbin I've become aware of suspected sex slavery in the basement of a Vietnamese restaurant in Renhe."

"Are you sure?"

"I'm not absolutely sure, but it seems more than likely. Like investigating triad, this has to be handled by an absolute incorruptible team. One bribe, one leakage of information, and these young women will be taken somewhere else to be abused – to be raped endlessly." Nuan sipped her water with her heart racing.

"Good point. How about we bring you and Constable Zhang in, and you lead Constable Zhang and a squad of officers to raid this brothel?"

"I sent Peng in to do a preliminary investigation, given he frequents massage parlours, and he told me something was wrong. I'll send Constable Zhang in as a customer to help me plan this raid."

"After that, you're out of that apartment in Renhe."

Nuan sipped her water. "Fine."

"How has it been?"

"At times it's been tough, but nothing I haven't been able to handle. Oddly, I think I'll miss it. The adrenaline rush of living by your wits, constantly dealing with the lies you tell, is – invigorating. Perhaps even addictive. Two people got me through – Dewai and Jia – Sergeant Xiong." Nuan looked at the floor. "I'm dealing with criminals so I've broken a few laws. I always assessed consequences and possible harm, before going ahead. I know from university that undercover operatives sometimes break laws, but the reality is different to reading and discussing case studies."

"Do you have problems with what you did?" Father asked.

"What surprised me is how easy it was. Unless you've been undercover you can't understand."

"You achieved a lot and I'm proud, as always."

Nuan thought about party girl's night with Peng, and that would change Father's pride to shame. That was where Jia helped her more than any man ever could.

"I'll go back to Renhe to brief Constable Zhang before sending him in. I don't want to raise alarm bells, so if he's comfortable the standard service is a massage with a handjob." Nuan realised. "Apparently that's not breaking a law but we're not certain about that."

"I'll brief Superintendent Ma on Monday, so you can come in on Tuesday ready to plan this raid for – Wednesday."

"Thank you Father, and you too Mother because I know you know."

"I know," she said.

Nuan stood. "I've got an undercover constable to discuss things with, so I better go. Zài jiàn."

They hugged, Mother especially, before Nuan headed out. Nuan realised she'd fucked this up a bit. Peng went in there and made a fuss over the handjob, so if a second customer that day made a fuss over a handjob; that would be suspicious. Fuck – she hoped Hu didn't mind.

By the time she reached home, Nuan knew clear and logical was the answer, which was Hu's style anyway. She let herself in to Hu sitting on his inflatable mattress, surfing the laptop on 4G. He looked up. Nuan decided good news and bad news was trite so she would play it straight.

"Can we talk?" Nuan asked as she sat in an armchair.

"Alright," as he sat on the couch.

Nuan went through the story, including Peng doing his thing and Father's decision to bring them in.

"Now Hu, there's only one undercover operation left for us here in Renhe. You need to investigate this massage parlour as a customer, and this is a lot to ask and I do understand if you don't want to, but I don't want to make a fuss or raise suspicions. Standard service is a massage with a handjob, as you know from our Beijing patrol days."

"You're joking?"

"Do you have a problem? No. These are sex slaves, being raped, so if you can deal with a handjob, even if you don't want it, we can save young women's lives. What do you say?"

"I'll do it. Really, the freaky part is you knowing."

Nuan wondered and then it hit her. "When I go home for a few hours with my boyfriend, is that any different?"

"Not really. You would have felt it with me when you came back."

"I sensed it but I wasn't embarrassed, because humans are sexual, like you and I once were."

Nuan knew, given Hu didn't have a girlfriend; he would be doing handjobs on himself. If he wasn't there was something wrong with him.

"I'll go now," Hu said.

"Thank you Hu."

He headed out while Nuan grabbed her pad and pen to write brief notes. Ten armed officers with radios, headsets and PTT. Body armour, radios, headsets and PTT for two. Photocopied sketch plans. Cars for police. A bus or something for victims. Somewhere to stay – police dormitory or cheap hotel. Translator – Vietnamese.

That covered it. Hu would be a while so Nuan decided to discreetly check out the restaurant. It didn't take long to walk there, where although the restaurant faced the street it was part of a small shopping arcade. Nuan strolled past a grocery store, a shoe repair shop, with three empty shops opposite and a staircase down to the basement. There was a corridor leading to a locked door at the back. Nuan then went outside to find a lane a couple of doors along, like at the cafe, leading to a lane running parallel at the back, similar to where she did her deals.

Nuan headed back to the apartment to sketch that out on a sheet of paper, just as the door opened.

"Fuck that's bad," Hu said shaking his head. "We have to do something."

"I had a look at the shopping arcade," Nuan said. "The massage parlour is down the staircase?"

"Yes it is, directly below the restaurant. Five other shops down there; all closed.

"The massage parlour?"

"An old Chinese woman in charge, with twelve cubicles formed from curtains hanging from the ceiling, each with a massage table. When I paid, the Chinese woman called, and a girl came from somewhere to the rear. For sure she was too young for that. I don't know how many girls but logically no more than twelve. Possibly some men to stop them from running away, but they wouldn't need many men for that."

"I'll put two armed officers at the front of the shopping arcade, two in the lane at the rear, and six go down the stairs with us. Does that sound reasonable?"

"That will be ample."

"Opening hours?"

"Eight to midnight."

"We'll go to the Office 1.10 on Tuesday to assemble a raid for Wednesday morning at – what time?"

"Not first thing in case they're running late and not everybody's there. Say nine."

Nuan noted that.

"That's it for undercover for us," Nuan said. "You ought to go home, while I'll definitely go home."

"I didn't do much; this was you and you were brilliant. The graduate with honours, third-highest marks for our year, and now you've run a remarkable undercover operation. I don't know how you did it."

Nuan shrugged her shoulders while vowing never to do undercover again.

Chapter Twenty Four

Jia strode to the young woman receptionist at the reception desk, dressed office-type in a black suit with a white blouse, and although hidden, she probably wore black pantyhose and black leather shoes with chunky heels. From the inside pocket of her leather jacket, Jia grabbed the folded page and her warrant card in its folder.

"Zao an," Jia greeted. *(Good morning).* Jia showed her warrant card. "I'm Detective-Sergeant Xiong and this is Detective-Constable Zuo. This is a summons for you to hand over any and all records on a possible member of your organisation: Chen Ru."

"I'll call my manager."

An older man in a suit came to the reception foyer. There introductions were made and hands were shaken, before Xia Xia asked Jia and Huang to come to his office. There Jia stood, so Xia stood too.

"How can I help you?" Xia asked.

"We're attempting to trace a qualified accountant or finance person in relation to a matter," Jia said. "Her name's Chen Ru and her date of birth is the tenth of October, 1988."

"Not all qualified accountants are members of the Chinese Institute of Certified Public Accountants."

"I am aware of that, but if she is I would like her details. If it will help, I have a summons in relation to this matter."

"I'll find out if she's a member first."

Xia went to his desktop computer to type slowly for a moment. He studied the screen while frowning. "I'm sorry but we don't have a member with that name and date of birth."

Jia thought that was a possibility. "Do you know of any way we can easily track a finance or accounting graduate from their name and date of birth?"

"You can check university records but that won't be easy."

At Office 1.10 they first rang universities in Guangzhou and Beijing, and now had a team ringing every university in China. "Thank you for your troubles," Jia said as she shook his hand.

He showed them out.

"Back to work, Huang. We've got almost a month to track her down, which I'm sure will be enough time."

* * *

Nuan swiped her security card for the lock to release, and then she opened the door to Office 1.10 which had a surprising air of busyness. All were on phone calls, although she caught Superintendent Ma's eye. He kept speaking for a moment then ended his call. Nuan went to where he stood to shake hands. She wondered how much he knew.

"My undercover operation took a dramatic turn," Nuan said. "I felt that sex slavery of teenagers in a brothel needed fast action, before those who trafficked them took them away. Unfortunately it seems you're busy too."

"We are busy, but we have space and time for this extra case. What do you need, Sergeant Shui?"

"My desk, my computer, Constable Zhang to help me, help from Lai Chun which I'll arrange, and ten armed officers to raid a brothel; leaving from here at eight tomorrow morning."

"I'll organise your officers if you organise everything else."

"That I can do."

"Sergeant Shui!" Superintendent Ma snapped, before saluting her. Nuan saluted in response.

He swept his hand around the busy room. "This is the result of your efforts."

Nuan understood. "We're a team and I'm a just a member of our team."

"For the next few days we're running two investigations, with you leading one and Sergeant Xiong leading the other."

"If these are trafficked sex slaves we need to get them into accommodation, interview them through translators, and get them home when the time is right for that, while arresting those we detain tomorrow."

"And prepare evidence for the case that will follow."

"Yes," Nuan said, with the implication that her investigation was more than a few days.

"I understand. Sex trafficking is a terrible thing."

Nuan spent several hours on the internet outside the firewall, which was nothing short of shocking. "Yes it is."

Nuan noticed Hu at his computer. "I'll get Constable Zhang started on his tasks; then speak with Lai Chun."

Nuan gave Hu his tasks of photocopying her sketch plan, checking-out their equipment from the armoury, and arranging cars, and a bus or a van. Then she left for Commissioner Shui's office, where Lai Chun was at her computer. She must have sensed Nuan watching, as she turned around.

"Sergeant Shui!" Lai exclaimed.

"Yes I'm back." Nuan sat on a chair next to her desk. "We're raiding an illegal massage parlour tomorrow where we may be releasing a number of sex slaves, possibly from Vietnam but they could be from other neighbouring countries. We're guessing about 12 women. Can you arrange accommodation and meals for about 12 women, perhaps at the dormitory, or if there's not enough room, at a modest hotel? They may be our responsibility for a few weeks. In time we'll work out where they need to be returned and make those arrangements."

Lai took a pad to quickly write those details. She looked up. "I'll let you know when it's done."

"Thank you."

Back at Office 1.10, Nuan used the staff directory to find officers in Guangzhou who spoke Vietnamese. She wrote two names and contact details on her pad for later reference; given Vietnamese was only Peng's observation. By the time she did that, Sergeant Yang in uniform was brought in by Superintendent Ma. Nuan explained the role for his men, gave him a copy of her sketch map which didn't have address details, to confirm his men to be ready to go by eight tomorrow morning. Then the lunch trolley rolled in. Lai Chun also confirmed the police dormitory was expecting these women.

Nuan served some chicken wings with rice, while wondering how best to help her team for the rest of the day. Jia was alongside and they hadn't even had a chance to talk.

"Everyone is so busy!" Nuan exclaimed.

"We had a meeting with the 435 and the 426 based on Commissioner Shui's idea of buying methamphetamine to sell to island nations."

Nuan nodded her head while thinking that was mostly her idea.

"After that meeting as we hoped, there was a phone call which led us to the village of Shalongba east of here, where I'm fairly sure the manufacture of our order of methamphetamine is underway. Meanwhile at that meeting, there was a woman in her 30s as their finance person, their 415, who I discovered has university qualifications. Now we're trying to track her down by ringing each university in China."

That explained their busyness. "Have you tried Hong Kong universities?" Nuan asked. "Triad are Hong Kong organisations, after all."

"I'll do that after lunch. If she's from Hong Kong that'll make life difficult."

"You'll only get her home address for the time she was studying, where her family may still live. We don't have jurisdiction in Hong Kong, but you can request assistance from Hong Kong police. Riots there are ongoing but that doesn't involve every detective there. Obviously you can't say your investigating a possible triad; maybe fabricate something minor yet dangerous, like a jaywalking violation which may affect this woman's ability to practice finance. What you need is an address to resolve this matter, which Hong Kong police can then ask on your behalf. If we find this woman studied in China and found her family somewhere here, a story like would work here too."

"I can see why you were good undercover."

"Everything we do here has to be kept secret, and what's more secret than a fake jaywalking violation?"

Nuan ate some chicken wing while thinking Jia was basically honest, while she was basically devious. That being the case, any future undercover operations requiring a female operative would be down to her which Nuan didn't want. She got by, Dewai was great, but the addictive nature of living on the edge could take over, like an ice addict needing their next hit. In time, working undercover could destroy a police officer's life. Nuan wanted to love Dewai forever, and to love their child in time; not a life of adrenaline-fuelled highs.

Chapter Twenty Five

Nuan straightened her body armour to feel more comfortable, but for sure it would never feel fully comfortable, as Sergeant Yang and his men climbed into the back of a Volkswagen Caddy van, in police colours of white with a blue flash. As the last officer climbed in, Nuan slid the side door closed before climbing behind the wheel. Although a relatively small van it was surprisingly truck-like, especially the big, flat steering wheel. She bucked-up before starting the noisy diesel engine, checked truck-like mirrors, indicated and eased away with Hu following in the second van, also white with a blue flash. Soon Nuan was on the roads to Renhe while concentrating on busy traffic. In the back behind the metal partition, Sergeant Yang and his officers had her map but they still didn't know the actual address. On and on without anyone taking the slightest notice of the two police vans travelling in a small convoy. Nuan spun the big, flat steering wheel right and then left, to ease to the shopping centre. There she double-parked with hazard lights flashing before switching off and climbing down. She slid the side door open for officers to climb out and separate as Sergeant Yang instructed. Two front, two rear and the rest following Nuan and Sergeant Yang into the shopping centre where their presence was generating a lot of interest, with startled onlookers either frozen or walking away very fast. To the concrete staircase, Nuan led the men down and down where Happy Massage was a beacon of light in the dull and dirty near-wasteland of that shopping centre basement. Nuan pulled out her pistol, racked it, and held it at arm's length ready, while marching to the open door where she strode inside.

"This is a police raid!" she shouted. "Everyone on the floor, face down with your hands behind your heads!"

Behind, Sergeant Yang shouted the same instruction as his officers came through the doorway and fanned out, pulling open multiple grey curtains. Nuan centred the old woman in her sights.

"Turn around now!"

The old woman did, to be handcuffed.

Two well-dressed younger men were handcuffed as curtains were slid away, revealing three older customers in varying degrees of nakedness. Nuan couldn't help but grimace, but Sergeant Yang knew customers weren't their priority.

Young women from late teens to mid twenties, were gathered by Hu into a group, literally cowering. Most were in barely-there black bikinis, but two had no bikini bottoms and one was totally naked. The younger men in proper shirts and slacks, big and bulky and handcuffed, were brought by two officers. Nuan contemplated the situation.

"Hu, can you find clothes for those who aren't decent?"

Nuan noticed Hu rummaging around tables now exposed, given all curtains were slid aside. There he gathered garments removed for fucking.

"Sergeant Yang," Nuan then said. "Those two and this one," indicating the two bodyguards and the old woman, "into my van.'

"Yes Sergeant Shui."

Nuan went to the young women where she counted nine.

"Do any of you understand Chinese?" she asked.

Blank looks.

"Understand Chinese?" Nuan asked more simply.

One of the younger women lifted her head a little. "Little," she said.

"I'll speak slowly and clearly. My name's Sergeant Shui Nuan; what's your name?"

Blank look

Nuan pointed to herself. "Shui Nuan." Then she pointed to the young woman."

"Ma Thi Mai."

"Ma Thi Mai, we'll take you somewhere safe now, later we'll speak with each of you, and then we'll send you home. Do you understand?"

She nodded her head but Nuan knew Mai understood only a fraction of that.

"Are you from Vietnam?" Nuan asked while pointing at Mai, to get a blank look in response. "Vietnam?" Nuan asked simply while pointing again.

Mai swept her arm around the group. "All Vietnam." She pointed to herself and, one by one, four others. "Hmong." She pointed to the remaining young women. "Kinh."

"I understand," Nuan said while nodding her head. Different ethnic groups which may mean different languages, but she would have to check.

"Come with me," Nuan said while beckoning. She led them to the street, bereft of pedestrians on one side, while on the opposite side, hundreds watched the unfolding drama, with many smartphones recording the incident for social media. Nuan led the young women to Hu's van where they climbed in the back.

"Hu," Nuan said. "Please take them to the dormitory, as we discussed."

"Yes Nuan. Well done by the way."

"Well done to you, Hu."

They were a team, and in this instance of regular policing they made a good team. Nuan peeled away the velcro on her body armour before seeking out Sergeant Yang, who had three officers holding three handcuffed criminals, heads hanging.

"Names?" Nuan snarled.

"Chao Kun."

"Sheng Xun."

"Pang Fan."

"ID cards," Nuan ordered.

They handed them across, one by one by one.

"Put those scum in the back of this van, and I'll drive us to Baiyun Detention Centre," Nuan calmly asked Sergeant Yang. "You can ride in front with me."

The three criminals were roughly pushed into the back to be joined by the nine constables, while the two sergeants climbed in front where Nuan tucked her body armour behind her seat. Nuan buckled-up, flicked off hazard lights before starting the engine.

She checked but not a car moved, as she indicated to pull out and head further north.

"Thank you for your assistance, Sergeant Yang," Nuan offered.

"I'm glad we achieved a good, clean operation."

"Your men won't rough up our prisoners too much?"

"I can't guarantee that. Those girls – terrible."

If those three didn't get beaten up by police officers for their sex crimes, then surely the guards at Baiyun would teach them a lesson! If not guards then other prisoners! As long as they survived for their trials. After a half-hour drive, Nuan reached the modern, factory-like detention centre. She indicated, turned right and stopped at a guardhouse adjacent to multiple perimeter fences of wire topped by coils of razor wire, with massive brick cell blocks and workshops spread inside.

Nuan reached inside of her jacket for her warrant card which she showed to the guard.

"Sergeant Shui with three prisoners to be arrested in due course."

The guard nodded before going to his guardhouse. The pair of wire gates slowly swung open for Nuan to ease her van along the short driveway. Nuan's prisoners would be detained based on their ID cards until they were formally arrested. It would take Nuan a few days to prepare her charges although she had seven days to actually arrest them. Eventually but usually before two months they would be tried, while in the meantime working for their keep in those workshops, before in this case being found guilty, given they were caught red-handed. Nuan braked to a halt at the administration centre where she switched off and climbed down. Nuan slid the rear door open.

"My word what a mess!" she exclaimed. "It must have been a rough drive!"

"Yes it was Sergeant," one constable responded flatly.

"Come with me," Sergeant Yang said, as he and three of his men led their prisoners to be detained for however long it took the Chinese justice system to get around to trying them.

Nuan strode along with their ID cards in her pocket, pleased with a good morning's work.

The young policeman led the women into an apartment-like building only the rooms were tiny, just big enough for a bed and a table. Each woman was given one room, side by side by side. There Mai sat on the bed of her room barely believing her luck. Literally in the middle of fucking, that man wanted her naked so Mai took her bikini top off, she was rescued by the police. Amazing! They came as if from nowhere but they knew what they wanted.

First Sua came into Mai's room, then Dawb, Huab and Kawm so all five Hmong were there.

"Are we safe?" Sua asked.

"We're safe," Mai said.

"How do you know?"

"I just know."

"That's not good enough for me."

Mai knew why she knew. "That woman police officer," Mai said. "She was in charge. She told the other police officers what to do."

"Are you sure?"

"I saw her pointing and ordering before the men did what she told them. The police officer who brought us here was told to get our bikinis. The police officers guarding those two men were told as well. Surely a woman police officer in charge will look after us women? If it was a man I wouldn't be so confident but with a woman in charge, a young woman wasn't she?"

"She was young and she was in charge," Huab said.

"Mai's right," Dawb said. "That woman rescued us. How could we not trust a young woman to look after us? This is simply a place for us to stay until they can send us home."

"That's right!" Sua at last realised. "We've been rescued and here we'll stay until we're sent home."

"What are you going to do when you get home, Mai?" Kawm asked.

"I'm going to hug my mother and my brothers and tell them I'm sorry."

"You have nothing to be sorry about, you were just tricked, and then other people took advantage of you like they took advantage of us. It's them, not you, who should be sorry."

"Now the police have Pang Fan and the men from the massage parlour," Sua said.

That was true and Mai was sure the young woman police officer would get them into big trouble. Then she realised.

"Those of us who came from families must tell the woman police officer about the families who abused us."

"Yes! They'll get into trouble too!"

Mai was so happy. She was rescued and she could make those who hurt her pay for what they did. That young woman police officer would make them pay; Mai was sure of that.

Chapter Twenty Six

Nuan rearranged one of the dormitory bedrooms with three chairs and a video camera. Her translator, Do Kang, who spoke both Vietnamese and Hmong, brought the first victim, the young woman Nuan spoke with when she detained the three at the brothel; Ma Thi Mai. Nuan shook hands with Mai who kept her eyes focussed on the floor.

"Please sit," Nuan said in Mandarin, translated into Hmong.

"Tell Mai my name's Shui Nuan."

Do Kang did that.

"Tell me your story from the beginning."

They spoke for quite a time where Nuan felt a growing rage. To listen to another language, totally incomprehensible, was bewildering. These women, when taken out of Vietnam, had to deal with that, beyond all those other atrocities inflicted on them.

Do Kang looked to Nuan. "Mai met a Hmong boy at her village, and later they communicated on Facebook. She came to the town of Lao Cai to meet this boy's family, only the boy sold her to a Chinese man as the wife for his son."

"What's the name of the man and his son?"

"Deng Wendong and Deng Yuanfu."

Nuan wrote those names in her notebook.

"Mai was taken to the village of Fusi, where she was married to Deng Yuanfu, but not really married."

Nuan understood that from her research. She wrote Fusi Village in her notebook.

"Her new mother-in-law was particularly hard on Mai. Her name's Ye Ru."

Nuan wrote Ye Ru.

"There were two other Hmong women there, also married but not married, but they didn't have bad mothers-in-law. Mai had arguments, she tried to run away but was brought back, and eventually she fell pregnant. After a time she was taken for an ultrasound where they aborted her foetus. This upset Mai so much that she was taken to an apartment in Guangzhou where they were guarded by those two men. Then she was taken to that massage parlour where she was shown how to do sex acts like masturbating men, sucking them and having sex with them. She was taught Mandarin words for oral sex, full service, and prices."

Nuan wrote a summation of that.

"How old is Mai?" Nuan asked.

Brief conversation.

"Sixteen, from Ta Van village."

Nuan wrote that.

"Her date of birth?"

Conversation.

"Third of October, 2003."

Nuan wrote that then thought. Probably the mother-in-law sold Mai as troublesome, and maybe even bought another Vietnamese pretend-wife. But Nuan had more pressing things.

"Tell Mai the two men and the woman in the massage parlour will be sent to jail for a very long time. I'll also send her husband, her father-in-law and her mother-in-law to jail for a very long time. Now we need to work out what comes next. If Mai goes home, she'll be blamed by her village for being a slut and nobody there will want anything to do with her. Can you tell her?"

The spoke but Mai shook her head.

"This has happened many times. One option for Mai is to start a new life in Sa Pa, amongst Hmong living there. There are tourist jobs in Sa Pa if she learns English, and generally she'll be better off. In time she can marry a Hmong boy living in Sa Pa, or even marry a Western tourist which isn't uncommon."

They spoke with Mai now nodding her head.

"Mai asked if this was true."

"Yes it is."

More conversation.

"Mai will go to Sa Pa."

Nuan was relieved, but she knew this should never have happened. She thought. "I need to interview all of the women we rescued, and then make arrangements with the

215

Vietnamese government. This will take a few weeks, living as she is now.

They spoke.

"Mai is happy here until she can go back to Vietnam."

"Thank Mai for me, I think she's very brave, and I hope she has a good future in Sa Pa."

"Do you want the next woman?" Do Kang asked.

"Yes please."

Do Kang took Mai away, while Nuan thought there were trafficking issues bigger than two men and that old woman in a massage parlour. Like triad, where arresting a low-level 49er like Peng would achieve fuck-all. People-smuggling gangs with a hierarchy of criminals were pulling the strands of this together. But the biggest issue was the shortage of Chinese women, thanks to China's ancient culture. Who could ever say that women aren't equal and daughters aren't precious? In Guangzhou people aren't obsessed about sons rather than daughters, but even in Guangzhou with Jia's succinct observation about studs and sluts, and that woman in the cafe thinking terrible things about Nuan that morning. Nuan then made a commitment: when they have their child if she's a girl, Dewai must agree that when she's old enough, she's independent in all ways including sexually. No double-standards and no shame.

Do Kang brought another young woman, or really a teenage girl, to sit. This one with darker skin and a jutting jaw was bordering on ugly.

"This is Yia Joua Huab, aged 16, date of birth 21st of July, 2003."

Nuan wrote.

"Tell Huab my name's Shui Nuan."

Do Kang did.

"Can you find Huab's story from the beginning, please?"

Once more they spoke for a long time.

"Huab met a boy on Facebook, who loved her," Do Kang said. "They agreed to meet at Sa Pa, only she was kidnapped and taken in a car and then a train to the apartment, and then to that massage parlour."

"Who kidnapped her?"

"A Hmong boy but not the boy on Facebook."

"Who took her to the apartment?"

"An older Chinese man, but not the men at the massage parlour."

Unlike Mai who was a wife before she was sold again, Huab was quite different.

"Who was first to have sexual relations with Huab?" Nuan asked.

They spoke.

"In a hotel in Kunming with the old Chinese man."

Fuck! Nuan will arrest Mai's husband who first raped her, but never will she find that old man who raped Huab.

"Is Huab from a village?"

"Yes."

"Can you tell Huab her options?"

They spoke for a long time and eventually reached an agreement.

"Huab will go to Sa Pa."

"Thank you, Do Kang."

"You can tell Huab she will be here for a few weeks before we can get her to Sa Pa."

They spoke while Nuan felt her eyes water. She wanted to hug Huab, and the others too, but the first rule of policing was not to get involved like that.

"Thank you so much," Nuan said to Do Kang. "Can you bring the next victim?"

Another teenager, who was asked to sit.

"This is Phi Nha Sen and she's Kinh. Her date of birth is the first of June, 2002"

Nuan wrote that down, and aged 17.

"Can you find Sen's story for me, please?"

They spoke in a language that sounded quite different.

"Sen is from Dong Ho Village near Hanoi. This is another Facebook scam but by a Kinh boy promising love, only to be trafficked by two Kinh boys to the border, where Sen was given to a Chinese man to be taken to Taishi Village, where she was married, but a fake marriage. Her husband at Taishi Village was Yin Wu. She was accepted by villagers, had an easy life with her husband, and eventually Sen fell pregnant. After Sen gave birth, her son was taken to be sold. Sen got very upset and refused to have anything to do with her husband, so those men took her to the apartment and then to the massage parlour."

"The men we detained at the massage parlour?"

They spoke.

"Yes."

Nuan jotted down those details.

"Her child was sold?"

"Yes."

"Don't translate this. I'm thinking this husband, Yin Wu, recouped the cost of his wife by selling their male child. When his marriage went bad because of this, he sold his wife, so-called, and bought another wife."

"I'm no expert but that sounds sensible."

Nuan thought in villages especially, a boy child would be worth a lot to a family who already had a daughter and didn't want the risk of their second child being a girl.

"Does Sen know who bought her child?" Nuan asked.

"Just a couple: a man and a woman."

"For Sen, the choices are her village which will see her ostracised, or Hanoi. The problem with Hanoi is if Sen can't make it, she may slip into sex work out of economic necessity, unlike Sa Pa where there's a support network of Hmong girls to help each other. How do I frame this? Hanoi where it might go bad for her, or Dong Ho where her life's effectively over?"

"You decision, Sergeant Shui."

"I say that we advise Sen to go to Hanoi, and we hope that's the best for her."

"I'll ask."

They spoke for quite a while Nuan jotted those last details in her notebook.

"Sen said she would like to go to Hanoi to live."

Nuan noted that.

"Can you tell Sen she'll be here for a few weeks, and thank her for me?"

They spoke while Nuan checked her phone.

"Do Kang," she said. "It's almost midday so we'll take a break to one, and then we'll speak with the next victim."

"Yes Sergeant Shui."

Nuan went outside for fresh air. She wasn't hungry but she needed something, so walked to a nearby cafe to have a flat white. There she thought. The prettier girls were sold as brides, while the ugly one went straight to the massage parlour. The massage parlour was the tip of the iceberg; the two Vietnamese women still living in Fusi village, showed that. For every trafficked woman released from sex slavery to an uncertain future, many more remained victims to be raped endlessly, although in some cases those marriages may even be happy, or at least not tragic. Nuan then realised when she detained the family in Fusi, she had to detain two other families and free the other two victims. First thing after lunch she would get Mai back to find their details. Everyone she could arrest she would, but really it was China's fucked-up culture that was to blame.

* * *

Nuan swiped the card on their door to let herself in. Dewai was watching the news.

"They had a story about an arrest of human traffickers at a massage parlour in Renhe, with the release of nine trafficking victims," Dewai said. "I recognised someone."

Nuan shrugged her shoulders before flopping on the couch. Dewai reached for the remote to turn it off, and given he was sitting at the end, Nuan lay down with her head on his lap.

"I discovered that when I was undercover, and I led that operation. I don't want to bring cases home because sometimes they're – gruesome. Today I've interviewed nine victims, and tomorrow the detentions start, although we can only detain those we can identify."

"Are you alright?"

"Not really. I'm doing my best but it's confronting, and more confronting that many more victims are out there. The big problem is women aren't valued as equals."

He rubbed her hair. "I love women in general and you in particular."

Dewai was a woman's man, lucky her. "As you know when a couple has children, the children take the family name of the husband. Preserving a family name has been seen as important, and in some places still is. This means they need a son, even under the one child policy. The other and bigger issue is Chinese culture is based on men lead – women follow. This was formalised by Confucius in his Book of Rites, which defined women as the property of their fathers until they marry, the property of their husbands in marriage, and the property of their oldest sons in widowhood, although this concept predates Confucius. When a family aborted a female foetus when that was legal, they weren't thinking about the Book of Rites, but rather this long-standing concept of women being lesser than men, which isn't the case. If anything, when Confucius wrote that in his Book of Rites, that showed he was scared of the power of women."

"You're a detective making arrests, while I write computer programs about feng shui."

"One's not better than the other, but I can do my job and still bring life into the world, which puts men under women's power. Women give birth to men's sons."

"That's where it started. Control women to control their children."

"I believe so. As a result we have a substantial gender imbalance, apparently 34 million more men than women, so criminal gangs are filling this vacuum with trafficked women. Often into marriage but sometimes into massage parlours like you saw.

"Men buy wives from these countries?"

"Trafficked women are the only way they can get a wife, especially in rural areas where the preference for sons was greatest."

"Ah."

"Talking with victims all day is bad enough, but to know those victims are just a tiny fraction and most victims will never be rescued, is quite terrible. I feel – suffocated."

"I'm glad I know what you're up to." He rubbed her hair which was nice. "I know there are secret things you can't tell me, but never feel afraid to share your burdens when you can."

Nuan felt embarrassed by that. "I guess I'm finding my way."

"We're both finding our way. Now, do you want a massage?"

"I'm enjoying lying on your lap, but I'm prepared to get up for a massage."

"We don't have to go further."

He was too decent. "I want to experience beauty to take away the ugly I've been exposed to these past days," Nuan said. "Does that make sense?"

He nodded his head while Nuan got up.

"It's been a long day," Nuan said, "so I'll shower to be fresh for your special massage."

"Take as long as you like."

Nuan got undressed in their bathroom while thinking her life was as good as it got, unlike too many in the world. But being a martyr didn't help anyone, while a massage and love would help her. Nuan flicked the tap on while looking forward to a shower, a massage, and love.

Chapter Twenty Seven

Nuan eased the Volkswagen Caddy van into the square of Fusi Village, oddly a village she knew well. Behind, Hu brought the Nissan Sylphy to a halt. Nuan climbed down to slide open the side door, where the six constables climbed down after an uncomfortable, hour-long drive. Sergeant Yang and Hu gathered close to Nuan.

"We know what to do," Nuan said. "You and you come with me," she said as she pointed to the two nearest constables. Walking along narrow, stone-paved lanes, she drew her pistol although she doubted she would need it. But like her body armour she liked to be prepared, as she led the way to an older-style house where she hammered on a sturdy, timber door.

"Open up, police!" Nuan shouted as she hammered again.

The door eased open a crack, where Nuan pushed at it with her shoulder. She forced her way into a dark living area, facing an old couple and a young couple. That wasn't what she expected.

"On the floor, face down with your hands behind your heads!"

Nobody moved.

"Now!"

One by one they lay face down on the stone floor while Nuan contemplated the situation. She put her pistol in its holster before kneeling by the older man.

"Are you Deng Wendong?"

"Yes," he said.

"Handcuff him," Nuan ordered.

A constable did that.

"You," Nuan snapped at the younger man. "Are you Deng Yuanfu?"

"Yes."

"Handcuff him."

The other constable did that.

Still kneeling, Nuan grabbed the hair of the older woman and pulled her head up. "You're Ye Ru."

"I am."

Nuan smashed Ye Ru's head against the stone floor.

"Did that hurt?"

"Yes."

Nuan felt like doing that again but handcuffed her instead.

Nuan stood. "Constable," she asked the young constable standing alongside. "What do we do to women who beat-up sex slaves?"

"We do this!" he said as he kicked Ye Ru, who grunted.

"Ye Ru?" Nuan asked.

"What?"

"This is for Ma Thi Mai," Nuan said as she kicked her hard.

Ye Ru groaned while Nuan smiled.

"More?" Nuan asked.

"No!"

Nuan backed away.

"So you have another Vietnamese sex-slave," she asked Deng Yuanfu.

No response.

Nuan kicked Deng Yuanfu – hard.

"Tell me her name!"

"Xy Thi Ko."

"Fuck you!" Nuan exploded in rage before kneeling by the teenage girl to put her right arm around slender shoulders. Gently, Nuan helped Ko to stand.

"Those three scum!" Nuan then ordered her constables. "Into the van!"

The two constables guided their prisoners out of the house towards the van, while Nuan followed with her arm still around the poor Vietnamese girl's shoulders. At the square, Hu and his two constables had Yeh Liang and May Thi Na, while Sergeant Yang and his two constables had Che Mu and Do Thi Hu.

"They've got another one?" Hu asked Nuan.

"Yes."

"Fuck them!"

"I know. Gather our prisoners' ID cards," Nuan ordered.

Constables did that, to hand the bundle of cards to Nuan.

"Prisoners in the van and girls in the car," she then ordered.

Order was sorted from chaos.

"Hu, once more to the dormitory."

He nodded before climbing into the car.

"Another good, clean operation," Sergeant Yang said.

"We're getting good at this," Nuan said

"We are."

"And as you know, more detentions tomorrow."

"Constables, get in the back of the van," Sergeant Yang ordered. "While you're there, don't rough up our prisoners."

"You know us," one constable said.

While they deserved to be roughed-up, Nuan worried that more than an hour's drive to the detention centre was something else.

"I'm your commanding officer," Nuan said firmly. "I don't want fatalities, regardless of what they've done. Do I make myself clear?"

"Yes Sergeant Shui," one constable said while contemplating at his shoes.

"Right."

Six constables and five prisoners in handcuffs climbed in back, where Nuan slid the door closed. Nuan removed her body armour to tuck behind her seat. She got comfortable, buckled up, and started the engine before spinning the big, flat steering wheel as she did a tight turn to get out of Fusi Village square.

"It's good to bring these people to justice," Sergeant Yang said. "This is a terrible thing though."

As she picked up speed on the road to Wuhe, Nuan wondered what to say. "Every woman we save is a small victory, as is every criminal we arrest."

"The fight against crime is always like that, but this one is more difficult than most."

"I know."

Nuan sped along a quiet road lined by lush rice paddies.

* * *

Nuan saw Taishi Village just ahead, south of Nansha Port on the Pearl River Estuary. Another poor village but larger than Fusi with a population of about 2,000; the home of peasants farming rice using methods unchanged for more than a thousand years, including using water buffalo to plough flooded paddies. As Nuan drove the police van along the main north-south road, it was clear that older buildings in Taishi had mostly been replaced by newer, brick structures, including simple, basic but not doubt decently habitable houses. That van didn't have a GPS so Hu was her guide with a map in his hand, as he told Nuan to turn right at the next intersection, and then the third house along on the left.

Nuan pulled up at one of those simple, brick houses. After Fusi, Nuan had planned for another sex slave just in case, as she climbed down to slide open the rear door for their two constables.

"I'll do this now," Nuan said.

Nuan hammered on the door. "Open up, police!" she shouted as she hammered again.

"Someone's in there," Hu said while peering through a window.

"'Open up, police!" Nuan shouted.

Suddenly the door swung wide open, and a middle-aged man came at Nuan with his hands reaching for her throat. Nuan grabbed for the extendable baton by her side, flicked it open, and beat the side of his body; hard, twice. He stumbled so Nuan moved to beat the back of his knees, for him to collapse. She beat his back with her baton then kicked his back so he was now flat on his face on the bitumen road.

Nuan stood over the prone body of her would-be attacker. "Are you Yin Wu?" she asked.

He groaned.

She collapsed her baton to put it back on her belt, before kneeling. She rolled him onto his back.

"One last time before I get dangerous," Nuan said calmly. "Are you Yin Wu?"

"I am."

"Your ID card?"

He reached into a trouser pocket to hand it to Nuan, who stood. "Constables, handcuff him and put him in the van. Hu, please search his house."

Hu went inside, to emerge a few moments later with a Vietnamese teen girl. Nuan was disappointed but not surprised. Yin Wu sold his troublesome wife to buy a new one from the people he dealt with before.

Nuan pointed to her chest. "Shui Nuan."

Nuan then pointed to the teenage girl. "Nguyen Truc Lam," she said.

"We'll look after you, Lam," Nuan said, even though she doubted Nguyen Truc Lam understood any of that. Nuan led Lam to the front seat of the van, helped her on, and pulled the seatbelt around her. By that stage Hu was in the back, so Nuan slid the door closed before removing her body armour for their drive first to the dormitory, then to Baiyun Detention Centre.

Chapter Twenty Eight

Nuan, dressed in her uniform, strode into the interview room alongside Hu, also dressed in his uniform. In the interrogation chair, a metal chair with ankle and wrist restraints, was the criminal she was most interested in. He hung his head like at Fusi when he was arrested. Silently standing next to the door was a prison guard in his green uniform.

Nuan switched on the video camera before sitting in her chair with Hu alongside. She looked down to her notes.

"Deng Wendong," Nuan said. "Today I arrest you for the following crimes: two counts of kidnap, two counts of illegal detention, two counts of slavery, one count of procuring a prostitute, and multiple counts of being an accomplice to the rapes of two victims. I have statements from these victims: Ma Thi Mai and Xy Thi Ko, which I'm certain will see you found guilty. What do you say to my charges?"

"I'm very sorry," he mumbled.

"Speak up so your response can be heard clearly."

"I'm very sorry."

"Given this is a strong case you will be found guilty, and you will be imprisoned for a very long time. Do you understand?"

He nodded his head.

"Speak up."

"I understand."

"Tell us your side of what happened?"

"My son needed a wife, so I contacted a man...."

"Which man?"

"Xu Shing at Zhaoqing."

"What's his address? What's his mobile?"

"I don't remember, but I have his details at our house in Fusi Village."

"How did you find out about Xu Shing?"

"He got Vietnamese wives for Yeh Liang and Che Mu."

That simple statement made Nuan feel sick. Deng spoke about Vietnamese women as if they were commodities.

"Then what happened?"

"The price was 10,000 yuan to Xu Shing, and 70,000 yuan for the woman. I paid the 10,000; then I was given an address in Hekou. I was told to wait at Hekou until they brought a woman, so I caught a train to Hekou through Kunming. The next day they brought Mai, I paid for her, and one of the Vietnamese men drove us to Kunming so we could catch the high-speed train from there. Later, we held a ceremony to celebrate my son's union with Mai. Xu Shing told me if we had a son we could sell it through him and get some of our money back, and then we could have another son for us, but Mai was carrying a daughter so my son arranged for an abortion. Then Mai wouldn't have sex with my son, so I spoke with Xu Shing and he paid 50,000 yuan for Mai. Not only that but he gave me a discount on the next woman, Xy Thi Ko. She was much better behaved."

"How much did you pay for Xy Thi Ko?'

"I paid 7,000 yuan to Xu Shing and 50,000 yuan to the Vietnamese men in Hekou."

"Do you know the names of these Vietnamese men?"

He shrugged his shoulders.

"Look at me!" Nuan demanded. Deng lifted his head. "The more you tell me, the better the judge will think of you when he sentences you. If you're lucky you may get out of prison before you die. Do you understand?"

He nodded his head.

"Tell me the names of the Vietnamese men."

"Hoang Van Long and Li Van Hong."

Beside Nuan, Hu wrote in his notebook.

"What was the address in Hekou?"

"It was a house at 42 Huancheng Road."

Hu wrote.

"Will I be tried for all of those crimes?" Deng then asked.

"You committed all of those crimes so you will be tried for all of those crimes. Your son raped both women multiple times; we have testimony for that, while you and your wife facilitated those rapes."

"Will my wife be tried?"

"Your wife Ye Ru will be arrested for two counts of illegal detention, two counts of slavery, multiple counts of assault, and multiple counts of being an accomplice to the rapes of two victims. No leniency will be shown towards your wife by me, do you understand?"

He nodded his head.

"Your son Deng Yuanfu, being a rapist on multiple occasions, will be arrested for his crimes. Both your wife and your son will serve long sentences, as will you, although you helped me in this interview so that may make a difference."

"I'm very sorry for what I did," he said with his head hanging.

"You should have thought of that before you committed these crimes." Nuan looked to Hu. "Do you have any questions, Constable Zhang?"

"No I don't, Sergeant Shui."

"Guard," Nuan said. "Please take this prisoner away and bring the next one."

Deng Wendong was unlocked from his shackles to be led away.

"Have you done this before?" Hu asked.

"Yes I have," Nuan said. "When I was on patrol I had a man and a woman go crazy at each other, before the woman took all her clothes off in the street. That was the same interview process, except when she was tried she got off with a fine, as did her husband. Later I arrested an ice addict who smashed-up a medical clinic and assaulted staff and patients. He was sentenced to five years."

"Those would have helped for today."

"They did."

"How do you feel?" Hu asked.

"He talked as if women are property. I'm a woman arresting him, interviewing him, sending him away for the rest of his life. Don't they understand women are real and equal? We love, we hate, we achieve; we despair. Don't they see that?"

"Do you despair?"

"This is a dirty case but I've come to terms with it. A number of women have been rescued, a number of criminals have been arrested, at least one more criminal will be arrested, and I'll liaise with Vietnam about their criminals. I know there are many sex slaves out there who won't be rescued, but we can only do what we can do."

"When we detain and interview Xu Shing," Hu said. "We'll have to get him to lead us to other trafficked victims, and arrest those now abusing them."

So right! "Xu Shing isn't running this on his own, so we need his associates."

"I don't think he'll freely give them up," Hu said.

Nuan thought. "Do we play this like a triad gang? Do we find Xu Shing's mobile, then get someone to buy a wife from him, and track Xu's contacts by who he calls?"

"Shen is in his forties and I'm sure he could play the role of a desperate bachelor who wants to buy a wife. That isn't as complex as what you did undercover."

"Shen is quite straightforward, so I think he could play that role and be believable."

The guard brought in Ye Ru, clearly showing the scars of her detention. Ye Ru was restrained in the interrogation chair before the guard stood by the door. Nuan was going to be quick with this one, and with the son.

"Ye Ru," Nuan said. "Today I arrest you for the following crimes: two counts of illegal detention, two counts of slavery, multiple counts of assault, and multiple counts of being an accomplice to the rapes of two victims. I have statements from these victims: Ma Thi Mai and Xy Thi Ko, which I'm certain will see you found guilty. Now I will ask you a number of questions, to which you will answer yes or no. Do you understand?"

"Yes," Ye Ru said with her head hanging.

"Were you aware your husband, Deng Wendong, paid money to buy Ma Thi Mai and later to buy Xy Thi Ko?"

"Clearly you know this, so yes."

"Were Ma Thi Mai and Xy Thi Ko detained in your village of Fusi?"

"They were free to come and go."

"But only within the bounds of your village of Fusi?"

"Yes."

"Did you instruct Ma Thi Mai and Xy Thi Ko to carry out household tasks?"

"Yes."

"Did you assault Ma Thi Mai when she didn't always understand your instructions regarding these household tasks?"

"Once she hit me with a saucepan."

"Did you strike Mai Thi Mai multiple times before she hit you with that saucepan?"

Ye Ru looked directly at Nuan, as if to challenge her

"I repeat I have a statement made by Ma Thi Mai regarding your treatment of her, including details on your assaults," Nuan said. "So I ask this question again; did you strike Ma Thi Mai multiple times before she defended herself with that saucepan?"

Still Ye Ru hesitated. "You know I did," she eventually said.

"Were you aware that your son Deng Yuanfu was raping Ma Thi Mai and Xy Thi Ko in his room?"

"They were married and sex is part of marriage."

"They weren't legally married because you purchased these women and they didn't have Chinese citizenship documents. I repeat my question. Were you aware that your son, Deng Yuanfu was raping Ma Thi Mai and Xy Thi Ko in his room?"

"I was aware they were having sexual relations."

"Who do you mean by 'they'?"

"My son had sexual relations with Ma Thi Mai and later with Xy Thi Ko."

"Did either of Ma Thi Mai or Xy Thi Ko have a choice in that?"

"I don't know."

"When Ma Thi Mai refused to have sexual relations with your son, what happened?"

"My son sold her to Xu Shing."

"Did you tell your son to sell Ma Thi Mai to Xu Shing?"

"You know I did."

"So that's yes?" Nuan asked.

"I instructed my son to sell Ma Thi Mai to Xu Shing."

"Did you know Mai Thi Mai was then sold to a massage parlour in Guangzhou?"

"Yes, I knew."

"Ma Thi Mai and Xy Thi Ko were coerced into having sexual relations with your son, Deng Yuanfu, or else they would be sold to massage parlours?"

"I suppose so, yes."

"By you?"

Ye Ru nodded her head. "Yes."

Nuan looked to Hu. "Do you have any questions, Constable Zhang?"

"No I don't, Sergeant Shui."

"Guard," Nuan said. "Please take this prisoner away and bring the next one."

Ye Ru was unlocked from her shackles to be led away. Shortly after, Deng Yuanfu was shackled in the interrogation chair while the guard looked on.

"Deng Yuanfu," Nuan said. "Today I arrest you for the crime of rape against two victims on multiple occasions. I have statements from these victims: Ma Thi Mai and Xy Thi Ko, which I'm certain will see you found guilty. Do you understand?"

"It wasn't rape," he said.

"That's your opinion. When your father brought Ma Thi Mai to the house you shared with your parents, shortly after that you took her to your bedroom. Answer yes or no."

"Yes I did."

"Did you push her to sit on your bed?"

"Why should I incriminate myself?"

"I repeat I have a statement made by Ma Thi Mai regarding your treatment of her, including details of times you had sexual relations with her. This statement will be tendered in evidence at your trial, regardless of what you say now. But if you show some remorse now then compassion may be shown when you're sentenced. Do you understand?"

Deng Yuanfu nodded his head.

"Do you understand; yes or no?" Nuan asked.

"Yes I understand," Deng Yuanfu said.

"Now, did you push Ma Thi Mai to sit on your bed?"

"I pushed her – yes."

"Did you ask Ma Thi Mai to have sexual relations with you?"

"I didn't understand her and she didn't understand me."

"Did you push Ma Thi Mai onto her back?"

"Yes."

"Did you attempt to remove her jeans?"

"I couldn't ask so I had to."

"Did she resist you?"

"Yes she did."

"Did you strike Ma Thi Mai?"

"Yes."

"Did you pull her jeans off?"

"Yes I did."

"Did you pull her panties off?"

"Yes."

"Did Ma Thi Mai put her hand between her legs?"

"Yes."

"Did you pull her hand away and hold it with one hand, while you used your other hand to penetrate her sexually with your penis?"

"Yes."

"Did you engage in intercourse until you ejaculated inside the vagina of Ma Thi Mai?"

"Yes."

"Did you subsequently have sexual relations with Ma Thi Mai?"

"Yes."

"Did you ever ask?"

"No."

"Did she fight you?"

"The first few times yes, but not later."

"Did Ma Thi Mai fall pregnant after a few months?"

"Yes."

"Did you continue to have sexual relations with Ma Thi Mai?"

"Yes."

"Did you take Ma Thi Mai to a doctor where he performed an ultrasound, determined she was carrying a daughter, and forced her to have an abortion?"

"I had to so that I could pay my parents for the cost of Mai."

"Did you force Ma Thi Mai to have an abortion because she was carrying a girl? Answer yes or no."

"Yes."

"The next time you attempted to have sexual relations with Ma Thi Mai, did she fight you?"

"Yes, she fought me very much."

"Did your parents intervene?"

"Yes."

"Did your mother then instruct you to sell Ma Thi Mai to Xu Shing?"

"Yes she did."

"Did you know Mai Thi Mai was then sold to a massage parlour in Guangzhou?"

"Yes, I knew."

"Did your father then buy Xy Thi Ko?"

"Yes."

"Like with Ma Thi Mai I have a statement made by Xy Thi Ko regarding your treatment of her, including details of times you had sexual relations with her. If you show some remorse about your treatment of Ko, then compassion may be shown when you're sentenced. My first question; when your father brought Xy Thi Ko to the house you shared with your parents, later that evening you took her to your bedroom."

"Yes I did."

"Did you push her to sit on your bed?"

"Yes."

"Did you ask Xy Thi Ko to have sexual relations with you?"

"Like with Mai, Ko didn't understand me and I didn't understand her."

"Did you push Xy Thi Ko onto her back?"

"Yes."

"Did you remove her jeans?"

"Yes."

"Was Xy Thi Ko crying?"

"Yes."

"Did you pull her panties off to penetrate her sexually with your penis?"

"Yes."

"Was Xy Thi Ko still crying?"

"Yes."

"Did you engage in intercourse until you ejaculated inside the vagina of Xy Thi Ko."

"Yes."

"Was Xy Thi Ko still crying?"

"Yes."

"Did you subsequently have sexual relations with Xy Thi Ko?"

"Yes."

"Did she cry?"

"The next time yes, but after that no."

"How many times did you have sexual relations with Xy Thi Ko?"

"Many times."

"Be more specific."

"At least 20 or 30. No, four or five times a week for two months."

"Would 30 to 40 times be about right?"

"About that – yes."

"Did you ever ask Xy Thi Ko to have sexual relations?"

"No."

"Could you have taught her the Chinese words or learned the Vietnamese words to ask that?"

"Yes I could have."

"Why didn't you?"

"I don't know."

"You didn't teach her a few words in your language, or learn a few words in her language, because you were going to have sexual intercourse with Xy Thi Ko regardless of what she wanted. Is that right, yes or no?"

"I suppose so, yes."

Nuan looked to Hu. "Do you have any questions, Constable Zhang?"

"No I don't, Sergeant Shui."

"Guard," Nuan said. "Please take this prisoner away."

Deng Yuanfu was unlocked from his shackles to be led away with his head hanging low. That was the worst.

Nuan went to the video camera to switch it off. She traced the lead outside to a computer on a desk, with a sergeant-guard monitoring it. He would have seen and heard that.

"Excuse me Sergeant," Nuan said. "Can you copy my interviews onto this USB?" Nuan asked while reaching into her pocket. She handed the USB for the sergeant to copy a number of files.

"You must have seen and heard things in your time," Nuan said.

"I have, and those were about as bad as they get, short of murder. Taking another person's life is the end of it, but your interviews were – quite bad." He ejected the USB before handing it to Nuan.

"Justice will be done," Nuan said.

"Any man who has a wife or especially a daughter...."

"Do you have a daughter?"

"We love our daughter very much."

Nuan left that sergeant to contemplate other daughters not as lucky.

Chapter Twenty Nine

Nuan reached home feeling down. She remembered a conversation from not long ago, and even if Dewai couldn't help there were things that could be understood. He was at his computer in the other room. Nuan pulled the other chair around.

"As you know my mother's an economist, and she's Deputy of Finance for the Ministry of Public Security; in fact she manages funds for where Father and I work. There isn't much she doesn't know about important things in Father's professional life, and now it's time for you. I know I don't have to say this is confidential."

Nuan plugged in her USB, then reached across to the mouse to navigate the folder and the first file. She double-clicked for it to play automatically. In total there were five files broken by time-slices. Nuan let the last file play to the end.

"That's terrible," Dewai said. "Are you alright?"

"I knew which questions to ask from interviews I did a few days ago."

"Ah."

"This is what policing is about. You investigate, sometimes by getting a lead through luck, you interview victims, you gather other facts, and then you arrest criminals like you saw and heard. Sometimes it's ugly like that."

"So you've been carrying this around for a while?"

"I came home and then I lay on your lap, if you remember. Since then I've come more to terms with it." Nuan thought. "I hope I haven't harmed you by sharing this?"

"No – well, it's not possible not to be affected. But you're the most important person in the world to me, so I can be like your mother with your father."

"Beijing is a horrible place. Crowded, dirty, smoggy and terrible weather. After my parents married, they moved from Beijing to here. Guangzhou was growing with opportunities for them, and a better environment for their child. Me, who came later. That's what family is about – thinking not about yourself but each other and your children, when children come. You and I are family, more and more each day."

"You've had a tough time, my love," he said. "Not just this but working undercover. Do you want to go away for a weekend to forget about ugly things?"

Did she? "That's a great idea!" Nuan exclaimed.

Dewai turned to his computer, restored his browser and searched. He scrolled while Nuan looked on.

"You're partial to a good massage," he said. "Does Zhuhai Imperial Hot Spring Resort sound interesting?"

"Yes it does."

"Let me book this weekend."

Nuan watched while Dewai typed. "It's done," he said. "I'll book a train too."

"This is going to be great," Nuan said.

"That's done too. Metro to Guangzhou South and the high speed train from there. Leaving Friday afternoon, that's tomorrow afternoon, returning on Sunday."

"I explained the Book of Rites, and how in a perverse way in the 21st Century, that's led to what you just watched. I can't forgive, I can't not wish that family not be imprisoned for a long time, but I wish there was an answer. Nothing comes close to the love of two equals, like you and me. Nothing." Nuan stood. "Do you want a good home-cooked meal so I can get my mind off bad things?"

Dewai didn't have to agree and he probably knew he didn't have a choice anyway. Nuan went to their kitchen to see what ingredients would go with that chicken in her fridge. From her kitchen the view was beautiful.

Chapter Thirty

Nuan swiped her card for the lock on the door to Office 1.10 to unlock. She entered to find Superintendent Ma alone, as she planned.

"Zao an Superintendent Ma," Nuan greeted.

"Zao an Sergeant Shui. How is your case going?"

"Hu and I arrested the first three yesterday. Later today we're going to arrest the three we detained from the brothel, and formally arrest three more criminals currently in detention. Unfortunately for you, our arrests have led us to a human trafficker who we should deal with. Reality is better than I can explain. Do you have some time?"

"I do."

Nuan booted her laptop. When it was ready she plugged the USB to scroll to file four of five. She slid the slider to where the interview with Deng Yuanfu looked like it started. With volume on her laptop speaker turned up, she pressed play. It was on the right spot, and even though she'd heard it twice before, and also when she interviewed the two girls a second time to get a more detailed version of the abuse they suffered, it still chilled her. At the end Nuan double-clicked file five. At the end, a moment's silence.

"Shit!" Superintendent Ma exclaimed; which surprised Nuan.

"Both were aged 16," Nuan said.

He shook his head.

"Two things come from that, Sergeant Shui," Superintendent Ma said. "That man will be in prison for many decades, and that's a fine piece of police work from you and Constable Zhang."

"At some point we'll arrest the trafficker: Xu Shing, and notify Vietnamese Police with details of their criminals. I'll supply the Vietnamese Police with copies of this recording which, in earlier interviews, convicts two Vietnamese nationals. Xu Shing should lead us to other trafficked Vietnamese women, and their abusers."

"Xu Shing isn't doing this alone."

"If we have the resources we can discover Xu Shing's associates with an undercover operation. It won't be complicated like me going undercover with triad drug-dealing."

"On that subject, I would like you to listen to the recording we took of the meeting to reach agreement with this triad gang. Come to my computer."

Superintendent Ma found a series of files, where Nuan listened first to Superintendent Ma and then Jia confirming quantities, prices and so on. The implications of that were obvious.

"This is pointless!" Nuan exclaimed. "The profits in making and selling methamphetamine are so massive we'll never make a difference."

"That's what Sergeant Xiong and I both feel. We'll arrest those involved seeing as we're on the cusp of doing that, and then I'll talk with Commissioner Shui. Do you think concentrating on human trafficking is more worthwhile?"

"Each trafficked victim is flesh and blood, and each rescued victim is a victory. The bigger problems are we can't unravel the tragedy of the one child policy which is the real reason for human trafficking for the purposes of forced marriage, nor can we unravel the tragedy of targeting relatively harmless drugs like heroin and cocaine in an unwinnable war on drugs, only to have methamphetamine fill the vacuum. There always will be addicts chasing their next highs."

"Sergeant Shui: I want you to help us to take into custody this triad gang leadership, and then I'll put resources into doing an operation on Xu Shing."

"Don't forget each day means more rapes."

"I'll make things happen as quickly as I can. He raped her while she was crying?"

"It was brave of that girl to tell the translator and I that. Superintendent Ma: I have more arrests for today, and then I'm at your disposal." Nuan thought her bigger picture wouldn't hurt. "I'm also going away this weekend to clear my head."

"Do you need help beyond that?"

"A weekend away with my boyfriend will help me enough."

Nuan noticed Hu, already in uniform, waiting.

"Constable Zhang and I will finish our arrests today, and then we're yours."

Nuan headed out to change into her uniform. She knew her uniform put fear into those she was interviewing. Fear was a worthy weapon.

Chapter Thirty One

Do Kang, the Hmong and Vietnamese-speaking Chinese police officer, escorted his Hmong charges onto a train to reach the station at Kunming, then to stay in a nearby hotel overnight. The next day they caught a train to Hekou, where they were walked across the border to a small bus for the last part of their journey to Sa Pa. It was more than wonderful, glorious, marvellous, incredible, to be home in Vietnam, but sad that Mai, like the others, couldn't go home to their villages. The Chinese police officer told them that and that made sense. Mai was forced-married, fucked by a husband she always hated, fucked by many other men, or sometimes did that other thing she never wanted to do again. Of course the people of her village would think she was a slut. In fact she was a whore, although she had no say in any of that.

"What are you going to do?" Sua asked Mai.

They had some money, courtesy of the Chinese police, to get by for a while. There was one thing beyond all others. "I need to learn English," she said. Do Kang said there was work for English-speaking tour guides who sometimes got married to the Westerners they guided. But even without marriage to a Westerner, if Mai didn't say anything specific about her past there were many Hmong men in Sa Pa. Apparently it was a big city, not crazy-big like Guangzhou but big enough to hide her past. Somehow the Chinese woman police officer knew that. She would have learned that from the internet.

Mai thought more clearly. "I need somewhere cheap to live, a job for now, and I need to learn English. Maybe I'll find a boyfriend when I'm ready."

"Do you want a boyfriend?" Sua asked.

"I want to like one man instead of hating all men."

"I want that without hate too. Maybe it's good without hate."

"So you hated your husband?" Mai asked.

"Yes I did. I'm sure we all hated our husbands, except those of us in the massage parlour who didn't have husbands before. Instead they hated the men who paid us."

Through the window were the mountains of Vietnam, and more and more houses. They were approaching their destination for a new start in life. Lots of Hmong in Sa Pa, that was for sure, which meant Mai had the opportunity for a decent new life. Mai stared out of the window at those houses, knowing this city was her best chance to put all the badness behind her and start again.

Chapter Thirty Two

Jia checked her inbox where she saw an email from the Hong Kong Police Force. They interviewed the parents of Chen Ru to obtain her address at Building One, Apartment 84, 14 Zhujiang East Road, Tianhe. Jia checked the satellite image to see a complex of buildings all in blue-tinted glass: a tall skyscraper, two smaller skyscrapers, and a large, squat building. Just then Nuan entered the room, she rarely was the first to work. That was good timing.

"Nuan?" Jia asked.

Nuan brought her chair around.

"How was your weekend?" Jia asked.

"Dewai and I went to the Zhuhai Imperial Hot Spring Resort."

Amazing! "That sounds lovely!" Jia exclaimed.

"It was lovely. And you?"

"I met Huang's parents as officially his girlfriend. We got to know each other."

"Are you really his girlfriend?" Nuan asked.

"I'm sorry you don't know," Jia said.

"That's alright; I've been mostly away. Huang's really nice," Nuan said.

"He's living with me now."

"I'm glad to hear that," Nuan said with a sly smile that Jia couldn't fail to notice.

"Now, can you do me a favour? Jia asked. "Hong Kong police found the address of Chen Ru, the White Paper Fan from this triad group. Your story about jaywalking worked. I don't want Chen Ru to see me sneaking around where she lives, so can you check out her apartment? Check for security cameras and take a few pictures with your smartphone camera."

"I can do this with Hu. When does this go down?"

"They're on target to ship before the end of this week. Once we get notification they've shipped, we'll take them out."

"Hu and I could detain Chen Ru seeing as we're checking out where she lives. Are you doing dawn raids?"

"Yes."

"Who's detaining the Deputy Mountain Master?"

"Huang and I."

"So Liko detains the Red Pole?"

Jia put her head down. "I hope that works given it's Liko," Jia said quietly, while wishing their equal second-in-charge was a better detective."

"Me too," Nuan whispered in reply. "What about identifying the ship?" Nuan asked.

"When they ring us to confirm production is complete, they will tell us the ship," Jia said. "When we take them into custody I'll get our coast guard to intercept and search that ship. Can I have your smartphone?" Jia asked.

Nuan handed it across for Jia to plug into her laptop. A few moments later, Jia ejected it. Jia then used her phone for a moment, for Nuan's phone to 'ting' with a new message.

"I texted you the address and transferred Chen Ru's ID photo," Jia said as she handed the phone back.

"Thanks. We'll head off now."

Jia had an idea. "Check if there are security guards in any of the buildings that make up that complex."

"Alright."

* * *

Building One was the taller tower; a residential skyscraper like where she lived, although this woman lived on floor eight so she wouldn't have had a particularly special view. Building One also had a long counter in the foyer with two security guards on duty. Nuan noted that as she walked with Hu to the lift foyer to press a button. A bell rang for doors to spring open, where they entered an empty lift.

"We're detaining this woman at dawn one day this week," Nuan told Hu. "Keep this in mind when we check things out."

He nodded his head as they came to a halt for doors to spring open. Nuan walked along the corridor noting smoke alarms but no security cameras, as she expected. She reached apartment 81 with 84 just along.

"What do you think?" Nuan asked.

"To detain one woman at dawn, at worst she'll have a male partner who could be armed. So at worst, two armed criminals in that apartment. You and I and five armed constables?"

"I want Sergeant Yang and four of his men."

"Agreed," Hu said. "We'll come in the one van, swarm across the foyer, and come up here in one lift."

"That will work. Jia asked me for details of security guards." Nuan noted the door of apartment 81 had security card access. "Clearly she wants a master security card."

"We should use a summons to get that card the day before."

"We can't be fumbling around getting a card when we arrive. We'll use the old excuse of a security training exercise, but it's unlikely a building complex as big as this would tip-off a triad. Across these buildings who knows how many apartments and residents they have? This place must be straight-up."

Nuan took her smartphone out to take a few pictures.

"Let's go, Hu," Nuan said.

Nuan returned to the lift to press the 'down' button. The door of the lift they recently arrived in sprang open. Nuan entered the lift, and pressed 'G' for doors to slide closed.

"Nervous?" she asked.

"Not really. Are you nervous?"

"I know it should be alright, but always I breathe easier when it's over."

Nuan knew when her father was a detective, guns were less common. He was often armed but not expecting to use his pistol. Policing now was different. She would breathe easier when it was over.

Chapter Thirty Three

Jia sensed something. She turned her head for her eyes to meet with Huang.

"I heard a call from the 426 to the 435," he said.

Jia came across to put on his headset. '426: merchandise loaded on ship. 435: which ship? 426: Hua Xia 68. 435: Will contact buyers.' Call ended.

To Jia the answer was obvious. "Superintendent Ma?" she called.

He came across where Jia gave him the headset before playing the short recording. He took the headset off.

"We should detain them all at dawn tomorrow," Jia said. Constable Zuo and me for the 435: Qiao He. Sergeant Liko and Constable Tang for the 426: Mo Feng. Sergeant Shui and Constable Zhang are currently checking-out the apartment of the 415 Chen Ru. Logically they should detain her. The China Coast Guard will intercept, board and search the ship Hua Xia 68 and detain all crew, while the People's Armed Police Force will arrest all inhabitants at Shalongba and surrounding villages: Shalongli, Chetiancun and Lichang, and search for signs of methamphetamine production, and arrest the mayor, the police superintendent, and the triad 49er at the address we identified. You and Sergeant Suo should be here on radio as our backup."

"That's good," Superintendent Ma said. "Come with me to speak with Commissioner Shui."

Jia was glad she had Nuan back. Nuan, Hu and Huang were officers she could rely on. Even though he was more junior, a sergeant grade three like herself, Jia would have had Shen leading the detention of the 426 with Liko as backup on radio rather than the other way around. Shen was straight-up, give him a task and he got it done, unlike Liko who put in a lot of effort for little outcome. The problem was hierarchy so Jia had what she had. Just then Nuan and Hu came through the door.

"Ah Sergeant Shui," Superintendent Ma said. "Just in time. You too, Sergeant Kam."

Within moments, Superintendent Ma, Jia, Nuan and Liko were at the big table in Commissioner Shui's office, with Commissioner Shui at the head and Lai Chun taking notes. Superintendent Ma invited Jia to outline her off the cuff plan, which she did.

"That should work," Commissioner Shui said. "What time do you propose?"

"Pre-dawn at five in the morning," Jia said.

"That will wake them up! Do you want me to arrange the China Coast Guard and the People's Armed Police Force for their parts in your operation?"

"Yes, but it has to be right on five for the China Coast Guard to intercept and board that ship, to prevent the crew disposing the methamphetamine overboard. Superintendent Ma; can you arrange for five armed officers for each of us three, fifteen in total, to meet us here at four tomorrow morning?"

"I'll do that."

"I recommend Sergeant Yang and his men," Nuan said.

"Anything else?" Commissioner Shui asked.

Silence. Commissioner Shui stood; they all stood and saluted, before leaving.

Jia swiped her security card at the door to Office to 1.10 where she and Nuan entered side-by-side.

"I'll prepare a summons for a master security card for 14 Zhujiang East Road, Tianhe," Nuan said. "Hu; you can get that from those security guards we saw?"

"Yes Nuan," he said wearily, which Jia noticed but Nuan didn't seem to. Nuan wore Sergeant Grade One like she was born to it, which in a way she was.

"Where's Liko?" Nuan then asked.

Jia looked around. "I don't know."

"Odd for him to disappear when everything's happening."

It was.

"Until I find him I'll work with Bo," Jia said. "Are you good for tomorrow?"

"I love getting up early," Nuan said sarcastically.

Nuan closed her eyes while counting with her hand. "Three vans, fifteen armed constables, a summons for security card access to our target, our equipment from the armoury tomorrow: body armour, pistols, batons, radios with throat microphones, earpieces and push to talk, and handcuffs. Is that it?" she asked.

"Headband flashlights to see in dark apartments pre-dawn," Jia said. "Like with the Axe Gang investigation, Liko and Bo will be Alpha One, you and Hu will be Alpha Two, Huang and I will be Alpha Three, while Superintendent Ma and Shen will be here as Alpha Four. I'll get Huang to book three vans."

"I'll do the summons, get Superintendent Ma to sign it, and send Hu to get the security card; then I'll go home. It's an early start and I can't think clearly anyway." Nuan came close. "You're brilliant," she whispered. "You should be sergeant grade one, not you know who."

Jia felt the same way but it was pointless to comment. "Before you go I'll type a list of who, what and when, including our call-signs, and print copies each of us."

"Including Liko for when you find him."

Just then he came through the door.

"He might have been in the mens," Nuan said. "He does look odd though."

Liko looked sheepish, if there was such a look. "I'll prepare the summation so you can go home," Jia said before sitting at her computer. Nuan was already at her computer doing her summons. Jia was carrying this operation, she had for a long time, and at that moment she wished she could just go home and relax. Nuan was entitled to do that, after working undercover for a month and then running another case in parallel, unlike some. Jia decided to get the key players on the same page and confirm everything was ready or in motion, and then go home with Huang. She and Huang needed to be fresh and clear for early tomorrow morning.

Chapter Thirty Four

Early not yet morning, the sun didn't rise until seven in late November, they gathered in the basement carpark of the Guangzhou Public Security Bureau where three Volkswagen vans waited. Jia appeared from the lift foyer.

"Right," Jia said in a clear voice. "I estimate it takes twenty minutes to drive to our targets, so we leave in five minutes. Alpha One and Alpha Two with five armed officers each. Get ready to go."

"You can come with me," Sergeant Yang," Nuan said. "You travel in the back, Hu."

Four constables and Hu climbed in back where Nuan slid the side door closed. Then she got ready behind the wheel before checking her watch. An engine started so she started the engine of her van. In the next van to Nuan, Huang was driving with Jia in the front. When they pulled out, Nuan put the Volkswagen Caddy into 'D' to follow. In her side mirrors she saw the third van of Liko and Bo. Nuan hoped they didn't fuck-up.

At four-thirty-five the streets of Guangzhou were eerily quiet with just a few vehicles moving, headlights showing the way beneath many streetlights, and rubbish trucks on the prowl. The steady drone of the Volkswagen diesel engine working up and down through the gears was strangely comforting. Beyond that growl there was silence; no need for small talk. Nuan exited left onto Xiancun Avenue to now head north, before taking the Huacheng Avenue exit to the left, and indicating right to 14 Zhujiang East Road. She indicated right into the apartment complex setdown and pickup loop, to pull up at the front door of the tower. Nuan checked her watch: four-fifty-five, before climbing down to open the side door of the van. They all climbed out, where Nuan led the way to the main entry door. Hu swiped their master security card on the sensor to one side for those doors to open, after which Nuan led the way across the foyer to the lifts. Once more Hu swiped a sensor to allow Nuan to press a button. A bell rang and doors sprang open, so they all gathered inside the lift. Nuan pressed 'eight'. Door closed before the lift climbed. Nuan checked her watch: four-forty-eight.

"Two minutes," she said. She removed her headband flashlight to switch it on, as did everyone else, then she removed her pistol to rack it, as did everyone else.

They arrived at floor eight, to gather in the corridor in silence. Nuan held her wrist visible as the numbers ticked down.

"Now!"

As agreed, Hu led the way to swipe the sensor on the door, with Nuan now holding her pistol at arms length, ready to aim and shoot. Hu opened the door to go inside. Sergeant

Yang and Nuan were next, followed by their constables all ready to shoot.

Suddenly lights blazed to illuminate many men in the room.

"This is the police!" Nuan ordered loudly. "Everyone on the floor, face down with your hands behind your heads!"

Suddenly a shot crackled loud and a constable fell. An ambush! Nuan centred the sights of her gun on the man who shot, and squeezed her trigger twice. Nuan's target fell as more and more shots filled the room with noise. Nuan sighted the next one and got him too. Another constable fell.

Think, think! Abandon the room and they would be shot from behind, while the only way out was the lift or the fire escape. They had to stay and fight.

"Pick your targets!" Nuan ordered; echoed by Sergeant Yang.

Even at close range body armour saved your life, but for sure you were badly hurt. Broken ribs or whatever. Nuan picked another triad to squeeze twice to miss. *Fuck!* A bullet skimmed past so close to her head, as she took a deep breath and squeezed her trigger twice to fell him. Their training, Sergeant Yang's men were a specialist unit, made the difference. With only three police down and just two criminals standing, Nuan held the upper hand.

She aimed her pistol at one of those two. "Drop your weapon."

He hesitated so she shot him twice. One left, who an armed officer took out.

Nuan pressed the PTT in her pocket. "Alpha One: we've been ambushed. All targets down but multiple casualties." She looked around the room. "No sign of Chen Ru. Send ambulances now!"

"Alpha Four: understood."

Nuan took stock: they weren't outnumbered; seven criminals for seven police officers. Three officers were felled: two constables and Sergeant Yang. Nuan knelt by Sergeant Yang groaning, and then the other two constables who were also alive. Battered and bruised but alive. Of the triad criminals she didn't know and she didn't care, other than they were mostly young and all in casual dress. Untrained they didn't stand a chance.

"Are you alright?" Hu asked.

"This is a fuck-up but I'm alright," Nuan said.

"Our training...."

Nuan, Hu and Jia were trained at university where they practiced for this many times. Then Nuan realised the others would be ambushed too. But she couldn't block the radio.

"Jia and Liko," Nuan said to Hu.

"Fuck, you're right."

Nuan leaned against the wall while waiting for ambulances to arrive. Their priority was their injured colleagues. She didn't care if triad bled to death in the meantime.

Huang dropped the master security card into the slot, where the red light turned green. Jia grabbed the handle to open the door to near-darkness only pierced by her headband flashlight. Suddenly the room was bathed in light while the first shot was deafening. Jia aimed and shot twice to get her target as she sensed constables entering the room from behind. Automatically she aimed and shot but missed while thinking through their situation. To abandon would mean chaos and casualties so they had to stand their ground. The triad she missed then aimed at Jia, who centred him in her sights, seemingly slowly, and squeezed twice. He fell. One more fell from the police onslaught. Jia counted three standing as she stood with her legs partly apart and her gun aimed.

"Drop your weapon!" she ordered the closest triad.

It fell to the ground with a loud thump.

"On the ground, face down."

He lay just as Jia heard two shots and another triad fell. Jia kicked her triad's gun away, to sense someone close. She spun around to see a dark figure and a gun. She brought her sights to him but he fell from another two shots. She turned back to her man on the ground now handcuffed by a constable. She looked over the scene to gasp in sheer horror! There, blood oozing from his head, Huang lay amongst two constables also shot.

Jia pressed her PTT. "Alpha Three: we've been ambushed. Multiple casualties. Send ambulances now!"

"Alpha Four: understood."

Jia knelt by Huang's neck to feel his pulse which was strong. One constable groaned while the other stirred. Jia stood.

"Gather their weapons and handcuff them," she ordered.

The three constables did that while Jia surveyed the scene, only to realise Mo Feng was one of their victims. She knelt to feel his pulse too. Good.

The three uninjured constables held six pistols from six triad, with five now killed or injured. Jia leaned against a table with her pistol still in her hand, hoping that Huang wasn't badly hurt, and hoping ambulances would be there soon. She had two victims she had to save: Huang her boyfriend, more important than life itself, and Mo Feng who could tell her what happened. Jia then realised Nuan and Liko would be stepping into the same traps. She pressed the PTT.

"Nuan and Liko?" she asked.

"Ambushed too," Superintendent Ma said. "Ambulances dispatched."

"Understood."

Jia took a deep, deep breath while her heart raced fast.

* * *

Four ambulance officers carried two stretchers into the room of carnage with a carpeted floor now soaked red with blood.

"Police officers only," Nuan ordered.

"But...."

"Do as I order."

They did that to depart, before another two arrived.

"One of you takes the injured police officer," Nuan ordered. "The other; check for any criminals still alive."

"This one's alive."

He was loaded to be taken away. Hu knelt amongst the victims.

"There are two more alive," he said flatly.

"Thanks," Nuan said.

Nuan and her team killed three boys sent in unprepared. What a needless waste. She pressed her PTT.

"Alpha Two update: three police officers injured but none seriously. Four triad injured, condition unknown, three triad killed. Request an update on Alpha One and Alpha Three."

"Alpha Three has three officers injured: two with minor injuries and one with condition unknown. Three triad injured, conditions unknown, three triad fatalities. Alpha One avoided a confrontation."

What the fuck?

Nuan pressed her PTT. "Understood and thank you." She thought and then pressed the PTT. "Have you dispatched officers to the hospital to guard these injured triad?"

"We'll do that now."

Two more ambulance officers arrived to take away their last victims. Nuan sat on the arm of a leather armchair to wait for investigators. Although she and her men were police officers, this was now a murder scene with all that entailed. She couldn't even use the bathroom there to wash her face to freshen herself although there was a way. She went to a corridor now buzzing, to spot an older couple in dressing gowns.

"Can I use your bathroom?" she asked.

They beckoned Nuan in where she half-filled their basin with water. In the mirror she looked terrible.

Chapter Thirty Five

Nuan sat at the table in Commissioner Shui's office, alongside Superintendent Ma, Jia and Bo.

"Can you report, Sergeant Shui?" Commissioner Shui asked.

"Hu was the first to enter, followed by Sergeant Yang and I. Lights came on and then we were under fire. I shot three triad while Sergeant Yang's men and Hu shot four more. Sergeant Yang and two constables were injured, none seriously."

"Your report, Sergeant Xiong?"

"Huang released the security sensor before I entered a dark room, followed by the rest of Alpha Three. Lights then came on and we came under fire. I made the decision to stand and attack, as backing away would have put us under a greater threat. I shot two triad while other officers and Huang shot three more. We took one uninjured triad prisoner. Two constables and Zuo Huang were injured."

"Constable Tang?"

"We approached the apartment of the suspect as I expected, when at the last moment Liko froze; then told us not to enter. We retreated. In the foyer I used my radio to hear from Alpha Four that Alpha Two and Alpha Three were ambushed. I looked for Liko, Sergeant Kam, but he was gone."

"Our injured officers?"

"A bullet grazed Constable Zuo's head," Superintendent Ma said. "His condition is satisfactory. The rest have suffered broken bones and bruising and are expected to make full recoveries."

"An alert should be posted for Kam Liko."

"Already done. I have Sergeant Suo Shen and two armed officers at his apartment."

"Triad leadership?"

"Mo Feng is under surgery as we speak. Qiao He escaped unharmed. The whereabouts of Chen Ru are unknown. Alerts have been posted for Qiao He and Chen Ru."

"This is my fuck-up by appointing Sergeant Kam Liko," Commissioner Shui said. "I apologise to you all."

"Until we investigate Sergeant Kam more deeply," Nuan said, "it's premature to apportion blame. Something may have happened since his appointment to Office 1.10."

"Do you have suspicions, Sergeant Shui?"

"Nothing factual as yet."

"All of you did well, as did every officer in Alpha Two and Alpha Three. I thank you all. Sergeant Xiong; do you wish to go home?"

"Thank you sir, but I prefer to be busy here than to sit at home or at the hospital."

"I understand."

They all stood, saluted, and left.

"I really need to be busy," Jia said.

Nuan thought. "Jia; you can track Liko's two mobiles: his police and his personal phone. I'll ring Shen to speak with Liko's wife to get his credit card number. We'll monitor that too."

They entered Office 1.10

"Superintendent Ma," Nuan said. "I want to interview Kam Liko's wife while Hu monitors his credit card."

"Alright."

"Hu?" Nuan called. "Can you ring Shen and get Liko's credit card details to monitor any purchases he makes, real-time?"

"Yes Nuan."

Nuan noticed something. "Why are you smiling?" she asked Jia.

"You're so – you!"

Nuan wondered what that meant.

"Detective-Sergeant Grade One Shui Nuan!"

"Really?"

"Really! It's not bad, it's good. It's great."

Nuan understood. Smiling to herself, she headed out to catch the metro.

* * *

Nuan sat while Liko's wife, Chien Ho, fussed about offering cups of tea and then glasses of hot water. Nuan wasn't in the mood for that.

"Please sit," Nuan said firmly.

Chien sat.

"We have reason to believe that your husband revealed details of a covert operation to an organised crime gang, resulting in many deaths and injuries. Do you understand?"

She nodded her head.

"Have you noticed any change of behaviour or any unusual activities by Liko during these past months?" Nuan asked.

"Liko has been working most weekends."

"We haven't been working weekends."

"He said he's been working weekends. Most Saturday mornings through to Sunday evenings."

"When did this start?"

"At odd times about six months ago, and then every weekend for some time. Then he stopped working weekends."

"Has he met anyone new or contacted people you consider strange or unusual?"

"He's received a few odd phone calls."

There was one thing which may shed light on what Liko was up to. "Do you have bank statements or credit card statements?"

"I'll get them."

Chien was gone for several minutes before returning with a bundle of papers. Nuan flicked through the bundle to notice credit card payments to China High Speed Rail almost every week for a while, and credit card payments to the Golden Dragon Hotel in Macau most Sundays for a while, obviously on checkout.

"Do you check your credit card statements?" Nuan asked.

"I leave that to Liko. Is Liko in trouble?"

"From these statements it's clear Liko was travelling to Macau to gamble. This may explain why he went rogue. Do you know where Liko might go for help? His family, your family, his friends, your friends?"

"Inside or outside Guangzhou?"

"More likely outside of Guangzhou."

"Liko has a cousin in Foshan. I'll get his address."

Chien Ho returned with an old-fashioned telephone card index. Nuan placed the card on her knee to take a picture. She handed it back to Chien Ho.

"What will happen to Liko when he's caught?" Chien Ho then asked.

Nuan quickly thought through her options and decided. "It's best that Liko's arrested by one of us who know him, than to be arrested by police officers who don't know him and may harm him. That's why it's important that you cooperate with Sergeant Suo Shen and other members of Office 1.10."

"In the longer-term?"

"Liko will be found and arrested, and then it's up to our courts to determine his punishment. Many police officers have been injured, some months of hard work by many of us has been destroyed, and serious criminals are now on the run and unlikely to be apprehended. You must realise the seriousness of what he did."

By that stage Chian was staring at the floor while nodding her head in understanding.

"I'm taking your credit cards and bank statements," Nuan said. "I'm sorry about what you must be going through but I have Kam Liko to apprehend. I must go."

In the corridor, Nuan scrolled her contacts for Superintendent Ma. She composed a text 'Kam Liko may get help from his cousin Kam Bolin on the attached address card picture'. Nuan attached the picture and sent it. Then another message to Superintendent Ma. 'I'm going home. If you need me, call me'. She sent that. Nuan scrolled her contacts to ring Hu.

"Wéi Nuan," he greeted.

"Wéi Hu," Nuan greeted. "Liko's been regularly gambling at Macau until recently."

"I understand."

"Now, go home Hu. It's been a long day so go home."

"Yes Nuan. Zài jiàn."

"Zài jiàn. You heard that?" Nuan asked Shen.

"That explains everything."

"It does. I'm going home now, too. Zài jiàn."

"Zài jiàn."

Nuan headed down in a lift and outside to catch the metro, to be home about half an hour later. She went straight to the couch and collapsed so hard that Dewai had to jump out of the way.

"One of our officers went rogue and fucked everything up," Nuan said. "It was really bad."

"Was anyone hurt?" Dewai asked.

"A few officers were hurt by bullets hitting their body armour and one officer has a head wound. Most likely he'll recover. We killed and injured several gangsters."

"You shot them?"

"We had to. It was us or them so we had to."

"Are you alright?"

Nuan knew what her problem was. "I think I'm in shock."

"Aah." Dewai lifted Nuan's shoulders to slip his knees under her head. He ran his fingers through her hair, massaging her scalp. Nuan knew he wouldn't stop doing that until she asked him to, which she wasn't going to do for a while. She needed that.

Chapter Thirty Six

Jia had never been in a hospital before. Just inside the entry doors was a foyer with a large, round reception counter. Jia asked for Zuo Huang where a busy, middle-aged woman used a computer before telling Jia to go to Ward 8B on the eighth floor.

The eighth floor, like the rest of Guangdong General Hospital, sparkled, yet a cleaner had a machine cleaning an already clean floor. Ward 8B was near the far end, and that sparkled too. Curtain rails hung from the ceiling at regular intervals surrounding beds spaced evenly. Part-way along was Huang. Jia went to kiss his cheek while contemplating the bandage on the side of his head.

"I'll have a scar," he said.

"You were lucky," Jia said. A few millimetres more.... She felt her eyes moisten and there was nothing she could do about that. "I love you, you know, so don't do anything like that again."

"Like what?"

"Get shot."

"What happened?"

"Liko's been gambling. We assume he ran up debts to triad and then he gave us up."

"The arsehole!" Huang exploded, while many heads turned to that commotion and bad language.

"We'll get him while you do what doctors tell you to do, to get better. Alright?"

"Alright."

"I love you," Jia said. "More."

"I love you more after this," Huang said.

Jia felt frustrated. "I can't put it into words. I love you more doesn't do how I feel justice. You're all of me, my reason, everything."

"Although it was me who got hurt, I would stand in front of a bullet to save you."

She kissed his cheek while thinking they were on the same page, as always.

Just then Huang's parents arrived to greet their son and Jia, who shook hands before taking Huang's hand. She wondered why she did that when they didn't hold hands. Then she knew: Huang was your son but now he's my boyfriend.

Huang's mother was terribly upset while his father was stoic. They didn't stay so long while Jia still held Huang's hand.

"It'll only be a few days," Huang said. "They said I'll be fine and I can even catch the metro home when I'm ready."

"I'll be waiting for you at our home."

Visiting hours ended so Jia had to leave. She kissed his cheek and then headed off. She loved him.

Chapter Thirty Seven

Nuan swiped her security card to enter Office 1.10, all busy but down on staff given Shen wasn't there, probably posted to Liko's apartment, Liko was on the run, and Huang was in hospital, according to hospital reception making steady progress. Nuan went to Hu.

"Zao an," Nuan greeted.

"Zao an," Hu responded.

"Any phone contact?"

"Nothing; not even from towers."

Liko knew they could trace him from towers so he had his phones turned off.

"Credit cards?" Nuan asked.

"Nothing so far but that's our best bet. Might even be our only bet."

"Liko probably doesn't know we can track many transactions real-time."

"That's right."

"The cousin at Foshan?"

"Superintendent Ma arranged for Foshan to post officers to watch out for Liko."

That was appropriate.

"Are you alright, Hu?" Nuan then asked.

He looked over his shoulder.

"Sometimes I get a bit focussed, but underneath I'm still the same."

"I know. Are you alright?" he asked.

"I'm better today."

"Me too."

Jia came in looking – not too bad. They greeted each other.

"This triad group, whoever they are, is your case," Nuan said. "You should find that arsehole Liko for us."

"I will."

"I'll take Shen, my laptop and a car, to see where that leads," Nuan said. She then got close. "If you're not promoted after your good work on this case, I'll be very surprised."

Jia nodded her head. "I'll find Liko first."

"Do you need Shen at Liko's apartment? A couple of constables can do that job given it's unlikely he'll return home."

"You're right Nuan. Call Shen in to investigate that trafficker."

"Thanks."

Nuan sat at her laptop to scroll contacts on her police phone to ring Shen. He said he would come in by metro, which was fine. She had all her trafficker's details, courtesy of a police constable at Wuhe who searched that house in Fusi Village. Jia liked typing lists which was a good way to do things. Nuan then started on her undercover list, or really a script for Shen to follow. Not hard to do given she'd interviewed four of these desperate, would-be husbands. Nuan typed and typed, totally focussed on her task.

* * *

"Jia," Hu called. "Liko just bought a train ticket."

Jia went to Hu's desk.

"Liko purchased a high-speed train ticket from Guangzhou South station booking office for 434 yuan," Hu continued. "Just now."

"Do we know where to?"

"No."

Jia looked around for Superintendent Ma but he still wasn't there. She had no choice but she knew he wouldn't mind as long as he had the time. Jia left Office 1.10 to walk to Commissioner Shui's office. Lai Chun was busy typing at her desk side-on.

"Excuse me Lai Chun," Jia asked. "Is Commissioner Shui free?"

"He hasn't any meetings scheduled so I'll ask."

Jia listened to Lai Chun on her phone for a moment.

"You can go right in, Sergeant Xiong."

Jia opened the big, big door to approach Commissioner Shui. She saluted, which he stood to respond.

"Commissioner Shui," Jia began. "Kam Liko just bought a high-speed train ticket from Guangzhou South station booking office for 434 yuan. I don't have the authority to find the details of this ticket, but I hope you may."

"Please sit, Sergeant Xiong, and we'll see how much authority I have."

Jia sat while Commissioner Shui rang Lai Chun to ask her to ring the chief executive of the China Rail Corporation. He then turned to face Jia. "This seems like progress."

"If we find his train, car and seat, we can intercept that train and detain him."

"That's correct. Beyond this detention, how are you coping?"

"Huang, Constable Zuo, is doing well," Jia said. "That's a big load off my mind."

"Anything else?"

Commissioner Shui was the father of her friend. "Last night I realised I probably killed some people. Until then it hadn't hit me. That's why I want to keep busy, so I don't focus on things that can't be changed."

"If you need help, let Lai Chun know and we'll do all we can."

"I'll be fine when Huang's home, which should be soon."

Commissioner Shui's phone rang for Jia to listen to a fairly one-sided conversation, where details were explained as well as the gravity of the situation. Then silence for a few minutes before Commissioner Shui wrote on a pad by his phone. Commissioner Shui thanked whoever it was, in fact the chief executive of one of the largest organisations in China, and ended his call. He tore the page from his pad to give it to Jia.

Jia read aloud. "Guangzhou to Kunming departing 15.51 from Guangzhou South railway station, arriving 23.04. Car E, seat 32. Kunming to Hekou at 08.10 the next morning." Jia looked to Commissioner Shui. "At Hekou, he plans to cross the border to Vietnam."

"Most likely. Now, what's your plan?"

Jia glanced at her watch to check the time, and she had time. "At Guangzhou South, Constable Zhang and myself will board that car from both ends to apprehend Kam Liko once the train is underway. Constable Tang will take a car to meet us at the first station stop."

"Kam Liko is likely to be armed."

"I don't expect an armed shoot-out with Kam Liko."

"I don't either, but be careful."

"The safety of civilians on this train is paramount," Jia said. "If he draws his weapon we'll abort."

"Agreed." Commissioner Shui stood, so Jia stood too. "I know this is in good hands."

Jia saluted before leaving for Office 1.10. There she gathered Hu and Bo to outline her plan. The details of Jia's plan were radios with earpieces, throat microphones and push to talk; pistols, extendable batons, handcuffs and body armour. Bo would check-out a car to meet the train at Foshanxi Station, scheduled for 16.12 or 21 minutes after departure from Guangzhou South. Jia remembered Commissioner Shui's admonition.

"If Liko draws his weapon to put civilians in danger, either on the train or at Foshanxi Station, we abort and let him go."

They both nodded their heads in agreement.

"Hu, you and I should depart shortly, given we need to find the platform and train at Guangzhou South Station. Bo, you should book a car now."

Jia and Hu headed down in a lift and then across the foyer of the Guangzhou Public Security Bureau, as always hushed but busy as many constables at many desks handled endless queries from members of the public. Uniformed officers came and went, often in pairs leaving or arriving from street patrols. Jia and Hu walked to Gongyuanqian Station, where soon they were on their way to Guangzhou South Station, the busiest station in southern China and one of the busiest in the country, although inconveniently located from the city centre. There, the interchange from metro platforms to the massive, modern, intercity station was quite easy. But the crowds! High speed trains departed to major cities at regular intervals, as well as regular speed trains. The waiting hall echoed beneath an arch-shaped, silver steel roof as rows and rows of seats had travellers waiting for departures. At both ends of the waiting area were a variety of shops and food outlets, while bisecting the waiting area was a bank of blue luggage lockers. Jia scanned the crowd in hope, but with so many there it was all but impossible to pick Liko, assuming he wasn't hiding until just before departure time.

"His train is departing from platform twelve," Hu said.

Jia's strategy was the same as following that drug-dealer Peng around. "As departure time nears we'll go to platform twelve, but we'll stay back until moments before. Platforms are roughly north to south here?"

"Yes."

"You board from the north end door of car E; and I'll board from the south end, to meet at seat 32."

"Too easy!" Hu exclaimed, but Jia knew he was joking.

"No need to hold my hand, but stay close like we're boyfriend and girlfriend, and we'll stroll around while keeping a lookout for Liko."

"No problem."

Shoulder to shoulder they circumnavigated the big waiting area, towards escalators that led to the upper walkway. Hu, like Huang, was as reliable as day follows night, absolutely trustworthy, and totally capable. Jia was glad to have him by her side as they circled the waiting room before she guided him from north to south parallel to the lockers; still looking for Liko but not seeing him. She glanced at the time on the departure screen where they had ten minutes.

"Hu," Jia said. "Stay close while we head to platform twelve."

"Alright."

Side by side they stepped onto an up escalator, before walking along the concrete-walled walkway with signs, in English and Hanzi, showing each platform number. At 12 – 13 Jia stepped onto a down escalator while realising that was an island platform. Twelve was on the right while thirteen was on the left. The Kunming train had docked where many were boarding. The carriage opposite was C which made E somewhere behind the escalator.

"Stay with me," Jia said just before they reached the bottom, where she veered left now mostly hidden by the escalator itself. Jia kept one eye on the current time on the departure screen. Ticking down, ticking down.

"Now," Jia said.

Jia strode ahead given she had further to go to reach the southern doorway. More entered car E now just ahead as Hu approached the northern doorway. There Hu stopped until Jia came to the southern doorway, to draw a breath and enter as Hu entered too.

That second-class carriage was in shades of blue, with three seats to the right of the aisle, and two seats to the left of the aisle; all facing north. Passengers stowed luggage, others got comfortable, some talked, some were silent, many had smartphone headsets in place. Jia noted seat numbers in the 90s, which meant Liko was closer to Hu now approaching, while being stopped by passengers forcing hand luggage onto overcrowded racks. Jia approached slowly for the same reason, as Hu got closer and closer. Hu's eyes were fixed to his right, to the seats in pairs rather than threes, but Jia couldn't see more than backs of heads mostly obscured by tall seat backrests.

Suddenly a man stood and shouted above the general commotion while grabbing another man beside and dragging that man to his feet.

"He has a gun!" one passenger shouted, which created a stampede of terror! Jia watched Hu so close to the standing men, for sure one was Liko, as passengers virtually swept Hu from his feet and dragged him towards the northern door. Jia took refuge at a pair of seats not yet occupied, to see Liko holding his pistol to the head of the passenger he'd taken hostage, while the shouting and screaming mob emptied the carriage in a mass panic. As the rush abated, Jia drew her pistol to place it in her left hand, and then she rested her right hand on the extendable baton clipped to her belt. Jia closed on Liko standing seemingly in shock. As she got close, Liko seemed to sense her. He spun around .

"Put your weapon down!" Liko ordered.

Jia held her pistol high and then placed it on a bag on the luggage rack.

"Back away," Liko ordered.

Jia walked backwards the length of the carriage while taking in the terror in that hostage's eyes. Jia kept walking back and back until she reached the vestibule, where she stopped.

"If you stay on this train they'll catch you at the next station," Jia said calmly.

She saw Liko's eyes flickering left and right, as if he was thinking his options through.

"Liko, give him up," Jia said. "You don't have a chance."

"Off the train," Liko said to Jia.

"If you stay on this train they'll catch you."

Silence for a moment. "Alright."

Liko went past still holding his hostage, but the narrow doorway meant Liko had to let his hostage go. As soon as Liko did that, Jia snapped her baton to full length and pushed the heavy handle hard into Liko's shoulders, to push him out of the train. Jia jumped out, and with her left arm outstretched for balance, she struck the side of his body as his pistol clattered onto the platform, and again and again and again. Liko crumpled to his knees, so Jia struck him across his back. He rolled onto his side where Jia bent her knees to strike his side more effectively. Jia struck him twice more before looking up to see Hu.

"Handcuffs Hu."

Hu, with Liko's pistol jammed into his belt, knelt and did that while Jia paused to think. She went into the now empty carriage to take and holster her pistol just as several uniformed officers poured off the escalator. Jia emerged from the doorway to a swarming mob of blue and Hu showing his warrant card. Jia went amongst those uniformed constables to show her warrant card too. Then she took stock.

"This train is safe to leave if you can get passengers from car E to re-board," Jia said. "Do you have somewhere to hold our prisoner in custody?"

"Come with me," a constable said.

Hu dragged Liko to his feet before roughly pushing their former colleague towards the escalator. Loudspeakers announced the train for Kunming was departing in one minute, which saw a mad scramble of travellers onto car E. In the meantime Hu, with Liko under custody, and Jia, followed the young constable deep into the bowels of Guangzhou South Station and a small public security bureau, including a steel-framed cell filled-in with toughened glass. Hu shoved Liko inside for the constable to lock Liko securely.

Jia felt for the PTT in her pocket. "Bo, it's Jia. We've taken Kam Liko into custody in a cell in Guangzhou South Station Public Security Bureau. Please come here to take him into detention."

"On my way and congratulations."

"Thank you Bo," Jia said. With Liko safe behind toughened glass, Jia paused to think. Could she have done that differently? Even if she flew to intercept that train at

Kunming, Liko could have taken a hostage while surrounded by disembarking passengers at that busy station, so there would have been a risk there. That mass panic was dangerous, that hostage was terrified, but short of not engaging with Liko at all, there was always a risk.

"How are you?" Hu asked.

"Just thinking," Jia said.

"We didn't expect him to take a hostage, nor could we plan a contingency for that. The rule was not to engage, which neither of us did."

"I know."

"Liko didn't realise you could beat the shit out of him!" Hu exclaimed.

Jia shrugged her shoulders while now thinking ahead. "You arrested a few suspects last week," Jia said.

"With Nuan who'd done that when she was on patrol."

"We'll get Liko's charges agreed with Superintendent Ma, and probably Commissioner Shui, and then you and I can arrest him."

"Giving us up to organised crime was bad enough, but drawing his gun and taking a hostage. Fuck, he'll be put away for a long, long time."

Jia contemplated their prisoner behind toughened glass. Kam Liko would be an old, old man before he next tasted freedom.

"Do you remember what we learned about addictions," Jia said.

"If you say addiction, people think drugs," Hu said. "But alcohol, which is a drug, gambling, sex if it becomes obsessive and destructive, internet, video games, cosmetic surgery, even extreme behaviour like jumping off buildings with parachutes. But gambling can be an addiction, especially here in China."

"Always they lose, and always the next bet will be the winner to clear their debts."

Drugs of themselves weren't a problem, nor gambling in moderation, nor sex, nor anything, unless it led to obsessive and destructive behaviour. Kam Liko, sitting with his head hanging, was proof positive of the dangers of addictions.

Chapter Thirty Eight

Nuan was glad to leave Guangzhou behind, to pick up the toll motorway to Zhaoqing.

"You seem to like driving," Shen said.

"Why?" Nuan asked.

"You're smiling."

"It's good to get away for a few hours, don't you think? Besides, I like driving."

"I can't imagine what you went through," Shen then said.

Nuan understood. "It was tough but I have my family and my boyfriend for support. I also have this new challenge. Really, I had one short burst of – bad things, while these women have had months and months of worse things. To rescue them is worthy, as is to break-up this trafficking gang."

"It's good you have a boyfriend to help you."

"My boyfriend's special for me in a modern way." Nuan glanced to Shen. "We live together. And you?"

"We're married 20 years this year."

"Congratulations!"

"We have a son in middle school."

"Has he made up his mind about his future?"

"Not yet."

"That will come. Maybe a police officer?" Nuan asked.

"If he wants to be a police officer I'll tell him about the university you went to. I'm impressed."

Nuan didn't want to comment on that but she appreciated the sentiment. There was a place for reliable and trustworthy experience like Shen, but to say that was patronising. Besides, actions spoke louder than words: Shen was now a key part of smashing this people trafficking group.

Every time Nuan drove to Guangning County she was always uplifted by the sheer beauty there. Vast plains of rice paddies green and lush, forests, looming forested mountains in the near distance, and the many waterways and lakes of the Pearl River Delta. Guangning County had to be one of the most beautiful places in China. Zhaoqing was a prefecture-level city of a bit more than a million, bisected by many waterways and with gorgeous views to those mountains. Their destination was Block A4, Shangcheng International, Number 19 Industrial Avenue, High-tech Zone, Sihui Shi. Sihui Shi contained vast blocks of modern, multi-storey apartment blocks in a newly-developed residential area bordered by the Suijiang River on one side, and a forest park on the other. Those apartment blocks could have been any modern development in China, right down to schools, shops, cafes, restaurants, day care centres; all necessities in place before first residents moved in. The car GPS was invaluable as it guided Nuan to their destination. There she parked in a visitors bay quite close to Xu Shing's apartment. They both climbed out of the Volkswagen Jetta for Nuan to go to the boot, where from her laptop bag she retrieved the transmitter and band. With her thumb she switched the transmitter on.

"Alright Shen," she said. "Inside you'll have to find a toilet to wrap this velcro band around your thigh; make sure the hole in the pocket is at the bottom, and then put the transmitter in that pocket with the antenna pointing down through the hole. The transmitter is already switched on, so I'll be listening and recording."

"I understand."

"Straight away or sometime later he'll ring the next link in the chain, but I'll be listening to his mobile, so we'll know the mobile number and the place where that link lives. And so it will go on from there. Good luck."

"Thank you."

Nuan took her laptop to the driver's seat of the car, and woke it from hibernation. With her headset on she restored the transmitter program where she heard a door buzzer, followed by greetings. It was so clear that Nuan could have been in the room, as Shen was invited inside. Shen repeated his cover story of being never-married, from Xia Jiao village near Wuhe, an area of Guangning County that Nuan was familiar with. Xu Shing repeated the price of 10,000 yuan for him and 70,000 yuan for a wife, which Shen agreed to. Then Xu Shing said he had to make a phone call.

Nuan reduced the transmitter program to restore her tracking program, where Xu Shing rang a number in

Wenshan not so far from the Vietnamese border. There a woman answered to confirm women would be available shortly, and to send the customer to Hekou on Friday. That woman then ended her call while Nuan put a trace on future calls to and from that number, before returning to the transmitter program. There she caught Shen paying the 10,000 yuan, to be given the address in Hekou for Friday. Shen thanked Xu Shing profusely, before being showed out. Nuan waited for Shen to climb into the passenger seat of their car.

"Was I alright?" he asked while he handed the transmitter and velcro band across.

"You were great," Nuan said. "Listen."

Nuan unplugged her headset, and restored her tracking program to play the phone conversation through the laptop speaker.

"That's it?" Shen asked.

Nuan thought. "Wenshan is in Yunnan Province so we don't have jurisdiction there, but we can still get her arrested by detectives in Yunnan when we give them this evidence. Meanwhile, we now have evidence against Xu Shing beyond a testimony, so we can arrest him when the time is right for that. Not now because an arrest would alert this woman in Wenshan."

"Given Xu Shing wanted to meet me after four, I think he works at a regular job and this is part-time."

"You're probably right, Shen.

Nuan folded her laptop to put it on the floor behind Shen's seat. She pulled on her seatbelt, started the engine, and set off for the one-hour drive. She had to leave that car at work before catching the metro home, where she wouldn't be home until around seven. She decided to eat out that night. Despite a long day, Nuan felt clearer and especially she felt calmer. She had to thank Dewai for his support during these past days. Words of thanks were too easily given, so her thanks would be a special treat. Nuan didn't know what her special treat would be, but she had time to work that out before she got home.

Chapter Thirty Nine

Jia sat at the table in Commissioner Shui's office, with Superintendent Ma, the Commissioner, and Lai Chun taking notes.

"Congratulations, Sergeant Xiong, for detaining Kam Liko without casualties," Commissioner Shui said. "What are your next moves?"

Jia glanced at her notes. "I rang the Macau Police Force who are currently reviewing camera recordings from the gaming room of the Golden Dragon Casino for the dates I gave them, where it's most likely Kam Liko has been gambling. If he's not there they will move to other casinos for those dates. I supervised a search of Kam Liko's apartment where we uncovered packing for a cheap mobile phone in a false name. Constable Zhang is tracing the use of that phone from its IMEI. China Coast Guard divers have recovered the 1,000 kilograms of methamphetamine thrown overboard from the Hua Xia 68 while it was still at berth. The People's Armed Police Force has detained all residents of Shalongba and surrounding villages, while collecting and cataloguing methamphetamine manufacturing equipment and ingredients. They also arrested the mayor, the police superintendent, and the triad 49er, and obtained bank account details for the mayor and the police superintendent for later charges."

"Good. Now charges for Kam Liko."

Jia checked her notes. "Fourteen counts of being an accessory to the attempted murders of police officers, one count of being an accessory to the manufacture and distribution of illegal narcotics, one count of the illegal use of a police firearm, one count of unlawful confinement of a person against their will, and one count of attempting to pervert the course of justice."

"Superintendent Ma?"

"Sergeant Xiong's list of charges is sufficiently comprehensive. I would like Sergeant Xiong to formally arrest Kam Liko."

"Agreed, especially given Sergeant Xiong is our most senior officer. On that note I'm promoting Sergeant Xiong to Detective-Sergeant Grade One, effective today."

Jia wasn't surprised given what Nuan said, and she knew Nuan played no part in that. "Thank you Commissioner Shui," she said. "For this arrest I'll use Constable Zhang, who arrested those involved in the human trafficking case Sergeant Shui is currently working on."

"What is Sergeant Shui up to?" Commissioner Shui asked while frowning.

"Sergeant Shui and Sergeant Suo are identifying members of the human trafficking ring she uncovered through her raid on that massage parlour," Superintendent Ma said.

"Ah."

"Every day we delay means more rapes of sex slaves."

"Good point."

Commissioner Shui stood. They all stood and saluted, before leaving for Office 1.10 just along the corridor. Superintendent Ma used his security card to let them in.

"Now that we've agreed the charges," Jia said, "I'll arrest Kam Liko now. I want to hear his side of what happened."

"Me too."

Jia asked Hu to check a car out, and soon he was driving to Baiyun Detention Centre. It was just as well that Jia had Hu because he knew exactly what to do. It took about an hour before they were led into a room with Kam Liko strapped into an interrogation chair, and a guard standing silently by the door. Hu switched on the video camera while Jia took her seat, followed by Hu beside. Liko had his head hanging in shame.

"Kam Liko," Jia said sternly. "Today I arrest you for the following charges: fourteen counts of being an accessory to the attempted murders of police officers, one count of being an accessory to the manufacture and distribution of illegal narcotics, one count of the illegal use of a police firearm, one count of unlawful confinement of a person against their will, and one count of attempting to pervert the course of justice. Do you understand?"

Liko nodded his head.

"Speak up for the camera," Hu demanded.

"I understand," Liko said.

"This won't change anything," Jia said, "but what happened?"

"An old friend came back into my life," Liko said while staring at his feet. "We went out a few times when he said he was bored, so we should go to Macau where there are prostitutes. I agreed because as a police officer I couldn't see prostitutes here where it's illegal, so we went."

"Why not Hong Kong?"

"He said Macau prostitutes were better. They gather at hotels where we can take our pick of the pretty ones. So we caught a high-speed train, and while I was there he loaned me 10,000 yuan to gamble, just for a treat. I picked mahjong but they were good players. He said not to worry, I could make it up the next time. That's how it started."

"Did you find a pretty prostitute while you were there?" Jia asked.

He nodded his head.

"Yes or no?" Jia asked.

"Yes I did."

"So you kept returning to Macau, kept losing, and ran up a big debt."

"Yes."

"Then what?"

"On one trip to Macau while I was having dinner, a man came to join me. He said I now owed a lot of money which could be a problem, unless I helped him. If he asked for information I was to tell him. If I didn't I would be in trouble and my family would be in trouble."

"Was he Macau triad?"

"I would suspect so."

"Did he ask about our investigation into methamphetamine?"

"He rang to ask me about our new cases but I said I was still working on the old case. Later he asked me again, and I told him there was an investigation into an unknown gang manufacturing methamphetamine in Guangdong Province. Later after we had that meeting, I rang him with the details."

"The meeting where we planned the raids on Qiao He, Mo Feng and Chen Ru?"

"Yes."

"So you knew we were going to be ambushed by armed triad, but you let us walk into those traps?"

He nodded his head.

"Speak up!" Hu demanded.

"I had to. Denying that investigation was one thing, but not telling them before those raids would have caused trouble for me and my wife."

"You should have told us and we could have fixed things," Jia said.

"How?"

"We're police and he's a criminal. We could have investigated him and then we could have arrested him."

"There will be other triad I don't know about."

Jia realised that was true. "You still should have told us and we could have done something. Instead you let us walk into traps, almost got us killed, all the hard work Nuan put in undercover was worth nothing, just because you couldn't control your gambling! Do you have any idea what Nuan went through pretending to be a drug-dealing prostitute? Do you?"

"I was with her," Hu said. "A lesser person would have broken-down. I don't know how she did it. You should be ashamed of yourself."

"I am ashamed."

"You'll have decades to contemplate your shame!" Hu exclaimed. Decades!"

"I know."

"Who was your old friend?" Jia asked.

"So Kai."

"Address?"

"I don't know."

"The contact in Macau?"

"Lor Desheng."

Jia thought that was most likely a false name, although the old friend must have been real. "You went to school with So Kai?"

"Yes."

"What school and year?"

"Middle School Number 22, graduating in 2003."

Jia stood. "Take the prisoner away," she ordered the guard.

The guard released Kam Liko's shackles to lead him away.

"I'll get a copy of that interview," Hu said.

Outside, Hu gave a USB to a sergeant-guard at a computer.

"When Nuan was on patrol," Hu said. "She did a couple of arrests for various violations. She would have learned how to do this from the constable she worked with at the time."

Jia couldn't help but smile at that. "Theory is one thing but experience is invaluable."

"That's right."

"Let's go, Hu. We have an old school friend to find if we can."

They headed out to their car.

* * *

Nuan swiped the card to their door, to let herself in. Dewai was watching television, which he switched off with the remote.

"I love you," Nuan said.

"I love you too," Dewai said.

Nuan came to face him. "No, no; I really love you! Today I realised all the time I talk about my boyfriend. My

307

boyfriend this, my boyfriend that, my boyfriend who I live with. People must be tired of hearing about my boyfriend but I just can't help myself."

"Shui Nuan; nobody could ever accuse you of not being passionate. You're passionate for your work, which I'm happy to support you with, and you're passionate in other and special ways. What's in that bag?" he asked.

"This bag is to say thanks for being you, but first I'll have a quick shower."

"Alright."

Nuan got as far as her journey home while still not knowing what treat to give to Dewai, until there it was. She quickly undressed, and quickly showered to be sparkling clean, before pulling on a new, black, lace bra, a new black, lace g-string, a new black, lace suspender belt, and then she sat on the closed toilet lid to carefully unroll new, sheer black stockings. She'd never worn stockings with a suspender belt before, just pantyhose, but the clips weren't that difficult. Then she went to their bedroom for her black stilettos. She walked towards their living room with her heart beating fast.

Chapter Forty

Nuan sat at her desk to switch on her laptop, still smiling. She never realised. Afterwards she decided each week to buy something new, until she had a proper collection. That shop just up from the metro station had racks and racks of colours and styles. All it took was imagination.

"You look happy," Jia said.

"I'm in love – still – more. When is Huang coming home?" Nuan asked.

"Today."

"I'm glad."

"Yesterday we arrested Liko."

That made Nuan's morning even better. "Good." She thought. "Although Liko fucked-up our drug case, by accident I found this case. So it wasn't totally wrecked."

"Oh another thing," Jia said. "Commissioner Shui promoted me to Sergeant Grade One."

That made Nuan's day even, even, even better. "I expected that would happen given what you've done. You deserve this."

"Thanks Nuan. What are you up to?"

"Thanks to Shen, I've tracked the next link in the chain. The sex slave guy in Zhaoqing rang a woman in Wenshan," and then it hit Nuan. "This woman in Wenshan must have other sex slave guys in other parts of China," she said. "Surely she's dealing women to villagers near and far."

"That's really off," Jia said.

"I know. Love is beautiful, the most beautiful thing in this world, and always has been, but buying and selling women is just awful. That's why I'm not too fussed about Liko fucking up our triad methamphetamine case, other than he's going to be punished for what he did."

"The charges!"

Nuan was happy about that before thinking there were more important things at play. "I'll find this woman's name, and we'll monitor her calls to expose more of her network. The problem is Shen will have to go to Hekou on Friday to pretend to buy a wife."

"That's more evidence for when this goes down," Jia said.

"True."

"I'll leave you to it."

Nuan logged into the mobile phone registration system to see if she could get the woman in Wenshan's name that way, while thinking if that if Office 1.10 took enough time, and because they were incorruptible again, this might end up being big when they took it down, all down to a chance meeting with Peng and Binbin. But this mobile phone was registered to a fake ID number, not unexpected for a possible career criminal. Low-level scum like Xu Shing weren't that clever but this woman was that clever.

Nuan sensed Superintendent Ma coming through the door, to turn her head to meet his eyes for a moment. He beckoned Nuan and Jia to his table, where Nuan wheeled her chair.

"Yesterday I froze the assets of Mo Feng pending his arrest and trial," Superintendent Ma said. "Sergeant Xiong, now that you've arrested Kam Liko, you'll need to prepare the brief for his court case. Later you'll arrest Mo Feng and the injured triad when they've recovered, and prepare briefs for their cases too. You'll need help for this."

"Huang will be in tomorrow so I'll use him."

"Sergeant Shui?"

"Sergeant Suo met with Xu Shing who then rang a woman in Wenshan in Yunnan Province. This woman could be the leader of this sex slave trafficking group, so by monitoring her calls we may find other links."

Superintendent Ma rubbed his chin. "This is getting outside our jurisdiction," he said.

Nuan knew that. "Xu Shing is in our jurisdiction, as are the villagers who bought women through him. How about we monitor his calls, and the calls from the woman in Wenshan, and when we uncover her human trafficking network I'll prepare documentation to give to other provinces to help them to arrest traffickers in their jurisdictions?"

"Good idea, Sergeant Shui."

"And of course at the right time we'll arrest Xu Shing, and then we'll arrest villagers in Guangdong Province and release women."

"Yes, I understand."

"Sergeant Suo had to agree to purchase a wife who will be available at Hekou on Friday. I propose that Sergeant Suo travel to Hekou with a translator, pay 70,000 yuan, and then take this girl home to Vietnam. In the meantime I'll use Constable Zhang and Constable Tang to monitor the various numbers we're tracing."

"Do that."

Nuan then thought of something. "Jia, does Superintendent Ma know?"

"Know what?" Jia asked. "Oh. Huang and I are boyfriend and girlfriend. We live together."

"That's great news!" Superintendent Ma exclaimed.

"We can work together or separately, that hasn't been a problem, while outside of hours is a different version of us."

"The work we do here is intense at times, but who better than a fellow officer who understands that? Congratulations and I hope you're happy together."

"Thank you.

Nuan was surprised by that easy acceptance, not so much of two police officers in a relationship which was common enough, but of living together which still wasn't common.

Maybe he had a close relative, nephew or niece, or even his own child, doing the same.

"On that positive note," Superintendent Ma said, "you two can get your cases underway."

Nuan then called Hu and Bo to her desk to explain the situation. They would monitor the two phones, Xu Shing and this woman in Wenshan, to build up evidence of this woman's human trafficking network. It wasn't long before Bo called Nuan.

Nuan went to his laptop where he gave her his headset. She slipped it on while Bo played the most recent call. She listened to a man calling the woman at Wenshan for a Vietnamese woman for a new client, as awful as that was, with the promise for Friday. Nuan handed the headset back.

"Here," Bo said as he brought up the map.

Lijiang City in Yunnan Province.

"Trace all future calls to that mobile and see if you can get his name."

Nuan watched as Bo logged into the mobile registration system to get the ID number for the registered user of that mobile, and from there he logged into the ID system to get a name, while Bo already had the address of that call. Nuan took her notebook to the whiteboard to write a diagram of names, addresses and mobile numbers she'd gathered so far, with the unknown name at Wenshan and her mobile number in the centre. She looked over Bo's shoulder to transcribe this new actor onto her diagram. Then she paused. This actor was trading a new girl on Friday, but three days wasn't enough time to break this gang. *Fuck!* This poor girl was going to be abused and there was nothing Nuan could do to stop that, short of jeopardising their bigger investigation. That was horrible. Horrible for Bo who wasn't stupid.

"Bo," Nuan called. "More calls will come through, more traffickers will be identified, to later be arrested, and ultimately more women will be rescued."

"Yes Nuan."

Nuan knew that was the best way to do things but that didn't make her feel better.

* * *

Jia unlocked her door, to catch Huang's scent when she opened it. He stood and somehow they fell into an embrace. Every day in hospital she kissed his cheek and held his hand, but she wanted more than that. Now she had more.

"I love you," Jia murmured.

"I love you too. Every day I looked forward to your visit."

Jia eased away to contemplate the stiches on Huang's head.

"I was unlucky that I was grazed by a bullet, then it got infected which took a few days to clear up. But I was lucky that it wasn't worse."

"When I saw you bleeding on the floor, I felt so – terrified. We have to get you and your colleagues trained to university standards in firearms. The three of us from university should do a few hours at a shooting range, to keep fresh. What do you think?"

"Yes Sergeant Xiong."

Jia nestled into his shoulder while he hugged her again. They were good together from their first date, and then love crept in like through the window, but after their near-tragedy came an even deeper love. Life would never be the same and that was a good thing.

Chapter Forty One

Nuan came early to work, fresh and clear after a great weekend. Dewai's family were lovely and she enjoyed it every time they visited. She went to her whiteboard diagram now more complete.

Jia looked at the diagram. "It's filling up," she said.

"This one here, Ruili, is on the border with Myanmar."

"So they're trafficking women from there. What's your plan?"

"Wait until new contacts tail off, and then brief Yunnan Province about those we've identified."

"Can you get this woman's call history for the past few months, and track her contacts that way?"

"Already done. But a call is just a call where we need is evidence of illegal activity."

"From her call records, how many do you think she has?"

"Eight."

"Did Shen buy that girl at Hekou?"

"Yes he did, and he took her back to her village. He noticed one Chinese man in the background at Hekou probably managing the Vietnamese. I would say the woman in Wenshan contacts this man and he gets young Vietnamese men to abduct women across the border. These two Chinese take the major part of the 70,000 yuan while Vietnamese get paid fuck-all, in a proportional sense."

"Probably a small fortune in a Vietnamese peasant sense."

"For sure. What are you doing, Jia?" Nuan asked.

"Liko's school friend So Kai has a work visa in Singapore so we lost him. I issued an alert if he returns but he would be stupid to do that. Mo Feng and three triad 49ers have recovered so I arrested them." Jia sighed. "They're triad, so I could put a gun to their heads during their interviews and threaten to pull the trigger, but they still wouldn't say a word."

Nuan knew the outcome. "Mo Feng will be executed based on your sting with the 1,000 kilograms of methamphetamine."

"One by one they're being arrested, to be tried in due course. Mo Feng will be executed, Kam Liko will be lucky to get out before he's an old man, while those three triad 49ers will spend years in prison the attempted murder of seven police officers."

"Me or you?" Nuan asked.

"Those three triad tried to shoot you."

"Serves them right," Nuan said with a big smile. "At least this human trafficking case will get us some success," Nuan said.

Jia shook her head in seeming exasperation. Nuan had another issue; there was a major gap of information on her diagram: the name of the leader of this group.

Nuan went to Hu's desk.

"Do you feel like travelling?" she asked.

"If you need me to travel, I can," Hu said.

Nuan wheeled her chair around. "I have a mobile number, and from that an address where a call was received in Wenshan. Satellite images show a modern skyscraper of twelve storeys and maybe 120 apartments. I thought a maintenance person dressed in overalls could visit each apartment. Rule out women who aren't likely to be traffickers, such as a twenty year old with a toddler, but when you're there with a possible suspect, use a burner phone to ring her once, and hang up. Get a phone from Lai Chun and make your bookings through her as well. It'll take all day to get there by train, so you'll need to book for two nights."

"It's not as if my nights are full."

Nuan had a thought. "Do you want a coffee?"

"Not really but I know you."

Nuan led Hu to the tearoom where she bought a milk coffee, while he filled a plastic cup from the water cooler. They sat at the table.

"Because of the one child policy there are many more men than women," Nuan said. "This is why we're dealing with these trafficked women. But outside of that, many women in bigger cities, in preference to love, want a fully-furnished, owned apartment, a car, a minimum income, and probably other things. Right?"

"Right."

"This is why village men are buying sex slaves. Now for you, keep an open mind during the time you're in Wenshan. Women there might not be so demanding. In fact, from Guangzhou, you bring something for them."

"You're expecting me to find love in Wenshan?"

"It doesn't hurt to look. Look like you're from Guangzhou. Leave your jeans behind and dress smart like you are now, even in your free time." Nuan sipped her bitter-tasting coffee. "You're a great guy Hu, so put yourself out there."

"I'll try."

"Be positive! Look at Huang and Jia! Huang's nice, a bit like you, and Jia's lovely. Something happened, I don't know what, and now they're living together."

Hu smiled while shaking his head. "I'll try, I promise, and you might be right about a Guangzhou man." Hu sipped his water. "Your problem is you're too much in love and you want everyone to be as happy as you."

Nuan understood. "Is there anything wrong with that?"

"Not at all." Hu threw his plastic cup at the bin. "I'll see Lai Chun now."

Nuan went to Office 1.10 to think, while Hu came in a few minutes later. *Maintenance, maintenance, maintenance – yes!*

"Hu," she said. "Find a pest control company website, and copy their logo to make an ID card with your photo, and get Lai Chun to laminate it. Wear it on your overalls with a clip."

"That's just too good!"

Nuan thought it was too.

* * *

Nuan wasn't wrong when she said it would take all day to get to Wenshan. The morning regular train left Guangzhou South Station at 9.46 to arrive at Puzhehei at 4.26. There a rental car was booked for Hu for the more than one hour drive to the Huaxi Hotel, which was more of a resort than a hotel. Brick buildings were spread across many hectares of lush gardens, while hotel itself – amazing. A towering foyer in two levels connected by a curved staircase, with the reception desk to the rear of the lower level of the foyer. There were two women in white blouses and black blazers, and she was the most beautiful woman Hu had ever seen. Taller, not very tall like Nuan but more Jia-taller. Lovely, melon-seed face with a V-shaped jaw, fair complexion, a gorgeous round nose, and her black hair cut short while parted to one side. It was her hair as much as anything; too many young women in Guangzhou dyed their hair brown or even close to blonde, where Chinese women were meant to be black, and nothing looked better than black hair against fair skin anyway. Hu went to this amazingly beautiful woman who looked up from a keyboard on a pull-out shelf behind the counter.

"Ni hao," she greeted in the sweetest voice Hu had ever heard.

"Ni hao. My name's Zhang Hu.'

She typed for a moment. "From Guangzhou PSB?"

"That's right. I'm here on business."

"What sort of business?"

Hu knew it wouldn't hurt to tell a small part of his story. "I'm a detective investigating a case here."

Big, big smile. 'You have a good imagination."

Hu didn't comment.

"That's real, isn't it?" she said.

"It is."

"You seem young to be a detective."

Hu wondered what wasn't trite, but everything was trite. "I never expected to arrive to such beauty," he said.

Silence. "Me?" she asked in a small voice.

"You."

She had one hand on the counter where even her long, slender fingers were amazing. Totally amazing.

"I would like to get to know you." Hu said, while hoping she wasn't taken.

"You're here for two nights."

"I could stay for longer. Do you think this would be possible?"

"Anything's possible but there are things," she said. "This isn't the place. Can I have your phone?"

Hu handed his personal phone across. She typed quickly before handing it back, where Hu saw he had a new contact: Chen Peijing, and an address.

"Meet me there at seven."

"I will."

She put a key on the counter. "Enjoy your stay."

"I already have."

Hu went to catch a lift to the third floor where his room was gorgeous. So new it looked unused. The view across gardens was gorgeous too. Hu unpacked his backpack including his overalls for tomorrow, before showering. Soon Hu was at the carpark where he typed that address in Baidu Maps. Not so far. It was an older-style apartment building close to the centre of that city of a bit less than half a million. Small Wenshan may have been, but that evening it was delightfully peaceful. Apartment 12 was on the second floor where Hu pressed a buzzer. In jeans and a t-shirt, Chen Peijing was just as startling as in her work uniform.

She beckoned Hu inside.

"We know each others names and we know what we do for jobs. You're a detective...."

"I'm a detective-constable grade one."

"How much does a detective-constable grade one earn?"

"Surely you're interested in more than money?" Hu asked while thinking he made a mistake. The plain-looking receptionist would have been a better option.

"Let's just set our ground rules."

"I earn 240,000 yuan."

"Hmmm."

"Not enough?" Hu asked sarcastically.

"Do you own your own apartment?"

"I've only been working for seven months."

"You don't have an apartment and you don't earn a lot for Guangzhou."

"I earn enough."   Hu then decided. "I earn more than a hotel receptionist in a shit-hole like Wenshan."

"Fuck you too!"

"Thank you."

Hu stormed out of her apartment and slammed her door. He definitely should have gone for the plain girl.

Chapter Forty Two

The central part of Wenshan had several skyscrapers interspersed amongst smaller, older buildings. Hu's target address wasn't far from Peijing's apartment, but a modern, multi-storey skyscraper. In the foyer Hu pondered, but decided a human trafficker would buy the most expensive apartment, which was the top floor, so he caught the lift to floor 12. At apartment 1201, Hu rang the buzzer to be face to face with a hassled housewife with a baby. He apologised before moving to apartment 1202, which had a very old couple, so that was unlikely. Apartment 1203 had no answer, for which Hu thought a return visit might be in order, if that was possible. Apartment 1204 had a possible suspect, as Hu told his story about checking for ants and other insects. Inside was gorgeous, with a living room which had a floor of parquetry leading to gorgeous city views through floor to ceiling glass, where one window had sliding glass doors to an outside balcony. Walls were finished in olive green wallpaper. There were built-in timber shelves and ample space for a dining setting and a large lounge suite. The main bedroom was massive as Hu pretended to search by using a torch, while at the same time thinking everything was so neat and clean it didn't seem like the home of a human trafficker. The second bedroom was equally massive with two timber-framed beds. There Hu dialled his phone, let it ring once, but didn't hear a matching ring. After announcing he'd finished, Hu went to the next door for apartment 1205 while thinking he could only do so many aborted phone calls, and certainly not enough to cover such a large building. Apartment 1205 was home to an older woman, maybe in her 50s, with blotchy skin and smoking a cigarette. He told her about searching for ants and other insects which she wasn't too happy about. Furnishings in this apartment were opulent including a cream-coloured leather lounge suite, a modern-looking, almost sparse timber dining table and four modern-looking chairs, also sparse-looking, while the built-in timber shelves held many bottles of wine. There were unopened letters on the counter separating the kitchen, addressed to Yi Baozhai at that address. Hu went to the main bedroom of grand views, pale yellow walls, and a big, built-in wardrobe with sculptured blue doors. Furniture was a king-sized bed with a cream-coloured sculptured bed head, unmade, and two matching cream-coloured bedside tables. Hu took his phone, dialled, and let it ring once, to hear the echo. Yes! Hu went to the living room where she was still smoking, to thank her and leave. Job done. He returned to his rental car. From his police phone he dialled Nuan.

"Wéi Hu."

"Wéi Nuan. I found her: Yi Baozhai in apartment 1205."

"Well done!"

"This was your idea and it worked well, although I was lucky to start at the top of this building."

"Now you're stuck there until tomorrow."

Hu wondered whether or not to blurt it out to Nuan, but decided not. Besides.....

"I'm going for a walk to see what I can see."

"Good luck."

"Thanks Nuan."

Hu knew it took more than luck for a man in China in 2019.

Chapter Forty Three

Nuan sat across the desk from Commissioner Shui, who had his glasses on while he read the third and final version of her report. Reading glasses showed his age in a nice way. He put the draft down.

"This is excellent work, Sergeant Shui. You've turned an unexpected lead into a well-formed investigation. Now politics come into play. I'll contact my counterpart in Kunming, Yunnan, arrange a meeting, and get Lai Chun to make our bookings. Dress really smartly, Sergeant Shui, not that you don't dress well, but be prepared to impress dubious men that you're the most professional detective-sergeant in China."

Nuan understood. "Yes Commissioner Shui," she said.

"What else do you need to tell me?"

"Once we agree a strategy and timeline with Yunnan, I'll detain Xu Shung on that day."

"I'll call Commissioner Li at Kunming."

Nuan listened to one side of his call, where there seemed to be agreement. Commissioner Shui hung up before ringing Lai Chun for their travel bookings, and a hotel booking. Nuan watched Commissioner Shui write on a pad.

"Right, Sergeant Shui," he said. "We're leaving tomorrow morning from Guangzhou South Station at eight-ten to arrive at Kunming at fourteen-twenty-two. We meet with

Commissioner Li and his superintendents at sixteen hundred. The day after, we leave Kunming at nine-twenty to arrive at Guangzhou South at fifteen-fifty-seven. We're staying at the Enjoying International Hotel near the railway station."

"Now I have some work to do," Nuan said. "I hate PowerPoint but it will work for this meeting, so I'll prepare a diagram of this trafficking network as well as printing ten copies of my report. On my way home I'll buy a suit."

"Are you sure?"

"I have white blouses and black stockings, so I just need a black jacket, a black skirt and matching shoes. I need a suit anyway." Nuan thought. "I know we agreed to be commissioner and sergeant at work, but while we're travelling in private, can we be father and daughter?"

"Of course, Nuan."

"This will be quality father-daughter time!"

"Indeed it will be."

"I'll get my details from Lai Chun."

Nuan stood and saluted, before heading out to get her travel details.

* * *

Commissioner Shui and Sergeant Shui waited outside a meeting room on the twelfth floor of the Kunming Public Security Bureau. The personal assistant to Commissioner Li beckoned both inside, where they were introduced to the commissioner and five senior superintendents. All men in their fifties, as Nuan expected. Commissioner Shui was invited to speak.

"Thank you for seeing us both," he said. "I'm sure you're all aware of Office 1.10 so I don't need to outline that, but Detective-Sergeant Shui, as a graduate with honours of the People's Public Security University, has been a part of Office 1.10 since its inception. Detective-Sergeant Shui: would you like to present your investigation into the human trafficking network headed by Yi Baozhai in Wenshan?"

Nuan wasn't expecting that, but she was prepared. She stood in front of those men while her PowerPoint slide was displayed on a screen behind her.

"As you can see from your notes, from our initial human trafficking contact Xu Shing in Zhaoqing, we monitored a mobile number in Wenshan in Yunnan Province, where a number of traffickers rang to order and confirm delivery of female sex slaves from Vietnam. These traffickers include Dai Duyi at Leizhou, Sun Fang at Lijiang and Shao Qing at Ruili. We also sent a detective-constable to confirm the identify of this contact in Wenshan, being Yi Baozhai. From historical call records of Yi Baozhai, we've also identified regular calls from Yang Zemin at Kunming, Bai Yongnian at Gejiu, Xia Weizhe at Yuxi, and Wei De at Chuxiong, but as yet we haven't intercepted incriminating calls from these parties. However, given the frequency of these calls and the way these men are dispersed well away from Wenshan, we strongly suspect these men are part of this human trafficking ring. My recommendation is these men also be apprehended and interrogated as suspected human traffickers."

"Detective-Sergeant Shui," Commissioner Li said. "How did you come across your human trafficking contact in Zhaoqing?"

"I was working undercover on another investigation when I became aware of a massage parlour with trafficked women. A raid on that parlour led me to Xu Shing."

"Who was your supervising officer?"

"Superintendent Ma."

"Is he aware of your investigation?"

"Yes."

"Who led your undercover operation?"

"Detective-Sergeant Xiong Jia."

"Another woman. What about Detective-Sergeant Kam Liko?"

"Kam Liko has been arrested for multiple counts of being an accessory to the attempted murders of police officers, one count of being an accessory to the manufacture and distribution of illegal narcotics, one count of the illegal use of a police firearm, one count of unlawful confinement of a person against their will, and one count of attempting to pervert the course of justice."

"Oh, I wasn't aware of that. How do you wish us to proceed with this investigation of human trafficking?"

"All suspected human traffickers and Yi Baozhai, located here in Yunnan Province, should be taken into custody on the same day at close to the same time, while we detain the human trafficker at Zhaoqing. At the same time, the Vietnamese members of this ring at the address at Hekou should be detained, as should any Chinese citizens there. The reason I recommend the same day and time is to prevent members of this network tipping each other off. When interviewed, these traffickers will then lead us to villagers currently cohabiting with sex slaves, so we can then detain these villagers and free their slaves. Time is of the essence. Many sex slaves are literally being raped every day."

"What would your ideal timeframe be?"

"I recommend coordinated detentions at 6am on Tuesday next week. That gives us the rest of this week to plan, and Monday to get officers into place for early morning raids.

"Can we do this at 6am on Tuesday?" Commissioner Li asked.

"We have all the details we need from Sergeant Shui's report," Superintendent Fan said, "so yes we can."

"Is that definite?" Nuan asked.

"That's definite," Commissioner Li said.

"Is there anything else you want to know from me?" Nuan asked.

"You've given us everything we need, thank you."

Nuan unplugged her laptop, folded it, and left the room with Commissioner Shui.

"That went well," she said.

"That went well, but that thing about Kam Liko...."

Nuan checked that nobody was in hearing range, then said under her breath, "Imagine two women being in charge."

"I know."

When she got home with her new jacket, skirt and shoes, Nuan realised her black stockings needed a garter belt. She doubted those men with old ideas realised that not only were they addressed by a young female university graduate, but a young woman wearing a black lace bra, a black lace g-string, and a black lace suspender belt holding her stockings in place. Then Nuan remembered a conversation she once had with Dewai.

"Some men are scared of talented women," Nuan said.

"That sums it up."

Those men held women down rather than riding the wave of that talent.

Chapter Forty Four

Nuan just loved early starts at 5.00, as she leaned against the Volkswagen Caddy van while Sergeant Yang instructed his three men to climb into the back. Nuan got behind the wheel to get ready, before Sergeant Yang joined her up front. She buckled her seatbelt, started the engine, then selecting 'D' to head up the ramp.

"You seem to like driving, Sergeant Shui,"

"I do actually," Nuan agreed. "These vans are quite useful for this sort of work and they drive nicely. I like to be focussed on traffic and the road so the rest of my mind is free. Not that we should worry, this should be straightforward, although saying that is asking for bad luck!"

"Like that dawn triad gang raid?"

"Don't remind me!"

They picked up the toll motorway to Zhaoqing, just cruising amongst sparse traffic.

"Driving doesn't get better than this," Nuan said.

"If you say so."

"This is good." Nuan thought now was the time. "You remember our raid at Fusi? That led us to a people trafficker in Zhaoqing, who we're detaining this morning. This trafficker led us to a network which our colleagues in Yunnan are bringing down in nine more raids this morning."

"Ah."

"This will lead us to more traffickers, victims and abusers; mostly in Yunnan Province, so mostly not involving you and your men."

After a lovely drive on the motorway, Nuan negotiated quiet, early morning streets of Zhaoqing. She parked close to where she parked last time, to gather her men around her.

Nuan flicked through the gallery on her police phone until she found what she wanted.

"Our target is Xu Shing," she said as she handed her phone around with his ID picture. "Apartment 84, after you follow me. Hammer on the door, and when he opens we'll take him into custody, hopefully not while being shot at!" Nuan took her phone back to slip it into her pocket. "Let's go!"

Nuan marched forward.

"You have a perverse sense of humour," Sergeant Yang said.

"Life's too short to be serious all of the time."

Nuan reached Block A4 where glass doors slid open for Nuan to stride across a rubber-tiled foyer to the two lifts, which were nowhere near enough for such a large building. She pressed the 'up' button for doors to spring open. They crowded in, where Nuan pressed for the eighth floor, before readying her pistol. There they arrived opposite apartment 89, with 84 down there. Nuan led the way to hammer on the door.

"Open up police!" while Sergeant Yang rang the buzzer.

Nuan hammered again while Sergeant Yang rang again, for noise to be heard inside.

"Open up police!" Nuan ordered

The only other way out was through the window, which wasn't going to happen. Nuan heard scrabbling, so she aimed. The door opened to a dishevelled wreck looking at the barrels of five police pistols.

"On the floor, face down with your hands behind your head!" Nuan ordered as Xu Shing backed away from police filling his apartment.

He hesitated so Sergeant Yang repeated that. Xu Shing slowly got down.

"Handcuffs," Sergeant Yang ordered.

One constable did that, to drag Xu to his feet.

"Xu Shing," Nuan said. "I'm detaining you for multiple human trafficking offences. Please take him to our van while Sergeant Yang and I search this shit-hole."

The three constables took him away.

"We're looking for bank statements, his mobile phone, address books, notebooks, computers; anything like that," Nuan said, as she went into a bedroom with a week's worth of clothes strewn everywhere. Nuan put a smartphone resting on a bedside table in her pocket before folding a laptop. Sergeant Yang came to the door with a bundle of papers.

"Just two statements but you'll get his account details from these."

"Excellent!"

They turned over most things in that one bedroom apartment, but there wasn't anything else incriminating, just mess.

"That's it, Sergeant Yang," Nuan said. "Thank you again."

Nuan put the laptop and bank statements under her arm before catching the lift to the ground floor, and then out to the van. She put the laptop, phone and bank statements into a plastic box waiting, before removing her body armour then climbing behind the wheel.

"I need to send a text," she said.

To Superintendent Ma: 'Xu Shing detained and some evidence gathered'. Send.

Nuan buckled-up and started the engine for her drive home. Now it was early morning with Zhaoqing stirring.

"We're good together," Sergeant Yang said.

"We're good together even when we get ambushed," Nuan said.

"We are."

Nuan pulled away from the kerb. "While most of this ring is in Yunnan Province, there will be more raids in this part of Guangdong Province."

Nuan navigated Zhaoqing streets with few cars, with their eventual destination being the Baiyun Detention Centre. That clean raid was a good start.

By the time they got to the detention centre, Nuan was an expert in their procedure. With his ID card handed over, Xu Shing was detained to be arrested in due course. Nuan then set off south to the public security bureau while missing country roads and toll motorways. City driving didn't please her anywhere near as much. After Nuan checked that van in, grabbed the box with their evidence and bid Sergeant Yang and his men farewell; she caught the lift to floor 18 and Office 1.10. There she left the box at her desk before seeking out Superintendent Ma.

"Ah, Sergeant Shui," he said. "Thank you for your message."

"Have you heard anything?" Nuan asked.

"The eight individuals you identified have been taken into custody, and one Chinese national and two Vietnamese were taken into custody at Hekou."

"EXCELLENT!" Nuan shouted. Then she realised. "I got carried away," she mumbled.

"That's fine Sergeant Shui. This has been an excellent morning."

"Now I'll check the computer and phone we recovered from the apartment of Xu Shing. I'll get Constable Zhang to investigate his bank account deposits and withdrawals, as further evidence. Then we'll prepare the necessary documentation to formally arrest him."

"I'll leave you to that."

Nuan set to instructing Hu on what he had to do while she started on her own tasks. Time was critical.

Chapter Forty Five

In the interview room at Baiyun Detention Centre, the guard shackled Xu Shing to the interrogation chair while Nuan switched on the video camera before sitting beside Hu, who was assisting.

"Xu Shing," Nuan said. "Today I formally arrest you on multiple charges of human trafficking. I have recordings of phone conversations between you and Yi Baozhai, and I have testimony from Deng Wendong, Deng Yuanfu, Ye Ru, and others at Fusi Village. Your conviction and punishment are only a formality. At worst you'll be executed, but you can cooperate with us and maybe courts will take that into consideration when they sentence you. Do you understand?"

As always with criminals Xu Shing hung his head in shame. Always false shame because for sure they would continue to commit crimes until they were caught. Xu Shing nodded his hanging head.

"Speak up for the camera," Nuan ordered.

"I understand," Xu Shing said.

"How long have you been referring men to Yi Baozhai in order to buy women?"

"About three years."

"How did you come into contact with Yi Baozhai?"

"I went to a massage parlour in Guangzhou and they told me I could make money rather than spend money."

"Which massage parlour?"

"Anshang Shuitang Spa Club."

"Did you buy a woman from Yi Baozhai for yourself?"

"I did but I later sold her to the massage parlour."

"Why?"

"It wasn't practical to work all day and lock her in a small apartment."

Nuan thought she'd heard it all but there was always something new. She sighed.

"Xu Shing, how many women did you trade to villagers for marriage?" Nuan asked.

"I don't know, maybe 20 or 30. No, more: 40 or 50."

"Do you know to which men?"

"I've forgotten most of them."

"Do you want to be executed for human trafficking?" Hu asked.

"Of course not!"

"Be specific with your answers!" Nuan demanded. "Do you remember which villages?"

"I'll try. Fusi of course, there were four women there. Taishi Village, Jinji Village, Hebu Village, Chayuan Village, Mabu Village, Liang Village, Jiangao Village, and Sizhe Village. I think that's it. No, the mayor at Nanjie, he bought a woman too."

Nine villages, two of which they knew, and the mayor of one town. "Are you sure that's it?"

"I'm sure.'

"Did you sell women to massage parlours?"

"Not normally, just my woman and the woman at Fusi."

"How did that happen?"

"I sold my woman to Anshang Shuitang Spa Club, and later that club told me they were after women, so I arranged for the Fusi woman to be sold there. I think she ended up at another massage parlour."

"I'll add an extra charge of procuring prostitutes if you're not absolutely truthful about these villages and massage parlours. For sure that will make things worse for you."

"That's all I can remember," Xu Shing said.

"Are you sure?" Hu asked firmly.

"I'm sure."

"Do you have anything else, Constable Zhang?" Nuan asked.

"No I don't, Sergeant Shui."

"Guard," Nuan called. "Please take this prisoner away."

He did while Nuan switched off the video camera. She didn't want to get up early to drive to Guangning County for as long as it took to arrest offending villagers and release sex slaves, and wondered if they could base their operation from a hotel in Zhaoqing. But they had to bring offenders and women back to Guangzhou each day so that wouldn't work. That was annoying, Nuan wasn't a morning person. She decided to get Jia involved.

Nuan greeted the sergeant-guard who copied that interview onto her USB. Soon Hu was driving to the public security bureau while Nuan composed a text to Jia with her thoughts. When they got to Office 1.10 Jia intercepted them both.

"I got your text," she said. "That information is a breakthrough, and I agree that you two, and Huang and I, should be involved in parallel. These villages have about 200 to 400 households where any of these may have sex slaves. We need to search every house."

Nuan hadn't thought that far ahead but Jia was right. "Do we get the People's Armed Police Force to do these raids?"

"I can't see any other way. That doesn't prevent you and I, and Huang and Hu, riding along to care for the women they rescue."

"That will work. Hu and I will detain the mayor at Nanjie."

"Shen and Bo can raid the spa club," Jia said.

"Excellent idea," Nuan said while looking around. "Shen?" she asked.

He joined this informal discussion where Nuan summarised her interview with Xu Shing. "Shen," she then said, "I'm only interested in detaining management of this club, and releasing any trafficked women they may have working there. Check IDs of hostesses, and if they're

Chinese citizens, release them. All women who don't have IDs, I'll make arrangements at the dormitory for their care."

"I understand."

Nuan was only interested in trafficked women, not women who chose that profession like Binbin. Once Anshang Shuitang Spa Club was closed down, those women would find work elsewhere easily enough.

Later that day Nuan was in a conference telephone call alongside Superintendent Ma, with General Yang, the commander of the Special Police Unit of Guangzhou, which was part of the People's Armed Police Force. There was always friction between the Ministry of Public Security, the regular police force, and the People's Armed Police Force, which Nuan wanted to avoid. The People's Armed Police Force had their speciality being weapons and counter-insurgency, while the regular police had different specialities, including some weapons skills. Nuan emphasised to the commander that their roles in her proposed joint operations were complimentary. This was reluctantly agreed, to start on Monday at 6am at the villages of Jinji and Hebu. Raids would then be conducted at 6am for each of the remaining villages. The PAPF would detain and arrest all criminals while the MPS would look after victims.

Later that evening Nuan felt more than simply burdened by what was going down. Now trusting Dewai absolutely, she told him their entire investigation and her plans for the next step.

"How does the People's Armed Police Force operate?" he asked.

Nuan knew from university. "In 1989 there was a student protest in Tiananmen Square that went on for quite some time, until the People's Liberation Army was called in, but they refused to intervene. At a second attempt the People's Liberation Army did quell this protest with some loss of protestors' lives, but were reluctant to do that again. Out of this was formed the People's Armed Police Force to deal with internal threats to security, while the People's Liberation Army deal with external threats. The People's Armed Police Force is like an army with generals, majors and so on. They're good with weapons but rarely do they need to use those weapons. Usually the sight of army-like officers in green uniforms causes civilians to surrender."

"I understand why you like to use them."

"I don't feel threatened by them. I investigate, and then they take over when I need that. This becomes their arrest, not mine, but the end result is criminals are brought to justice."

"You've had to hand over most of your investigation, to Yunnan and now to the People's Armed Police Force."

Nuan realised that. "That's unfortunate because we need to justify Office 1.10. I'll get our media people to attend the first of these raids and we'll publicise it that way." Nuan thought more. "I'll have us in uniform."

"I can picture that in the news and on television," Dewai said.

"This is absolutely truthful. This may be their arrests but it's our investigation." Nuan then realised. "I came home feeling terrible but now I feel lighter."

"I'm glad to help."

"This investigation is almost over and we should celebrate." Nuan had recovered from her weeks of working undercover in that nightclub. "Do you want to go to a nightclub? You can meet Jia's new boyfriend."

"Yeah, why not?"

Dewai wasn't overwhelming overjoyed by her nightclub proposal, but 'why not' was alright.

"If you want to really celebrate," Nuan offered. "We could have a weekend away."

"Ah yes. I'll look now."

Nuan lay on the couch feeling unburdened. Soon he would return with a relaxing, romantic destination for two, to which she would agree. That would make his day for sure.

Chapter Forty Six

As dawn broke, Nuan cruised her Volkswagen Caddy van through the quiet streets of Hebu Village, passing the facade of an old temple that had fallen into hopeless disrepair, and still bearing faded, anti-Confucian slogans from the Cultural Revolution. The characters across the lintel of this temple were still legible: *Serve The People.* On and on with decrepit houses interspersed with flash, modern, multi-storey houses telling stories of greed and corruption. Past a modern building in bright pink: the village committee. Then to the village square with a few bedraggled trees providing little relief from concrete and paving. On one side was a three-storey apartment block built many decades ago. Nuan parked near that building, to climb down to meet with Cui Meili, their photographer who followed in a Nissan car. Hu joined to make a threesome awaiting the People's Armed Police Force. Hebu was a big village where Nuan hoped upon hope that loser, Xu Shing, was right and they would find a sex slave there. To upend that village for nothing would be worse than tragic.

"Did you see the graffiti on that ruined temple?" Hu asked.

"Red Guards did many wrong things," Nuan said, "but with Confucius they were right. If it wasn't for Confucius we wouldn't be here now."

An olive green Volkswagen Jetta sped into the village square, followed by three olive green trucks. Even before that car stopped, Nuan was walking to intercept. As Colonel Yin climbed from the passenger seat, she was there.

"Zao an Colonel Yin," Nuan greeted while shaking his hand and hearing the camera clicking. "My name's Sergeant Shui of the Ministry of Public Security."

"Zao an Sergeant Shui. This is your investigation?"

"Yes it is."

"Shui is a familiar name."

"Policing runs in our family. This is our media officer, Constable Cui Meili."

Constable Cui hung her camera around her neck before shaking Colonel Yin's hand.

"Do you mind if Constable Cui takes a few pictures of your operation?" Nuan asked.

"That's fine."

Quiet turned to chaos as armed police climbed from trucks to seriously disrupt early Monday morning in Hebu Village.

"What's your plan, Colonel Yin?"

"Search for IDs at every house in this village. Bring those who don't have IDs here, and arrest all members of those households."

"We'll stay out of your way."

He nodded before heading off. The village of Hebu was very much disturbed by knocking and shouting, as early risers were interrogated and later risers were awakened; all to show their IDs before being let be. A young lieutenant led a young woman dressed in a nightgown to the square. There Nuan put her arm around this darker-skinned girl, before stopping to allow Constable Cui to take pictures. Nuan then led the girl to their van while promising to take care of her while suspecting she understood little of that, but at least she would recognise Nuan's soothing tone of voice. Two more lieutenants led a man, maybe in his 30s and in cotton pyjamas, to the nearest truck where he was bundled inside. They were in bed together, master and slave, before being rudely interrupted. Nuan felt easier; they had one victim which justified the chaos inflicted on Hebu Village.

Another girl was led to the square while a portly, older man was led to the nearest truck. Again Nuan posed with the girl while she asked Hu to ask who that man was. Hu rushed off while Nuan helped the girl to their van.

"He's the village accountant," Hu said.

"Oh," Nuan exclaimed.

There was much shouting and commotion now, as villagers were clearly angry about their village being invaded by armed police. The bigger principle would have been the symbolic invasion of their home. Hebu was a village with history when it came to protests.

Another girl and another prisoner, as Colonel Yin came to Nuan.

"Your men are doing a thorough and professional job," Nuan said.

"Thank you. Already this has proven worthwhile."

As they talked, Nuan heard Constable Cui's camera.

"How far have you gotten?" Nuan asked.

"About half-way. I'm surprised."

"Our investigation has shown that when one man buys a sex slave, other men get the same idea and then use the same trafficker."

Colonel Yin nodded his head as yet another victim was led into the square. Hu took charge to lead her to the van, while another prisoner was led to the truck, and Colonel Yin returned to his men. Nuan had an idea.

"Constable Cui, can you take pictures of those prisoners?"

She smiled before heading off. That was mischievous but this was Nuan's investigation. It didn't take long with the truck so close.

"That should come out well," Constable Cui said.

"Did the guard mind?" Nuan asked.

"I took his picture as well."

Ha!

"Do you know what to do when this is complete?" Nuan asked Constable Cui.

"Drive to the Guangzhou Public Service Bureau, write a media release, get it cleared through Commissioner Shui, and get it distributed with pictures."

"Try to make the evening news for those who are old-fashioned."

"That shouldn't be a problem."

"Remember, Office 1.10 for our investigation and uncovering this network, and don't downplay the role of our colleagues in the People's Armed Police Force."

"I'll put pictures of you and the colonel shaking hands, front and centre."

A girl in jeans and a t-shirt was led out of the nearby apartment building while a 30s man, also in jeans and a t-shirt was escorted to the truck. Slowly and steadily the officers of the People's Armed Police Force gathered in the square. In the midst of that was Colonel Yin speaking with his officers. Nuan decided to barge in, while pleased she thought of dressing in her uniform. In her blue uniform she looked like she belonged.

"Ah, Sergeant Shui. We're just finishing up. Five prisoners including the village accountant."

"I do thank you, Colonel Yin," Nuan said while shaking his hand. "Your men have been outstanding."

"Thank you."

"Tomorrow, Mabu Village."

"Yes."

Nuan returned to Constable Cui. "Five prisoners detained and five sex slaves rescued. You can go now. Zài jiàn."

Constable Cui got into her Nissan, to do a tight turn to then squeeze amongst trucks all but blocking the square. Soon she was out of sight. Nuan climbed into her Volkswagen Caddy van to get ready, while trucks manoeuvred out of the square. Soon Nuan was on her way to the police dormitory.

"Could you text Superintendent Ma with five arrests by the PAPF and five women rescued?" Nuan asked

Hu texted. Moments later his phone tinged with a message.

"Jia and Huang got six arrests and six women," Hu read. Another ting. "Shen and Bo detained three at Anshang Shuitang Spa Club, and are taking one woman without a Chinese ID card to the dormitory."

Nuan did quick arithmetic. "At this rate we'll get more than 40 women out of this series of raids. In total, more than 40 women handled by Xu Shing, which is what he said. He earned more than 400,000 yuan."

"That's not a lot of money to spend many years in prison, although a lot of money for a factory worker. Even a detective-constable grade one doesn't earn enough."

"How so?"

"I met up with a woman in Wenshan and my salary wasn't enough for her."

Nuan had heard stories like that. "There are women out there. Have you thought of where we work at the Public Security Bureau? You're a detective so that's got to be worth something."

"If I was working with a woman, like Jia and Huang, that would be easier."

That was true. "Today I had to publicise our good work and not piss-off the People's Armed Police Force, which is why we did pictures of me with their commanding officer. Later, we'll gather all of Office 1.10 with the women we rescued for a bigger story."

"That might help."

Nuan hoped so as she cruised north along the toll motorway to Guangzhou. Soon they were at the dormitory where Nuan put their five women under the care of Do Kang, seconded to Office 1.10 for a few weeks. Then to the Public Security Bureau where she checked-in the van, before changing out of her uniform and catching the lift to the eighteenth floor. There Nuan entered Office 1.10 while feeling terribly tired. She wasn't a morning person. She had a report to prepare, she read the draft of the media release which looked good, but by early afternoon she could hardly keep her eyes open. She was over her shift time anyway, so told Superintendent Ma she was going home, and told Hu to go home too. Nuan caught the metro to her home at Yue

Xiu where all was quiet. With grey curtains drawn, Nuan stripped off and slipped into bed for a few hours sleep.

* * *

Nuan woke with a start, before reaching for her phone which showed six-ten. She slid out of bed to find Dewai on his computer. He looked over his shoulder for Nuan to notice that look in his eyes. That look was why sometimes she was mischievous.

"There's a story about your raid," he said.

"What do you think?"

"This story is well done. You look good shaking hands like that. Who's idea?"

"My mind was clear in conversation with you, when I decided we should publicise this, which Commissioner Shui agreed with. He has issues like staffing and next year's budget, so the more publicity for us; the better it is for him."

"You look good in uniform."

"Better than now?"

"Absolutely not."

Nuan ruffled his hair. Then she felt sad about Hu.

"What's wrong?"

Nuan decided to blurt it out. "My ex-boyfriend where I work. He's a nice guy but he's having no luck. Zero luck." Nuan thought. "Do you know anyone?"

"For a blind date?"

"As his supervisor I shouldn't, but as his former girlfriend I can."

"Maybe. I'll ask her. I'll ring her now."

"Thanks. I'll cook dinner."

Nuan dressed; then went to the kitchen to decide she wasn't in the mood. She rang to have an Indian meal delivered instead. By then Dewai appeared, so Nuan got him to set the table. She heard a message come through on his mobile and shortly after she had a name and number on her mobile. By then their meal arrived, after which Nuan looked forward to an early night. She wondered if this friend realised that when you dated a police officer you dated their job. She would learn that soon enough!

Chapter Forty Seven

Mabu Village was closer to Shenzhen than to Guangzhou, while Mabu had an infamous policing past from about a decade previously. A traffic police officer, Sergeant Chen Lusheng, was invited to dinner with village officials where he drank himself to death, and was subsequently declared a martyr who died in the line of duty. His family even received compensation. Now Nuan waited early morning in Mabu Village square for the People's Armed Police Force to arrive.

"Despite my uniform I'm now Nuan, not Sergeant Shui, alright?"

"Alright Nuan," Hu said.

"Are you interested in meeting a friend of my boyfriend?"

Silence for a moment. "I suppose so. Yeah, why not?"

"I have her details on my personal phone. I'll text you when we get back."

"What does she do?"

"Information technology like my boyfriend. You're a university-level graduate of one of the toughest courses in China. From our first date, that was the common bond that Dewai and I shared. He's educated and he uses his mind like we do."

"We're different to most police officers."

"That's why you're in Office 1.10."

"Thanks for thinking of me, Nuan."

The green Volkswagen Jetta sped into the square followed by three olive green trucks. Officers dispersed while Nuan strode to greet Colonel Yin and shake his hand.

"Are there cameras this time?" he asked.

"No cameras today. Were you comfortable with what the Ministry of Public Security released?"

"I thought it was fair and balanced. I can also tell you're the daughter of Commissioner Shui."

Nuan sensed that was more an observation than a compliment or criticism. But 'fair and balanced' was a compliment.

"I'll leave you to your task while we're here to do our task," Nuan said.

"How are the women?" Colonel Yin asked.

"I left them in good care. Our investigation started at two villages where we rescued five women. Later I interviewed those women, where some were mistreated and some not. In fact, some thought their forced marriages weren't worse than being married to Vietnamese men. Despite that, they all wanted to go home. Their movements were restricted while they'd lost contact with their families. Here, we're giving some women their freedom, and in other cases we're releasing women from abuse and suffering." Nuan thought. "You're charging your prisoners with human trafficking-related offences?"

"Yes we are."

"Before the end of this week, one of us will use a translator to interview the women we rescue from these villages. I'll make sure you get video copies of these interviews as evidence for your cases."

"Thank you, I appreciate that."

Colonel Yin headed away.

"Sergeant Shui," Hu said. "You have certain political skills."

"It's just common sense," Nuan said. "We're working together now for a common outcome, so the more we cooperate the easier it is to get to that outcome. Later our paths may cross, where this cooperation will be remembered."

"Are these skills from your father?"

Nuan thought. "This might be from my mother, the economist who's a senior cadre."

"Ah, that makes sense. Maybe your father learned the same way."

"Maybe love comes from when you fit together like this," Nuan said with her fingers intertwined.

Already a prisoner was led to the first truck while Nuan led a young woman to their van. Like yesterday, more and more prisoners were led into the truck while more and more young women were handed over to Nuan and Hu. Some were girls, and really girls. Buying a slave was bad enough but buying a girl for a slave was revolting. Like yesterday, the raid gradually wound down as officers gathered at their trucks. This time there were six prisoners and six women. Once more Nuan congratulated Colonel Yin, not because she had to but because she appreciated the thorough way his men went about their tasks. Then she climbed into the Volkswagen Caddy for the drive to the dormitory, while Hu texted. Nuan heard a text arrive moments later.

"Jia and Huang got five arrests and five women."

That was good. Jia and Huang had two more villages on their itinerary, while Nuan had one village plus a mayor. Once more Nuan dropped their victims at the dormitory before checking-in the van, changing out of her uniform, and writing her report. Once more Nuan went home mid-afternoon to sleep for a few hours.

* * *

Nuan leaned against her van and yawned, even though she tried to stifle it. Jiangao Village was being thoroughly searched by the People's Armed Police Force, the officers of which were just as alert and on the ball as their first raid, even though Nuan could barely keep her eyes open. She wondered how they did it but then remembered all that military discipline. Unlike Ministry of Public Security regular police officers, armed police lived in barracks and generally had a shit life. Probably they got up at five every morning. A girl in a nightgown was escorted by an armed police officer for

Hu take her into his care while Constable Cui, back for more good publicity, took a couple of pictures.

Constable Cui came to Nuan. "This is heartbreaking," she said.

"I know. We all have a part to play. I'll make sure they get home for a new start to their lives, while you'll publicise our good work so we have the resources and the budget to continue the good fight."

"I never thought of that."

"You were good last time; Colonel Yin was impressed, so here you are."

Another girl so Constable Cui moved away to photograph a young armed lieutenant literally handing the girl to Hu, looking smart in his uniform. Nuan beckoned Constable Cui.

"If that's not a spectacularly good picture, I'll be surprised."

Constable Cui turned her camera end on to press a button. Nuan looked at the digital image. It was spectacular.

"I'll use that," Constable Cui said.

"That picture is worth getting out of bed at – what time?"

"Four-thirty."

"Do you know why we do this at this time?" Nuan asked.

"To catch them at home or in bed."

"That's right."

Another girl who Constable Cui took a picture. Nuan took over from Hu and had her picture taken with yet another girl, this one in jeans, a white t-shirt and cheap runners. And one more as the raid slowly ran down. Colonel Yin came to Nuan, clearly there was mutual respect, while Constable Cui moved away to take a couple of pictures.

"Four girls rescued and four criminals arrested," he said.

"Once more thank you very much. As you know, your colleagues have arrested more criminals and saved more victims in parallel with us."

"I know that."

Colonel Yin shook hands firmly while Nuan sensed genuine respect. Even armed police, trained to be ruthless, would have had enough heart to be moved by what they were involved with.

Chapter Forty Eight

To the north-west of Guangzhou lay the town of Nanjie, in hilly and forested countryside, interspersed with rice paddies. Those rice paddies was the reason for Nanjie, which had a river winding its way through the centre of town, long ago tamed by stone banks to protect ancient houses and other buildings nearby. Unlike a village, Nanjie would have been self-sufficient, except young women there would be drawn to Guangzhou. Guangzhou had jobs for women who were career-minded, and rich men for women who weren't.

In early morning's light, Nanjie looked poor. Old, brick buildings huddled narrow streets and lanes virtually unchanged for many centuries, except for electric wires visible in some places. Houses, shops, workshops, a blacksmith even, all squashed together. Brick buildings some cracked, others whitewashed now stained with mould, all with uneven, tiled roofs. In the distance was a single, high rise apartment complex amongst other apartment buildings some decades old, but the rest was quite ancient. Mostly older people up early, including a middle-aged woman in peasant clothes and a peasant straw hat, carrying two woven baskets from a pole resting across her shoulders. In an hour's drive they'd gone back in time 50 years. Beside the road were parked a few old cars, the odd modern SUV, while motorcycles were visible parked further along narrow lanes.

Nanjie was a town that young people left when they passed school.

As Hu drove, Nuan gave directions while she followed Baidu Maps on her smartphone. They left the old town to a newer development nearer that apartment tower building. New was in a relative sense. A two-storey concrete house in blue faded from many years of sunlight. Unless he was corrupt, the mayor of a town like Nanjie was a low-ranked cadre who didn't earn much. Nuan directed Hu to park out front before turning to check on Shen and Bo in their car behind. The two, new Nissan Sylphys, white with blue flashes, sparkled in early morning light. They gathered on the footpath.

"Shen and Bo," Nuan said, "go to the back door of this house. I'll give you a few moments to get into place before we knock on the front door."

Shortly after, Nuan strode to the dark blue door while reaching inside her jacket for her warrant card. There she hammered a tarnished, brass knocker; seemingly twice as loud on that early morning. Nothing so she hammered it again with thoughts of the mayor, Zhou An, hurriedly getting out bed while leaving his pretty young slave behind. A third knock before the door opened, where Nuan showed her warrant card to a middle-aged man with a receding hairline, dressed in a cheap flannel shirt and cheap, baggy jeans.

"My name's Detective-Sergeant Shui Nuan and with me is Detective-Constable Zhang Hu. Mayor Zhou; we have reason to believe that you have a trafficked woman from Vietnam on this premises."

"How did you come to this belief?" the mayor asked.

"We were told by a human trafficker now held in custody."

"There are no women here."

"Do you mind if we look?"

"Feel free."

"Go upstairs Hu, I'll get Shen and Bo to help."

Nuan went to the back door to let Shen in to search the ground floor living room, dining room, kitchen and what looked like a study, while she told Bo to search the garage. Upstairs had three bedrooms, a bathroom and a separate toilet, but no young woman. In the main bedroom with a queen-sized bed, Nuan opened wardrobe doors to note clothes more to one end and a gap to the left. She took a picture of that before rummaging through drawers under. Two of those drawers were empty so she took pictures of those. Otherwise, just men's clothing, underwear, socks and so on. Hu was going through bedside tables while Nuan then went to the bathroom. A glass with two toothbrushes, so she took a picture of that, toothpaste, shaving cream, brush and razor, deodorant. On the floor was a rubbish bin with a swing-top lid. Nuan put on a latex glove before rummage through used tissues until she spotted something: the packet of the Whisper brand of pads she once used before recent scandals. Nuan took a zip-lock bag from the pocket of her jacket before placing the packet inside and sealing it. Other than that, nothing. Nuan noticed Hu in the second of three bedrooms so she went through drawers and the wardrobe of the third bedroom, to find a photo album of faded colour and black and white photos of years gone by, letters which she browsed but were dated many years ago in Chinese seemingly from a girlfriend, framed photos of a middle-aged couple but again aged so she suspected they were the parents of the mayor. Of the belongings of a young Vietnamese woman there was no trace, other than the discarded packet.

Nuan met Hu in the corridor to show him the plastic bag. Hu knew Nuan as much as anyone and he wasn't a squeamish sort of man anyway.

"A woman has been here," Hu said, "but you'll need more proof than that."

Nuan knew that. She went downstairs where Shen shook his head. Bo then came in and shook his head too. Nuan went to Mayor Zhou, looking on. She showed him the bag.

"That doesn't prove human trafficking," he said.

Nuan scrolled through her pictures while pointing out that clothes seemed to have been removed.

"So?"

"Mayor Zhou," Nuan said sternly. "Evidence was given under interrogation, while there are abnormalities with what we discovered. Can you explain the reasons for this?"

"It's your responsibility to find evidence or proof."

"Tell me what you did with her. Tell me so we can rescue her."

"I don't know who you're talking about."

They were going nowhere.

"I'm ending this search now," Nuan said. "But I'm not ending this investigation. Expect to see more of me."

"I'll look forward to that," Mayor Zhou said sarcastically.

Nuan beckoned all outside.

"Now we'll speak to neighbours. Bo, opposite on the north side, Hu, opposite on the south side, Shen you go north on this side and I'll go south. You know what we're looking for."

Nuan checked her watch, almost eight, before going next door to the south. There she pressed a buzzer to be greeted by an elderly man with his smile showing a few missing teeth. That smile disappeared as soon as Nuan showed her warrant card. A woman's voice called 'who is it?' before she appeared behind her husband.

"Zao an," Nuan greeted. "My names Detective-Sergeant Shui Nuan. Can I speak with you both for a moment?"

Nuan was beckoned into a living room where time had stood still for many decades. An old television set, an old, floral lounge suite, and solid timber furniture from a past generation.

"I'm sorry to disturb you both, but I'm looking for a young woman who might have been living with Zhou An next door."

"There was his niece," the woman said, "but she didn't look like his niece."

"In what way?"

"She had darker skin and she didn't look Chinese."

Nuan took out her notebook to write.

"When did this niece come here?" Nuan asked.

"About two years ago."

"When was the last time you saw her?"

"We hardly ever saw her. It was as if she wasn't let out."

"Did you ever speak?"

"No."

"Even though this niece didn't go out much, when was the last time you actually saw her?"

"About two weeks ago."

Nuan wrote.

"How old do you think this niece was?"

"About 14."

"Your name, please?"

"I'm not going to get into trouble?"

"No, no; just to complete my record."

"Chang Huiqing. Mayor Zhou isn't in trouble?"

"We're just making enquiries. Thank you for your trouble."

"Do you want a cup of tea?"

That was sweet. "No thank you."

Nuan finished writing before heading to the next house to knock. There she was greeted by a young woman with a young child at her legs.

"I'm sorry for disturbing you," Nuan said while showing her warrant card. "My name's Detective-Sergeant Shui Nuan; I'm looking for a young woman who might have been living with Zhou An just along the street. This woman may have been referred to as his niece."

"I'm sorry I can't help you."

"Are you sure?"

"I don't know any niece. I'm too busy for nieces."

"I can imagine you're busy but this is important. This niece might be in danger which is why we need to find her."

"I don't know any niece."

Bang with the door.

Nuan thought the past generation, for all the pain of the Mao years they lived through, had a sense of community since lost. The third house along was empty, but the one past that had a younger couple. With prompting, they confirmed this young niece not often seen and not seen for two weeks. Nuan thanked them very much before returning to their cars.

There she sat on the bonnet of her car for her team to assemble.

Nuan started. "I have one report of a darker-skinned young woman not looking Chinese, supposedly aged 14, and known as Mayor Zhou's niece, not often seen, and last seen about two weeks ago. I have a second confirmation of this young niece not often seen, and last seen two weeks ago. Anyone else?"

"I also was told about a young niece not often seen," Shen said.

"You did better than me," Hu said.

Nuan thought. "We have three witness reports of a young niece, but age 14 might be a mistake given these Vietnamese women are more petite than Chinese and might seem younger." Nuan hoped that was the case.

"She could be anywhere," Hu said. "I'm quite sure Zhou An won't tell us anything, not even if we arrest him."

"I agree. Where would he sell her? Elsewhere in town?"

"Two weeks ago was about when we started detaining people," Hu said. "Did he hear?"

"I'll ring the superintendent in charge of this at Kunming, and ask him to question Yi Baozhai. Now we'll pay a visit to the local police."

Into their cars for the drive to the Nanjie Public Security Bureau; one of the few non-ancient buildings in that part of town, dating from the 1960s like the houses of the mayor and his neighbours. Built in the starkly, ugly functional style of that era. Inside, the desk constable looked half asleep as he slowly tapped at an old computer with a CRT screen. This constable wasn't aware until Nuan rang the bell on the counter, and was most apologetic when she showed her warrant card. Soon after, Nuan and Shen were with Superintendent Chang.

Although she remembered all relevant details, to look professional Nuan pulled out her notebook, to which she pretended to refer while she outlined the background of their human trafficking case before telling the story of this missing niece.

"Superintendent, has anyone commented on this young niece who cohabited with Mayor Zhou, or are you aware of a young woman with this description now with someone else in town?"

Superintendent Chang lit a cigarette and drew strongly before coughing. "No to both."

"Would you mind informing your officers that a young woman matching this description might have been sold to another resident of Nanjie, and ask them to look out for her?"

"That won't be a problem."

"Thank you." Nuan took out her warrant card folder for one of her business cards inside, which she handed across.

"If we come across something we'll be in touch," Superintendent Chang said, "but I don't promise anything."

"Thank you."

Nuan doubted the local police would find this young woman as she led her team to their cars.

"We don't have anything," Nuan sighed. "Not even a picture or a fingerprint."

"Could he have killed her?" Shen asked.

"For human trafficking? Better to sell her than kill her, but it's possible. If we find this young woman he'll go to prison for a long time." Nuan thought. "First I'll ring Kunming and ask them to interrogate Yi Baozhai, while you, Shen, should cross-reference his ID record to his Hukou to find brothers, sisters, or in-laws who might have nieces, and who those nieces would be. Anything else while we're here? No? Let's go."

Nuan buckled up in the passenger seat while Hu started the engine. Soon they were on their way to Guangzhou.

"You thought this was going to be a simple detention and rescue," Hu said.

That was true. "While I'm sure age 14 is wrong, this girl might be young, 16 or 17 even. To be caught up in sex slavery while you're still a child is just horrible. We need to find her."

"Any feedback from Yunnan on their arrests?"

"So far they've arrested 102 men and rescued 102 women, and they're about half-way through their list." Nuan counted. "Double that at 70,000 yuan each, plus Xu Shing's women, and that's more than one million, seven hundred thousand yuan."

"Fuck."

Exactly.

Hu drove to Guangzhou Public Security Bureau where he parked their car. Later in Office 1.10 there were joined by Shen and Bo, who soon were busy on a computer while Nuan was on the phone. The call didn't take long where Superintendent Fan promised to get officers to interrogate Yi Baozhai and email the outcome. Nuan then went to Shen's table.

"Zhou An has a brother-in-law and a sister-in-law who have a girl child," Shen said. "Mayor Zhou has one married niece aged 27. This is her ID photo."

She looked Chinese and she looked in her 20s. She was not the niece.

"Can you print a copy?" Nuan asked while noting Hu looking over her shoulder. "What do you think?"

"We've discredited the fake niece story but we've not proven his sex slave. We need evidence of a woman in his house beyond that packet. How about a forensic expert from the Hubei University of Police?"

Nuan thought that was a good idea. "Can you contact Wuhan and ask?"

"Yes."

Hu went to his desk where soon after he was on a call.

"Nuan?" Hu called. "Is Monday alright?"

Amazing! "Monday's excellent!" Nuan exclaimed.

"I'll get the expert to meet us here, and then we'll take them there by car."

Hu returned to his call for a few minutes while Nuan thought. Jia was raiding Sizhe Village that morning while Nuan had a case on her hands. It made sense for Jia, as a woman, to interview the rescued women over the next few days while Nuan continued her investigation. Jia could then send a USB with the videos of her interviews to the People's Armed Police Force. Shen and Bo should continue preparing triad case materials for court, and interviewing the remaining eight triad still recovering, when they were available.

Nuan sat with Superintendent Ma to outline what transpired that morning, and made her suggestion of who should do what, to which he agreed. Nuan then asked Hu to drive them both to Nanjie. Soon she was with the lovely couple and both she and Hu had cups of tea in a cosy kitchen with everything in its place.

Nuan reached into her pocket for the picture, carefully folded, and placed it on the table.

"This is the only niece of Mayor Zhou An," Nuan said.

"That's not the niece we saw," Chang Huiqing said.

"Thank you for confirming that."

Nuan put her cup down to write that in her notebook.

"Is there anything else?" Chang Huiqing asked.

"Only if you can think of anything."

"No."

"Thank you for the tea but we won't disturb you further."

"Always a pleasure."

Soon they were in their car on the way to Guangzhou. Nuan was curious. "Did you get anywhere, Hu?" she asked.

"Pardon? Oh! Yes; we're meeting tomorrow evening. Thank you for that."

"Dress up and look your best."

"Yes, Sergeant."

"I'm your best friend."

"I know. I think that old couple have a child or children, since moved to somewhere more prosperous."

That explained things. "You're probably right, Hu. They see their child or children, and their families, every New Year."

"That's right. When the time comes, Guangzhou may not be like that for us."

"You're thinking a long way ahead there, Hu, but you're probably right. You see your family?"

"Once or twice a month. It's not far after all."

Nuan thought Hu was a good man and would make a good husband, and dare she think it, a good father in time. When she got back, Nuan had paperwork, or actually had to log a report in their case file system along with the photos she took, and a photo of that sanitary pad packet. Then it was a case of waiting until Monday for help with specialised expertise.

Chapter Forty Nine

Near where Hu lived, the Lotus Lounge was a popular meeting spot and handy for a first date. Somewhat dark, with tall tables, tall stools, and a bar with many glasses above, fronting a wide array of drinks upside-down behind the counter, with dispensers for each shot. There Hu bought a beer before taking a seat to wait for Yan Qiu, a friend of Nuan's boyfriend. They'd exchanged photos so Hu knew he would recognise her, as he sipped his cool, refreshing beer. He saw her, their eyes met momentarily, before she came to his table. Hu stood to shake Yan's hand. Yan wasn't Nuan or Jia but she was pleasing. A little shorter than average for a woman, a round, goose-egg face, big eyes, shoulder-length hair dyed dark brown, slender but not thin in a white blouse, tight jeans and lovely suede boots. A bit older as Dewai apparently was; which probably meant she wanted marriage and children earlier rather than later. That was to Hu's advantage.

"Would you like a drink, Yan?" Hu asked.

"Yes please. A glass of white wine."

Hu bought one to bring it to their table. He sat while she sipped.

"I'm pleased you can meet with me," Hu said.

"I'm pleased this came about," she said. "I don't know how it happened, though."

"My friend is Dewai's girlfriend. Have you met her?"

"I've heard about her. She tamed the perpetual bachelor."

Hu was surprised by that comment. "Men and women aren't made to be alone," he said.

"I agree, so here we are. Are you a Guangzhou man?"

"There are two types of men here: Guangzhou men and those who aren't. I'm from Lufeng, after four years in Beijing. A job came up here, but beyond that I like this city very much. Guangzhou never stops, night and day."

"What sort of job?"

"I'm a police detective-constable."

She frowned. "Aren't you young for that?"

"My four years in Beijing was a university degree which led to me being a detective."

"Do you have a gun?"

Always gun questions! "If I'm on the streets investigating or doing a raid, then I'll be carrying a gun." Hu didn't want to go too far down that path. "Sometimes criminals have guns so we need to protect ourselves. That's all."

"Just one more question. Is that dangerous?"

"If it's a raid we wear body armour which lessens the danger. Substantially lessens the danger." Hu thought: *fuck it!* "I'm a police officer because for me it's the right thing to do. Every crime solved, every criminal arrested, every victim saved, is right for me. It's a job I enjoy very much."

"Interesting." She sipped her drink. "That's different to analysing computer systems."

"That's how you know Liu Dewai!" Hu exclaimed.

"As a detective, that's how you know the woman who tamed him."

"Yeah." To Hu, it was amusing to think of Nuan as the woman who tamed a man.

"What about your experiences?" Yan asked.

"Well, I had a girlfriend in Beijing for three years. It was her idea, but I agreed that it's best to end something that's not quite right than to make a mistake for life."

"That's mature."

"My ex-girlfriend is now dating – guess?"

"No!"

"Now, tell me your experiences."

"Something the same although it didn't end quite so peacefully. I felt used."

Sometimes Chinese women went to extreme lengths when they felt wronged. Hu decided to be mischievous.

"Did you stalk him?"

"A little."

"Slash the tyres of his car?"

Big smile. "He didn't have a car, fortunately."

"Stalk his new girlfriend?"

She laughed. "How did you guess?"

"You have that nice but naughty look."

"What's a nice but naughty look?"

"The sort of look I'd like to get to know more. Life can be boring when everything is too straight."

"Aren't you scared of me?"

"Do you want to take on a detective-constable?"

"So you're not scared of me?"

"If you're good, but not too good, I can teach you things."

"You're naughty, detective-constable."

"You can call me Hu."

"You can call me Qiu."

"Where have they been hiding you?" Hu asked. Qiu was quite lovely.

"With a boyfriend who dumped me."

"Maybe that was a good thing. Without that, I wouldn't have met you this evening."

"And I wouldn't have had so much fun stalking him! What do you like to do in your spare time?"

"At the moment I'm learning English. I should have done that in university. On our last case I realised English will help me at work when we cooperate with other police forces. I have family in Lufeng who I visit once or twice a month, and I have friends here where we meet in Yuexiu Park. Get outdoors, relax, talk, and admire pretty girls. And Weibo of course."

"How many followers?"

"I have almost 3,000. You?"

"I have a few thousand. Do you play computer games?"

"I do too much of the real thing to ever be interested in games. Now you."

"It wasn't until I finished stalking my ex that I realised how much effort I put into our relationship. Full-time work, sometimes long hours; then visits two or three times a week and most weekends."

"You had some spare time."

"I like shopping for clothes. I can spend hours trying things until I find the one."

Qiu and someone else Hu knew. "I'm used to that," he said.

"Ah, so you understand. I like movies too."

"Romance movies?"

"How did you guess?" Qiu said with a bright smile. "You're used to that too."

"Yes."

"Do you like movies?"

"There are some good Chinese movies these days. The Wandering Earth was good. I know there are many good Chinese romance movies."

"Lots!"

"To say China has changed these past decades is a serious understatement, but romance movies are one indication. At the revolution everyone had arranged marriages, now it's all about love. China seems to be the most romantic nation on earth when you look at box office sales or see queues at cinemas."

"Which is why we're here. Such things never would have happened 70 years ago."

"That's right. Here's to a new China and love, ganbei!" and Hu drank some of his beer.

"Here's to love, ganbei," and Qiu drank too.

Hu sensed Qiu's emotional closeness, so he put his hand on her hand. Just rested it there, and like most women she had gorgeous hands. Qiu didn't pull back or stiffen, just relaxed into it. Not just Qiu, Hu felt comfortable after just half an hour together. Comfortable enough to ask.

"I've not been there but I heard Baiyun Mountain is nice," Hu said.

"A mixture of calm, scenic and extreme."

"Are you interested in calm, scenic and extreme, Qiu?"

"Yes I am. Tomorrow?"

"Tomorrow afternoon please. This week I've been getting up quite early."

"What's early?"

"Four-thirty," Hu said flatly.

"That's early! What are you doing that early or can't you tell me?"

Hu pulled out his smartphone to search for Office 1.10, which led him to the second article written by Constable Cui.

"This is what we're doing," Hu said as he handed his phone to Qiu.

Qiu frowned before her face totally brightened. "That's you!"

Indeed it was a picture of Hu helping a young woman rescued by a PAPF lieutenant, who was still holding her. It was a great picture that captured the emotion of those early morning raids.

"Rescuing sex slaves," she read. Then she looked at Hu. "Really?"

"We did the investigation, armed police did the arrests, and we rescued many Vietnamese women smuggled into China. These women are now in our care."

"I'm impressed. So you can sleep in, you probably need to, and I'll be at the South Gate at two."

"I'll see you there."

Qiu gave the phone back, stood; they shook hands before he watched her leave. She had a nice bottom in those tight jeans. It was too early to say love but he liked her. That made sense: Nuan wouldn't have anyone other than a good boyfriend, who more than likely had good friends on his side. That totally made sense.

Hu headed home pleased with his Friday evening, while looking forward to a good sleep-in and their second date.

Chapter Fifty

Baiyun Park on a lovely, cool season afternoon was glorious. Spanning several mountain peaks just beyond the outskirts of Guangzhou, it was a park of manicured lawns, palm trees and greenery, lakes and watercourses, fountains with water sparkling on that sunny day, and pagodas to remind everyone that this was China. Best were the people, so many happy people enjoying themselves in that glorious setting.

"Have you been here before?" Qiu asked.

"I read about it online, before a date."

"Ha!"

"This is the best city park in China just as Guangzhou is the best city in China."

"You really mean that, don't you?"

"I've not been to every city in China, but compared to Lufeng, Beijing and Shanghai, Guangzhou is the best."

She grabbed his arm tight, so good.

"Are you interested in extreme?" Hu asked.

"If you are,"

Hu had memorised the way to the bungee jump, so they headed up and up the thousand steps, so-called. Still glorious as they climbed and climbed with views of the entire city.

"Look there," Hu said while pointing towards skyscrapers in the near distance.

"Beautiful."

"China is the best country in the world," Hu said. "We all know our great and glorious past, and now we're moving towards a new greatness. This is why I'm a police officer. To make China better and safer for the good people you see around us today."

"Really?"

"I did four years of hard work to make a difference."

Qiu held his arm even tighter as Hu spotted a lattice gantry up ahead. So that was it. They approached a short queue where a young man weighed each person and checked their blood pressure with a small machine.

"I'm nervous," Qiu said.

"Don't feel obliged."

"You're sweet. If I don't I'll regret it."

Hu stepped on the scale before having a band wrapped around his arm. He waited for Qiu to be checked, and of course she passed, before he paid 300 yuan for two. There he was led to the steel lattice gantry jutting out over the steep mountain they just climbed. Nothing below for hundreds of metres except trees, and in the near distance, glorious views of the best city in China. A young man at the end told Hu to remove his shoes before buckling the bungee jump harness around him. Then Hu was told to take a big step, which he did into oblivion. Down and down and down before he swung upwards – incredible. Swaying and bouncing for so long but probably not that long, before being hauled to the gantry. There the harness was unbuckled where Qiu waited while looking apprehensive.

"It's amazing!" Hu exclaimed. "Just go with it."

Barefoot she nodded her head while the harness was buckled in place. Hu had just pulled his shoes on as Qiu went over the edge, so he stood to watch. It was amazing! Hu stood and watched until she was hauled up; then he left the gantry to give room. Sometime later Qiu joined him smiling brightly. She smiled a lot anyway, but that moment she smiled extra brightly.

"That was awesome. You promised extreme and now I've had it."

"You enjoyed it?"

"I want to do it again!"

"Next time we come here."

"Alright. This is one of the best days I've ever had and I'm not joking."

"Me too," Hu said, and he wasn't joking either. The setting, the jump of course, but mostly his lovely companion, to who he felt really close on their second date. Now he knew what Nuan meant by love. Qiu was just – everything!

With Qiu holding Hu's arm once more they walked down the hill surrounded by manicured lawns and lush gardens, with many children playing. Hu suspected something about his companion. A relationship was important, like marriage, and to end one was serious, often with consequences.

Usually men ended relationships and women were upset, but sometimes women ended things and men took revenge. Another issue for was the traditional expectation that women had one sexual partner for their lives, which meant there was a sexual aspect to a long-term relationships that failed. Even though bigger cities, Beijing, Guangzhou and Shanghai had moved beyond women with one sexual partner for life, perhaps women still felt they were no longer sexually desirable after the failure of a long-term relationship. Whichever way a relationship ended, there were often hurt feelings.

"When you said you stalked your ex-boyfriend, you weren't joking," Hu said.

"No I wasn't joking. You two didn't get upset? Really, really upset?"

"I'd come to something the same realisation when Nuan spoke those words. I felt more relieved than anything else. She says we were too young but I think we were too alike. Same education, same skills, same careers. We seemed more like brother and sister, or good friends, which I felt wasn't enough, and she did too. Already I feel different with you."

"You're serious aren't you?"

"I think it's called love."

She smiled even brighter. "Me too, unlike before when it didn't work. That never felt like this. He was more traditional, if you know what I mean."

Hu knew what that meant. Most men when they became boyfriend and girlfriend, took over and ran their girlfriends lives, as was traditional but not in 2019. That probably drove a wedge between them. Qiu was clever and vivacious, a 2019 woman, not a woman to be ruled. In fact Hu liked women to be independent; sharing life as a couple but balancing mutual independence. Hu then saw a bench by the side of the path. With Qiu still holding his arm he guided her there to sit.

"Let me ask you a few questions," Hu said. "How do you analyse computer systems?"

"I won't tell you how but why. Information is critical for business success, so what we do is determine what information a business needs to succeed, determine methods to capture that information, and determine how it should be presented. It's all about information. Now detective-constable, how do you solve crimes?"

"Reality isn't like television! Actually we use a lot of data to investigate crimes and suspects, and while I can't tell you what data we use, part of our university degree taught us how to acquire and use this data. Another part is old-fashioned policing, like following suspects in cars or following suspects on foot, talking to witnesses; in many ways like you, gathering information to prove who committed a crime."

"We're similar?"

"I think we are. You have a degree?"

"Like you, yes."

Hu had an idea. He pulled out his smartphone to search once more for Office 1.10. There he found the earlier article with the picture of Office 1.10 in a line, the arrested leadership of Axe Gang triad group kneeling in front, with police officer hands on criminal shoulders. Hu tapped the picture twice to make it bigger.

"That's all of us," Hu said.

"That's you again. Who's the woman who tamed Dewai?"

Hu pointed her out. "Detective-Sergeant Shui Nuan."

"Which criminal did you arrest?" Qiu asked

"Nuan and I worked as a team for that arrest. She shot our target so he was in hospital, recovering."

"Oh. Have you shot anyone?"

"Yes."

"Did you kill them?"

Hu couldn't lie. "Yes I did," he said.

She gasped. "When?"

"Not long ago." Hu looked around to spot a boy playing with a plastic water pistol. He asked that boy's mother to borrow it for a few moments. Back with Qiu.

"Stand up, please."

She did.

"Spread your legs a little for balance, and stretch your hands out for stability and accuracy. You're right-handed?"

"Yes."

Hu put the plastic pistol in her right hand with her fingers over the grip, and wrapped her left hand around.

"Pretend there are sights on this pistol, where stretched out like this, these sights are more accurate from your right eye or your primary eye, to your target. This pistol will recoil when you squeeze the trigger, which is why you hold it at arm's length with both hands."

"You do this every time?"

"If you're under fire, every shot has to count. If you do this every time, your shots will count."

"So you killed someone like this?"

"They would have killed me."

She lowered the pistol to look at Hu with her eyes super-big.

"Our investigations and arrests make China better and safer. Sometimes criminals fight back, so you must be trained and prepared. But this is for China, the country we love."

Hu released the pistol from her grip to return it to the boy's mother. He sat beside Qiu again.

Hu had a thought. "I know something good that we can do together to round out this lovely day," he said while trying to be oblique but not too oblique.

"I'm sure you do but not quite yet. But I'm interested in learning more about you, Hu."

"How about we go out for dinner?"

"Alright."

"I know a place close to where I live which isn't the most expensive, but it has great food and great service."

"I'm in your hands."

"Good."

Hu and Qiu walked the almost 15 minutes to Meihuayuan Station, and from there they caught the next train to Renhe Station. It was a five minute walk to Hu's favourite Cantonese restaurant.

"Ah Hu!" Chang greeted loudly. "This way."

Chang led them to a table for two.

"Are you good with Chang's recommendation?" Hu asked.

"Yes."

"A meal for two and a bottle of white wine."

"Yes Hu."

Chang hurried off where moments later, they had a cold bottle and two glasses. Hu twisted the metal cap off and poured.

"When you said great service, you weren't joking," Qiu said.

"I come here a couple of times a week," Hu said. "Now, let's talk. "I'm aged 23, I graduated seven months ago, I've been working since that time, and I earn 240,000 yuan. Obviously that will increase over time." Hu leaned forward. "Most police officers are graduates from middle school, where it's just a job that pays well enough and has good job security. The highest they'll be promoted is constable grade one, or maybe a sergeant on street patrol, which is where most officers need to be anyway. With my education and already being a detective, it's almost a given that I will rise to a high rank."

"So the talented outshine the basic?"

"Invariably."

"I earn 300,000," Qiu said. "Do you own your own apartment?"

"I've only been working for seven months. I rent an apartment but it's only 800 a month, which enables me to save for a deposit."

"I've been working for four years. I'm 26 by the way."

"Nice."

"Really?"

"You have more life experience."

Chang brought out their first dishes, rice with stir fried beef, which Hu allowed Qiu to serve. He then served.

"This is nice!" Qiu exclaimed.

"I told you good food and good service. Renhe is like this. You live at home?"

"I do."

Hu thought. "My home can be your home, as much or as little as you want it to be."

"Maybe. I'll see you tomorrow for yes or no."

Hu was fairly sure that was yes.

"I know a cafe where we can meet tomorrow," Hu said. "Als Gong Cha in Baiyun Qu does great coffee."

"I'll see you at ten at Als Gong Cha."

Chang brought out their next dish, fish, which was also excellent. Hu thought with two good incomes, a modest rent and other expenses, they'd have a deposit in no time. Qiu was friendly, good company, and they fitted well together like Nuan described the other day, while at age 26 she had the burden of her parent's expectations. Little things like not yet owning an apartment and not yet reaching maximum earnings potential, mattered less when that clock to age 27, and a leftover woman, was running.

* * *

Hu got to Als Gong Cha a little before ten, to order and pay for a flat white which he noticed Nuan preferred. He took a table near the window to wait. His coffee arrived, then Qiu came to his table looking quite delicious in tight jeans again. As always: jeans, a blouse and proper shoes with feminine heels. She sat.

"I'll get you a coffee," Hu offered.

Hu ordered and paid for another flat white.

"How was your morning?" Hu asked.

"Good. And you?"

"Good."

"Are you sure age 26 is alright?" Qiu asked.

Hu put his hand on her slim hand. "I think you're in your prime, and you have life and relationship experiences. I think 26 is a good age."

"You seem older than 23."

Hu sipped his coffee while thinking. "This might have been our degree; it was tough for sure. If not that, then these last six months at work have been intense. For whatever reason, your age seems to match my age."

"You killed someone. Surely that made you grow up?"

Hu wondered. "Maybe it did. Can I call you girlfriend?" Hu asked while still holding her hand.

"Only if I can call you boyfriend."

"You can call me boyfriend. Try your coffee; it's nice."

She did.

"This is great! You know all the important things, Hu. Where to eat, what to drink; I'm in good hands."

She sipped her coffee while Hu finished his.

"I know other important things for when you're ready," Hu said.

"I'm ready," Qiu said. "You live near here?"

"I do."

"Beyond that important thing, I really need to pee."

"Come with me."

Hu had never been into holding hands and certainly Nuan wasn't, but that didn't stop Qiu always slipping her hand inside his arm, now to be girlfriend and boyfriend as they headed through sparse Sunday morning crowds.

"I have a surprise where I live," Hu said. "An Asian toilet."

"It's an older-style apartment."

"But renovated."

"I'm sure it's nice."

That was a lovely, Sunday morning. Not too hot, not too cool, and not too crowded.

Chapter Fifty One

Nuan was really curious but at work she knew she shouldn't. As Nuan usually got to work last, Hu was there and she thought he looked – satisfied. Now she was totally curious.

"Zao an Hu, how was your weekend?" Nuan asked.

"Zao an Nuan, fine thank you."

He turned to his computer to check emails, then turned back.

"I'm being mean to you. Yes, I have a girlfriend. She's great and I'm sure we'll be good together. Thank you for your assistance."

"I should have thought of this earlier!" Nuan exclaimed.

"Don't worry. If you thought of this earlier, this wouldn't have turned out the same way. This was the right time."

Nuan was surprised. "You really like her?" she asked.

"We're like this," Hu said with his fingers intertwined.

Nuan understood. "That's great."

"I'm meeting her family this weekend, and the next weekend we'll meet my family."

Nuan glanced at her watch. "Now, sorry to interrupt your good news with work. When's our forensic investigator due?"

"Around eleven. I'll keep busy until then."

Nuan had to book media people for later that week and liaise that with Jia, so she set herself to that task of emails and texts. Only then was she aware that Hu had a young woman with a big case. Their investigator.

"Detective-Sergeant Shui Nuan, this is Detective-Constable Jin Bao."

Nuan shook hands. "Thank you so much for coming all this way to help us!" Nuan exclaimed.

"Constable Zhang explained your problem, so let's investigate this possible crime scene."

"Hu?" Nuan asked.

"A car's booked and the mayor is expecting us at midday. Get your weapons and we'll head off."

Nuan noticed they had batons, pistols and Hu had handcuffs, so she quickly got the same from the armoury to meet them in the basement carpark. Soon they were on their way to Nanjie. There they stopped at the Mayor's house where Nuan pictured the lovely couple next door, children long moved away, quietly observing.

"Now we'll do this," Nuan said.

Nuan hammered using the worn, brass knocker, to be greeted by the mayor, although not exactly greeted.

"Mayor Zhou," Nuan announced. "We're here to search your house more thoroughly. Hu, can you stay with the mayor?"

Constable Jin placed her suitcase on the kitchen counter to open it to remove a small zip-up bag, a spray, an oblong light, a camera, and a couple of zip-lock bags. "If this was fresh I'd use a body suit and shoe coverings, but this crime scene, if it is one, is already contaminated, so I'll just use latex gloves. Bedrooms are upstairs?"

"Three bedrooms and a bathroom," Nuan said.

"Let me see what I can see."

Nuan followed at a distance where Constable Jin went to the bathroom, to unscrew the shower drain. She used tweezers to put long hair tangled on the drain into a plastic bag to seal it.

"This hair is fresh," she said. "Irrefutable evidence of someone with long hair recently showering here. If we had DNA we could match it. If this was a murder it may have happened here. She looked up at the window.

"Sergeant Shui, can you hold a blanket over that window?"

Nuan stripped a blanket from one of the single beds to hold it in place, darkening the room. Constable Jin sprayed from a bottle before shining a blue light. As stains on the floor glowed bright, she took two pictures.

"This dark patterning is blood. There's a lot of blood here, as if this was the murder scene."

Evidence was growing: no young niece, long hair, and now blood.

"I'll check the bedroom they shared."

This room had curtains which Nuan drew. Again spray and blue light, and again that dark pattern, captured by camera.

"More blood here and a shoeprint. See?"

Constable Jin took out a small recorder to record her observations. Then she went to the hallway to close all doors, with Nuan hanging back out of the way, before spraying the timber staircase. Again the blue light and capturing little, glowing specs by camera.

"Blood splatter on the treads," Constable Jin recorded. "Consistent with traumatic blood loss before being wrapped in a blanket or other article and carried down these stairs." She switched the recorder off before going downstairs. There all curtains were drawn before more spraying, the blue light and the camera.

"More drops, diagonal from the stairs to the French doors." Recorder switched off. "Does the suspect have a car?"

"Mayor Zhou?" Nuan asked.

He nodded his head.

"Keys please," Nuan demanded.

"Given these French doors lead to the back yard, let's check the boot of his car."

The garage was dark enough to show staining on the carpet of the boot of an old Toyota Corolla. Again more pictures.

"Here, blood has soaked through the blanket or whatever the victim was wrapped in, to soak into the carpet in this car boot. Since then this carpet has been scrubbed clean."

Recorder switched off. "I believe we have a murder scene here. The next step is to find the body."

Nuan returned to the house while removing her handcuffs from her belt. "Zhou An, I'm taking you into detention for the suspected murder of a person as yet unidentified." She clipped her handcuffs on his wrists. "Your victim was murdered in your bathroom, wrapped in a blanket or something similar, carried to your car, and then taken away. If you would like to tell us more, feel free."

"How can you prove this?"

"We already have," Constable Jin said. "If you tell us where her body is, we can give her family some relief."

"You told your neighbours that you had a niece staying here, they said she was in her teens, yet your only niece is 27 years old and married," Nuan said. "There's other evidence like long hair and the sanitary pad packet I previously recovered. Now this so-called niece has mysteriously disappeared and we have proof of blood everywhere."

"I refuse to tell you anything," Zhou An said.

"Do you need anything else, Constable Jin?" Nuan asked.

"We should match his shoes to that print. Mayor Zhou, please sit on that chair."

He did, for Constable Jin to remove one black leather shoe. Upstairs, Nuan checked his wardrobe to find another pair of black leather shoes, one pair of brown leather shoes, two pairs of runners and a pair of boots. Constable Jin placed one of each upside-down near the staining, before spraying and lighting. She took a picture then took out her recorder.

"The shoes of Mayor Zhou An are the same size as the shoeprint in blood, but none match the tread pattern." She turned the recorder off. "Later you'll have my pictures, so if you find the right shoe you can match it."

"I understand. Is there anything else?"

"Not at this scene. Just make sure that when you find her body, you get a proper post-mortem performed to determine her cause of death. At a guess, massive blood loss from something like her throat or wrist being cut."

While they went downstairs, Nuan wondered if he could get out of that by making up a story of suicide and panic disposal of the body. If he did then he had to give up the body's location which might incriminate him. But first came detention, but before that.

"Thank you very much for your assistance, Constable Jin," Nuan said.

"Thank you for inviting me."

Nuan suspected many sergeants and even superintendents didn't want their thunder stolen by a detective-constable with specialised knowledge and skills, like she and her fellow graduates had a different set of knowledge and skills.

"We could do with someone like you in our team," Nuan said. "Can you do regular investigating, beyond this?"

"Of course."

"Would you or any of your colleagues be interested?"

"I might be interested."

"What's your grade?"

"Detective-Constable Grade Two."

There was room there. "This isn't my decision but I'm impressed, given the paucity of evidence here. If I can make things happen, I will."

"Thank you, Sergeant Shui."

"Let's get Zhou An into our car for a ride to Baiyun Detention Centre," Nuan said, while Constable Jin refitted his shoe and tied his laces. Nuan planned to leave Zhou in detention for a few days to see if that would loosen his tongue. As they trooped out, Nuan imagined that lovely couple peeping from behind closed, but not fully closed, curtains.

Once their passengers were in place, mayor under detention immobilised by his handcuffs. Nuan got in front.

"Hu, on the way out can you take us through the town centre to see if there are surveillance cameras here?"

"If you wish, Nuan."

Nuan knew what the outcome would be in regards to surveillance cameras, not yet if ever. She wasn't disappointed. Where would he bury his former sex slave's body? Somewhere that body wouldn't be discovered. More than likely somewhere he knew. For now they had to get back to

Guangzhou, but the next step would be to find that place. There was something else in the meantime.

"Constable Jin, are you staying overnight?"

"Yes, at the Hongcheng Hotel in Yue Xiu."

"I live near there. Are you interested in raiding our superintendent's entertainment budget? You too Hu, given this was your idea?"

"Yes," they both agreed.

"We'll meet at your hotel foyer at seven, for good Cantonese food which I'm sure you'll agree is the best food in China."

"Hang on," came the voice from the back, while Hu chuckled.

"I understand. We'll have a nice meal together."

Indeed they would.

Chapter Fifty Two

Just as Nuan parked in front of the town committee building, she heard a message on her phone. From Hu: Yi Baozhai refused to cooperate. She texted to thank Hu before going inside. There she asked to speak with the personal assistant of Mayor Zhou, who was Fang Jinjing. When the middle-aged Fang appeared, Nuan showed her warrant card.

"Can we talk, please?"

"Come this way."

'This way' was an office outside a larger office, where Fang sat at a desk with a computer on a return while Nuan had an uncomfortable little chair in front. She felt like a naughty schoolgirl with the stern headmistress.

"Mayor Zhou has been arrested?" Fang asked.

"Zhou An is currently being detained, so I'm here to clarify a few things so that we can resolve his detention. Firstly his wife."

"She died of cervical cancer about five years ago."

Nuan was surprised as she wrote that. His wife was infected with an STI which killed her. Next question.

"Were you aware that a young woman was staying with Zhou An?"

"I was aware his niece was there."

"Did you meet this niece?"

"No."

"Did Zhou An have anywhere special he liked to go in his spare time? Maybe fishing or hiking?"

"Not that I'm aware of. His friends might know."

"Do you know who Zhou An's closest friends are?"

"Assistant Mayor Su Tao, Town Accountant Li Zedong and Police Superintendent Chang."

Nuan wrote while thinking it was always the mayor, other committee members and the police superintendent who formed power cliques in small towns.

"Is the assistant mayor and the town accountant in today?"

"They're both in. I'll show you to the assistant mayor now."

Soon Nuan was with Su Tao where she repeated her questions to get much the same answers. Finally with Li Zedong, again with the same answers. This time Nuan was frustrated.

"Are you telling me you're one of Zhou An's closest friends and yet you have no idea of what he does in his free time?" she exclaimed.

"Ah."

"Well, what? Work, watching television, what else?"

"Playing cards with us, playing table tennis with us, watching sport on television together."

"Anything outdoors? Hiking for example? Hiking is popular in many parts."

"No, not really."

"Fishing?" she snapped.

"Yes, fishing."

"Where?"

"I don't know. Superintendent Chang will know."

"Did they go fishing together?"

"I think so, yes. For sure yes."

"Are there good fishing spots near here?"

"Speak with Superintendent Chang."

"Alright I will. Thank you."

When Nuan got to her car, an idea hit her. Behind the wheel she scrolled through her phone contacts to ring Hu.

"Wéi Nuan," he greeted.

"Wéi Hu. Zhou An's closest friends are the assistant mayor, the town accountant and the police superintendent. I'm questioning them now."

"That will be like questioning the three wise monkeys."

Hu was totally right. "I wound up the accountant and I'm going to wind up the superintendent. Can you find and monitor the mobiles of Su Tao, Li Zedong and Superintendent Chang? You'll have to look up our database for his given name."

"As soon as I find their records, their calls and locations will be under surveillance."

"Thanks Hu. Zài jiàn."

Nuan ended the call while thinking she was glad she had Hu as her regular partner. Really, he should be a sergeant and probably will be one day. She drove to the Public Security Bureau nearby, to be with Superintendent Chang who lit a cigarette while Nuan tried not to breathe his fumes.

"I've taken Zhou An into custody for charges that are yet to be finalised," Nuan said. "I was told you're a friend of Zhou An and you go fishing together."

"What charges do you propose?"

"Most likely human trafficking although there's the possibility of murder."

"The young woman you were talking about."

"I'm interested in finding more about Zhou An. You go fishing together."

"Amongst other things."

Nuan referred to her notebook. "Playing cards, playing table tennis, watching sport on television."

He drew on his cigarette and coughed heavily. "Yes."

Nuan couldn't imagine Superintendent Chang playing much table tennis.

"Where do you normally go fishing?" Nuan asked.

"Why do you want to know?"

"Please answer my question."

"Various places."

"Such as...?"

"Just various places."

"Please be specific, this is important for my investigation."

"Sergeant Shui, I'm a superintendent and a superior officer."

"If you want, I can get my superintendent grade one to ask these questions."

A heavy silence. "That won't be necessary. Take the road north out of town for about three kilometres and then turn left. Further on are a couple of lakes where we fish."

Nuan wrote.

"Anywhere else?" she asked.

"Usually there."

"Thank you. Gào cí." *Goodbye.*

Bank to her car to drive north out of town parallel to the river, amongst peaceful rice paddies. The river shimmered in sunlight as Nuan glanced at the trip meter. At just over three kilometres was a narrow road on the left where Nuan turned. Now she was heading due north rather than north-east, and into forest. A little further on, the road ended at a sizeable lake. Nuan stopped, got out and surveyed what once may have been a natural formation but was now largely man-made and surrounded by ancient stone walls. The lake was in a number of parts separated by weirs, which Baidu Maps showed to be about a kilometre long and 50 or 60 metres broad. *Would he bury her here?* Nuan thought he could but to find a body there would be a challenge. She walked around the lake looking for recently disturbed earth, about human body size, while thinking she little chance. The further she went the less likely it seemed. By the time she was heading south, Nuan knew what she should do. Back in her car, Nuan rang Superintendent Ma.

"Wèi Sergeant Shui."

"Wéi Superintendent Ma. I believe I've found the general vicinity of where the sex slave murdered by Zhou An could be buried. Can we get some search and rescue sniffer dogs to comb this area?"

"Like they use for earthquakes?"

"Yes. The scent's the same, especially as this victim was killed two weeks ago."

"Leave that with me."

"In the meantime, Constable Zhang is monitoring the phones of Zhou An's closest friends. With me on this trail, if they know something they may respond. I'll come in now."

"Alright Sergeant Shui."

Nuan ended that call before heading back to Guangzhou Public Security Bureau. By the time she got back to Office 1.10 it was about time to go home, but there was good news from Superintendent Ma. Three handlers with their dogs would be available the day after tomorrow. Nuan booked a car and a van for the day after tomorrow, checked Hu where only personal calls had been made and received, told him to go home but he said he was going to visit his girlfriend instead, while Nuan went home as well.

At home she poured a mineral water cold from the fridge, to sit with Dewai.

"How's your work?" Nuan asked before sipping a glass wet with condensation.

"Fine, the usual. And you?"

"I'm searching for a body so I can arrest a murderer. Justice must be done even if the victim's life was short and tragic."

"Do you get jaded?"

"Tragedies like this redouble my efforts. It's likely we won't find her family although we'll give what we find to the Vietnamese police. If they can't find her family and if we find her body, she'll have a funeral where at least one person cared."

"Make that two."

"Hu as well, and maybe...," Nuan had forgotten her name.

"Qiu."

"Four people might care." There was one reason, and one reason only for sex slaves, and now the murder of a sex slave. "I wish we had women's equality," Nuan said. "With you we're absolute equals, and I know from experience, Qiu will have the same with Hu. If we have a daughter I want her to be equal in all ways. I don't want double-standards."

"I'm not like that but I know what you mean. You're a bit young but about 12 years ago there was a film, Lust, Caution by Ang Lee. It was a story during the war where a young, female espionage agent had to engage sexually with a collaborator, only the sex became so intense and eventually so loving that she fell in love with him. The sex scenes were explicit but to tell that evolvement of emotion they had to be. The actress Tang Wei, a former model, was then officially ostracised. She had sponsorships from her modelling days cancelled, and she wasn't allowed to work for quite a few years."

"For playing a role?"

"The collaborator knew she was an enemy agent but he couldn't help himself."

"That role was about the sexual power of women. That scared the old men in power."

"For sure."

"I don't respect that. Those old men will bed a beautiful young woman, as long as she knows her place. Or if a woman is in a place of power then she must be virtuous, even though men aren't held to the same standards. I don't like these mis-matched gender expectations especially after this investigation."

"Our daughter can be a police detective, if she wants."

"Our daughter can be as free as any son.'

"Yes."

Nuan was going to hold him to that, if they had a daughter.

Chapter Fifty Three

The three Labrador dogs each with a handler, one male sergeant, one male constable and one female constable, were surprisingly well behaved. Nuan slid the door of the van for them to climb inside. After closing the door she climbed beside Shen to get ready for another drive to Nanjie, and beyond to that lake. Following in a Toyota Corolla were Hu with Bo and shovels in the boot, just in case.

"You're in your element, Nuan," Shen said.

"I like driving as long as it's not too early. I don't like early starts."

"I don't think anybody does."

Nuan knew the way; it wasn't that far, where they parked at the southern end of that lake separated into a number of smaller lakes. Nuan went to the dog handlers to admit she didn't have a clue where the body might be, if there was a body at all. They didn't mind, they simply had a job to do. Under the direction of their sergeant they commenced their search while Nuan and her team trailed. The dogs were in their element as they pulled at their leads and barked, seemingly not under control although Nuan as a city person knew nothing about dogs. She was totally in the hands of those dog handlers as they tracked deeper into forest alongside that oblong lake. On and on with much barking loud enough to be heard from villages nearby. The further they went the more Nuan knew they were in the wrong place, because nobody would carry a body that far. On and on around the lake and heading south, following Nuan's walk from a few days previously. Past a concrete building before returning to forest, then to open ground almost opposite to where the van and car were parked, when one of the dogs started pawing at the ground. Another joined in while Nuan went forward. There, overlooked by Nuan the other day, the ground had been turned over. With the team gathered around, all Nuan had to do was give the order. Dig but be careful.

At the car, smart casual wear was protected by grey overalls, shovels were retrieved, and soft ground was dug centimetre by centimetre. The sight of dark material caused Nuan to gasp involuntarily. She beckoned Shen, Hu and Bo away before kneeling to brush dirt from a delicate hand. She took a shovel to use it like a broom to uncover a face and a neck with long, black hair, partly concealed by a grey blanket. Nuan stood and cried without being at all embarrassed. Hu called Superintendent Ma to send an ambulance.

* * *

Nuan never imagined a place so clean. The mortuary in the basement level of the Guangdong General Hospital in Yue Xiu sparkled with stainless steel. On a stainless steel trolley lay the corpse of an unknown female aged 16 to 18, as described by the pathologist Dr Lee, who had suffered an injury across her throat leading to massive and certainly fatal blood loss. Nuan in her gown and mask, gloves and overshoes, watched with her mind as blank as she could make it, as the poor girl was cut open and her organs removed. This was the final insult although there was no way out of it. After removing, weighing, checking, reinserting, sewing, the result was known for certain. Her throat was cut and she bled to death.

"Can you send a tissue or a hair sample for DNA testing to compare to the hair we retrieved from the murder scene?" Nuan asked Dr Lee.

"I'll send a sample of this victim's hair to our laboratory."

"Thank you."

"What do we do with this victim?"

"Can you email me a copy of your facial pictures so we can contact police in Vietnam, where this victim most likely came from. If they can't help us, the Guangzhou Public Security Bureau will make arrangements. I'll do that personally."

"Alright."

Dr Lee unbuttoned his white jacket so Nuan unbuttoned hers, and removed her gloves, mask and overshoes. Freed, she gave him her business card with her email address for pictures and the DNA results. At least justice would follow. Already there was sufficient proof, but the DNA match, when that happened, would be absolute proof. Nuan then caught the metro to the public security bureau although she totally lacked focus. Instead Nuan went to see Lai Chun. Soon she was with Commissioner Shui.

"Congratulations for solving this case," Commissioner Shui said.

"It's congratulations to our team," Nuan said.

"Are you alright?"

"I was expecting this so I was as prepared as possible. The pathologist thought aged 16 to 18 which is a tragically short life. Old enough to be looking forward to love and all that follows, but never realised. When we got stuck, Constable Zhang recommended a forensic expert, and he arranged for Detective-Constable Jin Bao to travel from Wuhan to help us. I was impressed. Not that she found blood spatter and hair fibres but that her overall approach was methodical and thorough, and she carried that blood spatter to a logical conclusion and a detention. With a fresher crime scene I was sure she would have come up with more. I spoke with Constable Jin and she would be interested."

"Really?" Commissioner Shui asked with arched eyebrows.

"Constable Jin does general investigating as well as forensic investigating, and we're one person down."

"You think she was that good?"

"She carried a case with all her equipment, she knew how best to approach this examination, she was methodical as I said, and although this isn't essential, she was personable. We all got on well together."

"Well, forensic investigating is new here."

"I'm converted."

"What we could do is offer Constable Jin a position in Office 1.10 under the supervision of Superintendent Ma, to work alongside you and your colleagues, while providing forensic services to the Criminal Investigation Bureau. So, Office 1.10 is more a home than a position, but you can use her on your cases like everyone in CIB."

Amazing! "That's really good!" Nuan exclaimed. "Our crime scene was about two weeks past, which was what it was, but if forensics are going to be useful then it's important detectives learn not to contaminate crime scenes until after examination. Cordon it off and don't trample it to death."

"I'll make sure that's well known before we get this established."

"Nothing can bring a victim back to life but we will get justice, thanks to that forensic evidence we uncovered."

"Thanks in part to Constable Zhang."

"There's probably nothing available for Constable Zhang now, but don't overlook him in the future. He's good."

"I've heard the same."

"Now Constable Jin is constable grade two, so you have room to move there."

"You have all the answers," Commissioner Shui said with a big smile.

"This is your decision, of course."

"I'll do background and reference checks, but I can't see why a university graduate would be anything less than scrupulously honest. So that's just a formality before I ring with an offer of a promotion to constable grade one, and something close to her own department."

"Alongside us she'll have colleagues to help her to settle into her new home, and friends of course."

"Are you all friends?"

"Absolutely! Jia loves nightclubbing and so does her boyfriend Huang, as does Dewai but not as much, while Hu and his new girlfriend are joining us tomorrow night, and Heng and her boyfriend. Hu's new girlfriend is a former colleague of Dewai, which isn't a coincidence."

"You're all grown-up, Nuan."

"Nightlife in Guangzhou is just great. I came home for my family but I also came home to the best city in China."

"Enjoy tomorrow night."

"We'll celebrate justice, and if the Vietnamese police don't find anything, we'll arrange a funeral in the weeks ahead. I'm sure all of Office 1.10 will be there."

"I'll be there too."

"Thank you Father."

"Thank you for carrying a difficult case through to justice, Nuan, and thank you for the many victims you've saved."

That was true. Jia did the second round of interviews while Nuan was stuck with this other case. But Father was right; there were many former victims now saved. Something she should always remember.

Chapter Fifty Four

All members of Office 1.10 were in uniform while waiting for Do Kang to bring the Vietnamese women. Constable Cui waited, this time with a proper camera. Nuan noticed Jia talking with Huang. When they stopped, she went to her colleagues.

"Zao an," Nuan greeted.

"Congratulations for solving your case," Jia said.

"Thank you. When I get back to my computer, I'll get Do Kang to email pictures of the victim to Hanoi. If they don't have a matching missing person, I'll get a quote for a modest funeral and take a collection to cover that, if you're interested."

"Yes, I'm interested," Jia said.

"Me too," Huang echoed.

"You'll attend?" Nuan asked.

"Of course," Jia said.

"Yes I will," Huang said.

"Thank you. I'm sure all of us will be there, Dewai said he'll come, and Commissioner Shui too."

"Don't lose sight of the good things that came from this case."

Nuan looked across as the van pulled up, and a group of young women climbed out.

"How many?" she asked.

"Forty-three. Add to that the 219 they rescued in Yunnan Province."

"That's a lot of rapists who'll be serving prison time, and one murderer."

"Have you charged him?"

"I'm waiting for DNA analysis and comparison to a sample we took at the suspect's house."

"That's high-tech for China."

Absolutely that was high-tech thanks to Constable Jin, and thanks to Hu.

"Are you two good for tomorrow night?" Nuan asked.

"I can't wait!" Jia said.

Nuan really looked forward to dancing without dealing ecstasy and all of that shit from her undercover days. But beyond that she was really, really curious. She knew she had to bide her time.

In the background, Do Kang led the girls they rescued onto the lawn. This was the same as the girls from the massage parlour, and the two girls from Fusi. At first cowering and emotionally beaten, but already coming good. Friendly girl chatter, smiles; straight and tall and recovering. Amazing.

Constable Cui gathered the women together to take a few group shots, before getting the women to kneel while the members of Office 1.10 stood behind, with Superintendent Ma in the centre, and Do Kang at the end. A few pictures were taken like that before the women were taken aside for Constable Cui to photograph police officers only.

"That's it," Constable Cui said.

"When will this be out?" Nuan asked.

"This will be online this afternoon; it will be on television news tonight, and in tomorrow's newspapers."

"Thank you."

Then they were on their way to Office 1.10 where Nuan had a busy day coming up. First get Do Kang to contact police in Hanoi, then finish her report on the investigation of Zhou An in their case file system, and start the brief of evidence for his eventual trial.

Chapter Fifty Five

Nuan waited for her filter coffee machine to do its thing. Once coffee finished dripping she poured a mug, added milk before putting the carton back in the fridge, and took it to the table next to the lounge suite. There she curled up with her smartphone to visit Weibo. Nuan went to her timeline to scroll posts from those she followed while sipping from her mug. It was delightfully decadent to be curled up on the coach at 11 in the morning, still in her pyjamas, drinking coffee while surfing Weibo. This time though the posts she read were more serious than entertaining. Something about a virus originating from a Wuhan wet market. Doctor Li Wenliang posted details about this virus on WeChat and then disappeared. This followed a post on WeChat by Ai Fen about the same virus. Nuan frowned as she read theories of a cover-up in Wuhan. Local cadres saving face by denying the existence of something bad in their city made sense, except 2019 was the year of WeChat and Weibo.

"What is it?" Dewai asked. He wasn't a WeChat or a Weibo man; instead using VPNs to visit discussion forums beyond the firewall.

"Rumours of a new virus originating in a wet market in Wuhan," Nuan said. "Covered-up of course."

"A virus like SARS?"

"It's unknown at this stage, but after SARS we know we can't take risks."

"What do you think?"

"This is local cadres saving face, except such a thing doesn't exist anymore. If I now know I'm sure President Xi now knows. He'll take action." Nuan put her phone down to look up at Dewai. "Whatever this is, we're in good hands." Nuan sipped her coffee. She wasn't so naive as to take notice of the books, cartoons and songs honouring 'Xi Dada' *(Papa Xi)*, although those less educated than her did, but she knew in recent times China had taken her final steps to be a true global superpower, while Chinese living standards had never been better. Whatever this virus was, for sure China was in good hands.

* * *

At ten in the evening on Saturday, the queue into True Color was already growing. Nuan and Dewai slotted themselves on the end; Nuan in her party girl outfit of a gold-coloured silk blouse, a short, white skirt, and knee-high, black, stiletto boots. Men had it easier when it came to dressing up for a nightclub, except many single men wanted to party but only a few would get that privilege. Any decently-dressed single woman was welcomed inside.

Nuan felt a tap on her back to turn and face her friend Heng and Heng's boyfriend Matt from Australia; as always holding hands like he didn't want to let her go even though

Heng wasn't going anywhere. Nuan greeted them both as did Dewai.

"How's your Mandarin?" Nuan asked Matt.

"Getting better. I have a good teacher."

"You pronounce it well."

"Did you have trouble learning English?" Matt asked Nuan in English.

"Yes I did, until I realised our language reflects our culture while English reflects Western culture. When I made that breakthrough that made a difference."

"I'll remember that," he said in Mandarin.

"Ni zài jiào yuè yu ma?" Nuan asked Heng in Cantonese. *Are you teaching Cantonese?*

"M hei, m hei!" Heng exclaimed in Cantonese while looking horrified. *No, no!*

"What was that?" Matt asked in Mandarin.

"I'm just having fun," Nuan said with a smile.

"I know you."

They all did.

They were beckoned inside where Dewai went to the bar. Soon he had a beer and Nuan had a gin and tonic, which she sipped through a straw while looking for Jia and Huang. There she spotted them. Nuan grabbed Heng close, because of the loud music.

"Let's go to the balcony," Nuan shouted in her ear.

They went to the Pearl River side of True Color while Nuan asked Jia and Huang to join them. Outside, conversation was possible. They all sat except for Nuan.

Dewai, Heng and Matt," Nuan said. "You all know Jia from a few times here now, and this is Jia's new boyfriend Huang from where we work. Huang, this is my boyfriend Dewai, and my friend Heng and her boyfriend Matt."

They shook hands in turn which was really complicated.

Nuan thought she would put things in perspective. "You met here?" she asked Heng.

"We did," Heng said.

"Matt's from Australia and he's in love with my best friend. Matt's here for another year or so, but after that he's going to stay in Guangzhou."

"I love this place!" Matt exclaimed.

Nuan knew Matt loved Heng more than he loved Guangzhou, but if he loved both then that was good. Nuan sensed a presence to see Hu with his new girlfriend. She was a few years older and totally beautiful with a lovely, round, goose-egg face, big eyes, and a nice figure: busty and a nice bottom where Hu rested his hand while she held his arm as a definite sign of possession. Nuan was taken by her big, bright smile as Hu eased her close.

"Yan Qiu," Hu said. "This is Shui Nuan, and you know Dewai."

Nuan shook hands to receive an even bigger smile.

"Over there are Xiong Jia and her boyfriend Zuo Huang," Hu said. "Both are police officers."

More hands were shook.

"Yan Qiu," Nuan said. "This is my oldest and best friend from school, Chen Heng, and her boyfriend Matt Blake from Australia. Matt's learning Mandarin to make Guangzhou his home."

More hands were shook.

"Please sit," Nuan offered while admiring Qiu's outfit. A tight, red blouse, a black leather mini-skirt, and gorgeous boots in black suede with pointy toes and a bit of heel. They were like pixie boots.

"We're all connected through Nuan," Qiu said.

That was observant – yes they were.

"I'm really pleased you all came to my special night out," Nuan said. "I planned this a while ago, but since then we've finished the major part of our most recent case so this is a celebration of that."

"I warned Qiu that when you date a police officer, you date the job," Dewai said. "For me that's been a good thing."

Qiu was holding Hu's arm again while his hand was on her bottom again. Definite attraction there. But more important things.

"I love your boots!" Nuan exclaimed. "Where did you get them?"

"Tianyu Shoes," Qiu said.

"I must go there."

"Do you like shopping for clothes?"

Nuan remembered her fun time with Binbin. "Very much."

"We'll have to do that one day."

How sweet? "Yes we will. Can I have your phone please?"

Qiu reached into her bag to hand her phone to Nuan, who made a contact while making a contact on her own phone. She handed Qiu's phone back.

"Now we're officially connected!"

Qiu laughed brightly.

"I've heard things about you," Qiu said.

"Only good things I'm sure."

"I heard there's only one Shui Nuan in this world, who seems to bring everyone into her orbit."

"Have you been talking about me?" Nuan asked Hu.

"That was me," Dewai said.

"Ah. The most important things in this world are your lover and your friends," Nuan said. "Friends while you're working together, friends when you go shopping together, and your best friends and your lover at True Color on a Saturday night."

"Best friends, new friends and my lover," Qiu said.

"Now my friends, old and new, and my lover, we're here for a reason," Nuan announced. "Let's dance!"

Nuan followed Heng and Matt holding hands; Matt liked dancing which he particularly liked about Guangzhou. Following were Jia and Huang, and Qiu and Hu, she holding him and he resting his hand on her bottom again.

"That's a lovely outfit," Jia said to Nuan.

"I bought this when I was undercover," Nuan said, but she wasn't going to say more than that. Nuan wanted to leave that night in her past, except for that outfit.

The dance floor was busy with inevitably more women than men. Even though Dewai didn't like dancing that much he always joined in, which Nuan appreciated. It was clear Huang liked dancing. When there was a moment's break of music, Nuan grabbed Jia.

"Huang's great!" she exclaimed.

"Yeah," Jia said with a big smile. "I love him in all ways."

"Good for you."

Dewai went off to get a drink. He'd done three or four dances and he would return for more, but Nuan had Heng and Jia and their boyfriends, and Qiu who enjoyed dancing as much as anyone there, and Hu who seemed to like dancing more now than before, so she didn't mind. There was nowhere better in the world than a Guangzhou nightclub late at night or in the early hours of the morning, as she danced with her best friends and a new friend.

Epilogue

A 2018 report by the Vietnamese National Committee on Crime Prevention and Control found from 2012 to 2017, law enforcement agencies rescued about 7,500 trafficking victims (1,250 per annum), where over 90% were female and 80% were from an ethnic minority. Most victims were trafficked internationally (90% to China), and 80% were sexually exploited in marriages or in the sex industry.

In mid-2019, the Chinese Ministry of Public Security conducted a joint operation with the police forces of five neighbouring countries to rescue 1,147 foreign victims of human trafficking, including 1,130 women and 17 children, while detaining 1,332 suspects, including 262 foreign nationals. This was the biggest in a series of Chinese policing operations targeting human trafficking. Despite these successes, the problem of human trafficking into China, especially for sexual exploitation, is ongoing.